The Girl and the Wolf

The Girl and the Wolf

once upon a time

Fiona Drechsler

Book 1 in the ***once upon a girl*** *series*

Fiona Drechsler
Rathenaustr. 56
99085 Erfurt
fiona.drechsler@gmail.com

ISBN: 978-3-910642-01-0

For all my dreamers out there!
Follow your heart and you will achieve your goals!

ONCE UPON A TIME THERE WAS A GIRL. AND THERE WAS A WOLF. THE GIRL WAS BRAVE, THE WOLF WAS LOVING. THEIR ADVENTURES STARTED HERE...

Prologue

(One year ago)

Her steps slowed and her heart pounded faster. Ruby wished she could make out who it was she had spotted in the distance. But even with narrowed eyes, she was still too far away to make out their face.

And then suddenly she knew who was leaning against the tree, and she stopped, frozen in space. Was this a dream? Was she imagining it? It couldn't be him!

It couldn't be Leo.

And yet this boy looked exactly like Leo. Leo, who had been forced out of his house, out of their village, and whom she had not seen for almost two weeks. Thirteen days, *she thought.* It's been exactly thirteen days since we last saw each other.

Maybe she was just imagining it. Why should she see him again now of all times?

Slow steps carried her closer to him, and each step made it clearer. It was him. It really was him!

When she was only a few feet apart from him she stopped; he hadn't moved an inch. "Leo?" It sounded like a question, because she had to make sure her brain wasn't just playing a stupid trick on her.

"Hi Ruby." The familiar voice removed all doubt. His dark brown hair was a little longer than it had been back in the village, but the same brown eyes beamed at her.

When he didn't move again, she walked towards him with certainty. Relieved, she pulled him into a hug, but Leo hardly moved. Only after a few moments did she feel him tentatively place his hands on her back, pressing her against him.

She heard him take a deep breath. "Aren't you afraid of me?" he asked softly.

Her own voice was as quiet and careful as his. "Why should I be?" Ruby couldn't even remember how long they had been friends. Probably for most of her life. Why should she be afraid of him?

"I'm a wolf."

ONE

Once Upon a Time...

Ruby was on her way to her mom's house *again.* And she was late. Although she knew the way through the big, beautiful forest very well, that happened many times. Today it was absolutely not her fault.

Ruby's grandmother, affectionately called Granny Annie by the whole village, hadn't wanted to let her go that day until everything had been extra clean. And boy, had her house been clean in the end! All the floors had been swept, tables wiped down, dishes washed, and windows cleaned. And that was even though no one would see it! After all, Granny lived in the middle of the woods and was only visited by her best friend Lisette and her granddaughter Ruby. What a waste of time!

Now Ruby was hurrying through the woods in her red leather jacket and with several bags over her shoulder, careful to stay on the path. She heard her mother's voice in her head: *Don't stray from the path! There are dangerous wolves out there, and you have to be careful.*

And suddenly...

"Boo!" a boy's voice yelled from behind a tree near her. Ruby almost dropped one of her bags. She hated that she had been so obviously surprised. After all, she knew the voice.

Said *dangerous wolves.*

Alright, dangerous might not have been the right word.

"Damn it, Shawn! Do that again and you'll regret it!" she shouted in his direction. The eight-year-old was standing by the side of the path with a sly grin, while Ruby was furiously stroking her straight auburn hair. Her braid had loosened as she worked, and the long strands fell wildly in her face.

Ruby would describe this wolf in particular as rather annoying, but not dangerous. None of the pack were dangerous. And they really didn't look it, either. Although everyone seemed to know they were wolves, Ruby had never seen them in anything but their human form.

Laughing, eight more boys and girls emerged, some as young and small as Shawn, others considerably older. Corey, at seven, was the youngest, but didn't let on. He ran around acting like he owned the whole forest. So did Shawn. Corey's brother, Will, was also their age, and the three of them got up to all sorts of shenanigans.

Nikki, at fourteen, was one of the oldest and one of Ruby's best friends. The athletic girl with dark brown hair came up to her and rolled her eyes. "I told him not to do that. But you know boys. They think that kind of thing is totally funny." Nikki was also one of only three girls in the pack, and was probably pretty happy to see Ruby every once in a while. Just as glad as Ruby was, conversely, to be able to walk the long way between Granny's house and the village with her friends.

With a sigh, Ruby's gaze roamed over the three bullies. Some of the others also enjoyed such things. Mike, for example, who at sixteen was actually too old for this. Or Philippa, Will and Corey's oldest sister, who was nowhere near as grown up as she would like to be. They would just play pranks all day if they could. Ruby's gaze lingered on one who wouldn't let that happen: Leo. Another one of her best friends. He caught her gaze and she smiled at him.

Nikki nudged her shoulder briefly, gesturing to her right with a small movement of her head. Shawn, who was trying to climb a tree with no tangible branches, paused briefly as Ruby just happened to arrive beside him, checking to see if his rowdy friends were catching on to his action. Her chance! She playfully put her arm around his shoulders and pushed him forward as she walked along. Although she was eight years older than him, she was only a little more than a head taller. But while she still had that advantage, she had to use it. With a firm grip, she controlled the direction they were going, making sure he couldn't get loose. "Now tell me again what was so funny about that," she demanded, playfully offended.

But the little guy didn't understand what she wanted. "I wanted to scare you. And that was really funny..."

Mara, undoubtedly the smartest of the pack despite her age, quickly interrupted him. "That was sarcasm, Shawn. You're not supposed to respond to that. Just apologize." She was eight and had the same round face as her sister Philippa.

The others laughed and Ruby joined in. Shawn's cheeks turned slightly pink, but he was already opening his mouth again, certainly ready to reply angrily.

"Go ahead, Shawn," urged Leo now, who was still walking farther back, giving him a good view of his entire pack. "Apologize." His voice was calm and determined, so calm in fact that Ruby didn't know how his words could have come through to them so clearly up front. But evidently, they were doing their job.

"I'm sorry," the boy at Ruby's side now mumbled. Satisfied, she let him go.

"Apology accepted." Shawn quickly moved away, and Ruby looked after the somewhat too defiant boy. She wondered involuntarily how he would be doing in the village right now. Much had changed for him since he and the rest of the pack had been banished. He no longer went to school, ran around the forest all day, and spent most of his time only with Corey and Will, with whom he got into way too much mischief. Would this all be different if there hadn't been a witch traveling through their village back then?

Then Nikki brought her out of her thoughts again. Still walking beside her, she glanced unobtrusively at the bags over Ruby's shoulder. "Hey, want me to take something off your hands?" she asked.

Ruby couldn't help but grin. "It's okay, it's not that heavy." Still, she played conspicuously with the straps of her pouches and peered inside. Inside each was some food. Granny's fruits and vegetables and her popular pastries. She could feel the eyes of the whole pack on her.

Ruby thought she could see the children lift their noses. As if they could smell the pastries through Tupperware, boxes, and the fabric of the bag. Maybe they really could, but Ruby was having fun pretending not to notice.

"What did Granny Annie bake today?" asked Philippa, Mara's older sister, in a very interested tone. She suddenly walked close behind Ruby, trying not quite successfully to catch a glimpse into her bags.

"Oh, all kinds of things," Ruby answered immediately, turning so that the bags were again farther away from Philippa, and grinning at her. "Bread, cookies, cakes, and even some rolls. She let me taste one, and wow! They are soooo yummy!"

Everyone looked at her with wide eyes. It was mean that she was teasing them, but Ruby just couldn't help herself today. Her day had been long, and she had missed her friends the whole time. Having their attention pleased her. "And not only that, she made her famous apple pie. Even with cinnamon! The house smelled so nice!"

She laughed when she saw their faces, and had to pause for a moment as she opened one of her bags and looked inside. There were bread, cake, some fruit and vegetables. Enough for the pack and their parents for the evening. Ruby handed the bag to Nikki.

"Give the bag back to me tomorrow so Granny won't wonder."

"Thanks," she replied with a grin, and the others looked relieved, too. Nikki had seen through her game long ago; after all, Ruby gave the pack a bag every day. Still, her joy was genuine.

The pack would never ask her directly for food, but it had become a bit of a routine with them. They would get some food, and Ruby almost never walked through the woods alone. Ruby's mom and she herself gave away most of it to people from the village anyway, so she didn't see it as a big deal at all. And so far, no one had really noticed that there was always something missing.

While the others scattered along the path and in the surrounding forest, Nikki stayed beside her. "I meant it," she said, "I can take something off your hands." It was sweet how Nikki cared.

The auburn-haired girl looked at her four remaining bags. In fact, they weren't very light, and Ruby's back hurt already from all the cleaning that day. "Thanks, that would help," she finally said, handing her friend two more bags. Nikki accepted them and continued walking just as fast as before, despite the extra weight.

For a few moments they walked silently side by side, then Nikki giggled. "Something pretty funny happened today. I was strolling through the woods with Mike and Luke, and then we came to a place where the creek was pretty deep..."

Ruby could hardly listen. While she loved it when Nikki told of her adventures, it also made her incredibly melancholic. When Ruby was a child, she had always played pirates or circus with Leo, Luke and Nikki. They had had adventures and fought evil. And promised each other that they would still do that when they were grown up.

For Ruby, that was still just a wish. But Nikki and her brothers were constantly running through the forest, always discovering something new while she went about her daily chores, never seeing anything unknown. Ruby loved her friends, but envy was hard to suppress some days. She also wanted to get out into the world and see and experience new things that she could only dream about now.

At some point, Nikki drifted further forward to Mike and Luke, with whom she had been hanging out a lot lately. Ruby's gaze wandered wistfully, smiling at the group that showed up every day just for her, taking a half-hour walk. And suddenly she saw Leo coming toward her, with his tangled hair as usual and his calm brown eyes in complete contrast. Her smile grew bigger and happier. There wasn't much left of the boy she used to go on adventures with. With whom she had fought monsters and defeated pirates. Not so loud. Not so self-assured anymore.

But she probably wasn't like she used to be either. In the past, she definitely wouldn't have kept such a big secret from her mom. That she was walking through the woods with a pack of wolves. And had been doing that for a year.

Involuntarily Ruby thought back to how she had wanted to tell her mother, shortly after it had happened the first time. How she had imagined beforehand that her mother couldn't be angry anymore, once she knew that they were still her friends, and not bloodthirsty monsters like everyone said. But, alas, it had never worked out that way.

TWO

Lies and Secrets

(One year ago)

Ruby was terribly anxious when she entered the house. Her mother's bicycle was already in the front yard, and her shoes were on the shoe rack. As usual, Ruby found Catherine in the kitchen.

"Hey Mom." Somehow her voice trembled. But if Catherine noticed something was going on, she didn't show it. She calmly put plates and glasses on the table, and got butter and cheese from the refrigerator.

"Hello, sweetheart. Did you have a good day? How's Granny?" She finally sat down in her chair. Walking around made Ruby even more nervous than she already was.

Catherine looked expectantly at her daughter, but she didn't put down her bags as usual, nor did she sit down in the empty seat. "Um, it was pretty good." Understatement of the century. She had seen friends again whom she had thought lost forever. But even though Ruby herself was so incredibly happy about it, she knew what her mother thought about the wolves.

"Come on, sit down, you must be hungry," her mom urged. Reluctantly, Ruby moved to her chair. Carefully, she took the bread that was meant for her out of her bag and placed it on the table.

"Mom, I..." She cleared her throat. The lump in her throat just seemed to swell immeasurably.

"Yes, sweetie?" She was already distracted again with cutting up the bread and dividing it evenly between both plates. But maybe that wasn't such a bad thing. Maybe there was something good about Catherine not hearing every word that came out of Ruby's mouth.

"Do you really think the wolves are so terribly dangerous?" Ruby spat out; she was talking fast so she couldn't change her mind. "I mean, all the ones that disappeared used to be our friends. Do you really think they would attack us?"

Just after her first sentence, Catherine had already set her knife aside. Her eyes spoke volumes, and despite all her hopes, Ruby already knew what was coming. "They're not our friends anymore, they're wolves. And wolves are inherently dangerous. You can't trust them." She sighed. "I know you want to see the best in them, but Witch Casmira said it very clearly: this kind of magic is dangerous, and witches who use it don't care about innocent victims."

Ruby looked down at her hands. "Nikki ... and Leo..."

Catherine, who remembered her former neighbors too well, and how close Ruby was with them, reached her hand out to her daughter. "They can't control the curse. We had to banish them. We can't let them attack any of us."

The girl squeezed her mother's hand and looked into her eyes. "They wouldn't. Never. They would never." Her voice almost broke, and she herself heard how desperate she sounded.

Catherine's gaze softened. "You can't know that. A curse like that shouldn't be underestimated. You're not yourself anymore." Her mom brought Ruby's hand to her mouth and pressed a kiss to her fingers. For a moment she closed her eyes, then sighed. "If I could, I wouldn't send you into the woods anymore," she admitted. "But Granny needs you, and she doesn't want to move back to the village. And I trust you. The forest shouldn't be a place you're afraid of. The wolves are probably not even there anymore." It was like she was talking more to herself than to Ruby. As if she needed those assurances more than she cared to admit. "Please promise me you'll always stay on your path. And if you ever see any of them, stay away."

Ruby couldn't. She couldn't tell her mother that she had met them. Catherine would never allow her to go into the woods again. Ruby would never see any of her friends again. And her mom wouldn't change her mind. "Yes," she agreed, then. "I'll stay on my path. Don't worry about me."

And with that, a year of lies and secrets began.

THREE

In the Forest

"Did Nikki ask you about Greta again?", Leo snapped Ruby out of her thoughts. His voice was deeper than before. Which was probably normal, considering he was seventeen by now.

"Not today, for once," Ruby replied, trying to make her voice sound light. Her thoughts were still circling around the secrets she kept from her mother. And how she rarely told anyone. "But we were just talking about it yesterday, too." It made her extra nervous to talk to Leo about his sister. Especially when it was such a sensitive topic. All wolves handled their banishment from the village differently - even a year later - and Leo always wanted to make sure everyone followed his rules anyway.

With long strides, Leo walked beside her. He tried to make his voice sound almost indifferent, even though he actually cared. "Any news on that front?"

"No." Ruby knew he was trying to find out if Nikki had snuck into the village, but she didn't ask Nikki that because she didn't want to come between the two siblings. They were both her friends, and she would not betray either of them to the other. She wanted to change the subject, but the only thing she could think of was the conversation she had with her mom about the wolves. Although that had been a year ago.

For a while, they were both silent. Ruby looked over at Leo, wishing the walk was a little longer. But alas, it wasn't much longer. "Did you find out why Corey hid his food?" she asked him. One of the more exciting stories going on in the pack. Shawn ate everything no one took from him, and Corey hid his ration in a box under his bed. For reasons still unknown.

"I don't know. He wouldn't talk to me about it. Maybe Mike will get it out of him." Even though Leo was the leader of the pack, some of the kids just had a better relationship with the other older pack members. Sometimes simply because they were siblings. Mike wasn't Corey's brother, but Shawn's, but he was sixteen and didn't make any rules in the pack, so the younger ones saw him as cool.

"Kids are weird," she said softly so the others couldn't hear. But she didn't mean any harm. She herself remembered all the stupid things she had done as a child, and for which she had no explanation today.

"You can say that again," Leo grinned, as quietly as she did.

They were approaching the village, and Ruby realized too quickly that this meant goodbye once again. At the same time, she was glad that it wasn't pitch dark yet, and the shadows between trees and houses wouldn't swallow her up.

She turned to the group, which had also slowed down. "Thanks for coming with me," she said, taking her bags from Nikki. "See you tomorrow!"

Smiling, Ruby watched as some of them were already running deeper into the forest, with a seemingly endless energy. Only Leo, still standing next to Ruby, appeared calm as usual. He looked longingly for a moment to where the first houses were beginning to appear, and then turned to leave. Before he disappeared for good, however, he turned to her once more.

"See you tomorrow, Red."

She smiled. "See you tomorrow, Leo."

FOUR

Fairy Town

It was not far from the edge of the forest to her house. And today Ruby was quite happy that no villager ran into her and wanted to start a conversation. It was already late. Ruby just wanted to get home.

Mom's bike was in the front yard when Ruby ran to the front door. It was no wonder, today she arrived later than usual, of course her mom had already come home from work. Even on other days, her mom was usually home earlier than Ruby.

The girl entered the small hallway where the shoes and jackets of the two women were. There weren't many, two pairs for each of them. Her mom's in neat rows, Ruby's in less than perfect order. Sometimes her mom would try to tidy it up, but somehow it would get messy again pretty quickly. And that, even though Ruby actually always wore the same shoes.

"Ruby?" she could already hear her mom calling from the kitchen. Of course. She had probably heard the front door slam.

"Be right there," Ruby called back, rolling her eyes. Who else walked into this house without knocking? As she peeled out of her beloved red leather jacket and hung it, not very carefully, on a hook on the wall, she heard her mom in the other room tapping her fingers on the tabletop. It was a beat that always reminded Ruby of her mother. *Cha. Cha-cha. Cha. Cha-cha.*

She only did that when she was impatient. So Ruby hurried to run into the kitchen with all her bags and hug her. As expected, she stood between the table and the kitchen counter, looking not very relaxed.

No sooner had Ruby placed the four bags that had been hanging over her shoulder neatly on the kitchen table than her mom propped her hands on her hips. "You're late." It wasn't a question, but a statement. Still, her look demanded an explanation.

"Sorry, Granny Annie was in a good mood. She baked quite a bit today." A sweeping gesture of her hand pointed to the bags and backpack she had now removed as well. "I ended up helping her clean up." It was the truth, even if she hadn't done it entirely willingly. Ruby would have preferred to leave on time, too, but Granny was hard to disagree with. At least, if you didn't want a fight. In the end, Granny would still have done everything on her own, and Ruby would have heard about it for the rest of the week. At least.

Her mother's shoulders slumped slightly. "It was a good day?" she asked again. Ever since Granny had fallen and hurt her hip a few months ago, Catherine had worried about her mother even more. She would love to get her out of the house in the woods and have her live with her, but Granny Annie was nothing if not stubborn. And she was adamant about not leaving her house.

"She's only complained about my hair twice," Ruby nodded. Sometimes when Ruby helped her Granny out, her reddish-blonde hair would fall in her face. Then Granny Annie would always complain that (A) she couldn't do a decent braid and (B) her hair was so different from the blonde locks of her ancestors. Ruby had once been really annoyed by the latter, but now she loved the rather straight hair, which, along with her red leather jacket, had earned her the name Little Red Riding Hood.

Meanwhile, Ruby was pulling more bags out of her backpack and placing them next to the others. She and Catherine couldn't eat that much even if they wanted to. "She didn't even take a nap, she was in such a good mood," Ruby continued, finally dropping into one of the chairs next to the table.

There was a smile on Catherine's face. Then she sat down at the table as well. "Have you eaten?" she asked her daughter.

Nodding, Ruby ran a hand through her hair and looked out the window. It was getting late, and they had things to do. She saw that realization in her mom's eyes, too.

It was Catherine who finally said "We should hurry." When Ruby tried to stand up, however, she said "Sit tight. Sort the food." Then she went to the large kitchen cabinet and pulled out more bags.

Ruby, who already knew the whole game, purposefully took some cans and bags from individual bags and put them in different piles. There were nine servings for eight families and themselves, which were again packed and divided between the two women. Since it was late that evening and would soon be dark, the two split up and set out on their own. Ruby took on four families, and Catherine the other four.

Ruby knew everyone in the village. She had helped out or been helped by almost all the families at one time or another. It had always been that way here. At least before the curse. They always brought the food to the families who needed it most.

Her first stop was just a few houses away from their own. The parents had two children who were skinnier than any other child in the village, and a small baby they didn't care much for themselves. "Little Red!" called Greta, a petite girl with light brown hair and her six-month-old brother in her arms, as she opened the door for her. She immediately shooed her inside, into the kitchen, where her other brother was stirring in a pot. It looked like soup. A very thin soup.

"We were beginning to think you weren't coming today," the girl said with relief, lifting the baby to her other side. "Didn't you, Hanni? Didn't I tell you she wouldn't be coming for sure? Usually, you're always here when it's still quite light."

It wasn't an accusation, and Ruby didn't see it as such. Greta didn't think her family was one of the poorest in the village. She was an optimist. Even if her parents obviously weren't.

"Are you kidding?" retorted Ruby. "You guys are my favorite stop." And they were - assuming their parents weren't yelling so loud you could hear it from the front yard.

She handed Hannes the first bag, and the boy immediately peeked inside. "Cookies and cake!

Greta look!" he exclaimed with wide eyes. His sister bent over the goodies with a furrowed brow.

"You didn't have to do that, Ruby. Mother won't let us eat cookies." Greta wanted to reach into the bag and hand the cookies back to her, but Ruby wouldn't allow it. Instead of accepting it, she put the cookies and cake in a compartment of the kitchen cupboard, where – to Ruby's knowledge – the children's parents never looked.

"Do you want some soup?" asked Greta as Ruby turned back to her, grinning, and held a bowl out to her guest.

"No, that's okay," she waved it off quickly. It hardly seemed like enough for the whole family. "I have to get on before it gets dark. But hopefully I'll have more time tomorrow."

It wasn't easy for her to leave the two of them alone. Or the three of them. The baby certainly wasn't having an easy time of it either. With a heavy heart, she walked out, back into the cooling air.

She wrapped her arms around herself. Ruby didn't like the next part as much, because it took her a long time to get to the next house. But her mom had been at work all day, so she volunteered for the longer walk. Plus, this way it wasn't noticeable if she chatted a little longer.

Five minutes later, she knocked on the next door.

A boy, a few years older than her, with wild black curls and a dark complexion opened the door. Matteo absent-mindedly wiped his hands on his pants, but his eyes lit up when he saw Ruby. His reaction to the pastries was similar to Hannes' and Greta's. And he invited her in.

Matteo's mother was sick, but cheerful. She was sitting in an armchair in the living room. "Would you like some tea, my dear?" she asked, trying to push herself up out of her seat.

Quickly Ruby replied, "Sit down, please." The poor woman could barely walk, let alone stand, and unfortunately that had been the case for a while. "I don't need tea. I have to go soon." Normally, Ruby would have loved to chat with the two of them. At least five minutes. Or ten. And settled in for tea.

But today? As she noted with a glance out the window, it was already dawn, and she had two more houses to visit. By the time she got back to her house, it would surely be dark.

His mother sent Matteo along to accompany Ruby, and although she had meant for him to stay with her the rest of the way, Ruby said goodbye to him at the next house. She was not afraid of the dark.

She was in a village where no one went outside at night. And those who did anyway, she knew. Ruby trusted everyone in the village, even after the whole wolf thing. Especially since she was friends with the oh-so-dangerous wolves.

Her path led her to a very lonely house. An old woman lived in it. When Ruby had holes in her clothes and Granny Annie was too sick or stubborn to take care of them, she would ask Holly for help.

Just as warmly as the others, she greeted her. But this time it was not hard to leave again. Holly was tired, too. In fact, she was already in her sleeping clothes. Had put on her reading glasses and a book was lying next to the place where she always sat.

"Did you eat enough today?" asked Ruby again before she went on her way again.

"Yes, yes, my child, what you bring me is always enough, after all I'm alone and I'm not very hungry anymore," she replied.

The girl had to go on but couldn't quite pull herself together. Instead, she carefully placed Holly's food in her storage cupboards, set aside the used dishes, and drew the curtains.

Holly waved at her to come over. She had watched the girl with a smile. "Be on your way, my child," the old woman finally said. "It'll be dark soon and you have one more ration to deliver," she continued, glancing at the bag at her side.

The girl could only nod. "Sleep well, Holly." She said goodbye and went back outside.

To her surprise, Matteo was still waiting for her, "I thought you went home already?"

"Hey, I promised my mom I'd walk you home, and I will do so." Ruby liked his sense of duty. And the smile with which he looked at her. They'd been friends forever, but with his sick mother and everything that had happened before, it could be hard to meet up with him. He practically worked day and night. Tailored clothes and took care of broken shoes. Everyone described his hands as nimble and talented. If Matteo wasn't so compassionate with penniless villagers, he could have made a small fortune from his work long ago.

With him at her side, Ruby walked to the last house. It wasn't as close to the edge of the forest as Holly's, but it was still far enough from her own that it couldn't be seen.

"They're probably asleep by now," Ruby explained as she just looked at the dark windows for a moment and didn't knock right away. Instead of going inside, she walked around the small grey house, placing the bag of goodies in front of the kitchen window. In the morning, the young father would find it and be able to make his wife and their children something delicious to eat.

Together with Matteo, she now also walked the longer way back to her house. And although it was getting colder, Ruby did not shiver. Instead, she talked to him and passed the time that way.

"Did you read about Feenburg Castle?" asked Matteo before she could even think of a topic. "Yesterday in the newspaper?"

Confused, she shook her head. The kingdom was supposedly not far away, but when you came from a village like Fairy Town, everything was pretty far away. Just getting through the forest to the nearest town took two hours on foot.

"So apparently the princess broke into the royal library, stole some books, and then took off."

This really was news! "Run off? Where to?"

He shrugged. "To the city? The next kingdom? No one knows."

"Poor thing! All alone out there."

"I feel more sorry for the queen. She has no one now that the king has died."

"Right..." She playfully punched him in the arm. "Seems we're better off here in the village."

Matteo laughed. "I guess so."

"So, has anything exciting happened lately?" she inquired.

"In this village? No," he laughed. "I'll tell you this: when my mother gets better and we have enough money, we'll go out into the world and try our luck there." She couldn't see his face as she walked beside him, but there was no doubt in his voice. No doubt that this was not going to happen. And Ruby liked that.

"I'd like to get out into the world, too," she replied, "even if things like this happen there." She imagined herself traveling beyond the forest that surrounded the entire village. Beyond the town where her mom and some villagers worked. Maybe to the next kingdom from where exciting stories reached them. Or even further. To places she couldn't even imagine.

"Are you kidding? You're already getting out of Fairy Town! Every day you go into the woods and fight your way through the bushes to get to your Granny. It's so exciting!" His voice almost rolled over, he was so excited.

"You make it sound like I'm Tarzan or something," she laughed. Then a hesitation. Should she tell him the truth? He obviously had the wrong idea about the forest altogether. "It's not one bit dangerous out there," she finally did explain with a nod to the trees behind the houses. "And all I do is go to my Granny's and help her around the house. Not exciting at all."

He laughed at her throwaway way of answering him. "It's more than most of us see. And hey, you could run into a bloodthirsty wolf at any time," he joked, bumping his shoulder against hers.

"Don't start that with me!" she groaned, wanting to slap her hand over her mouth right then and there. Of course, she didn't tell him that she knew wolves, and that they weren't a bit bloodthirsty. Who knew if he would even believe her. But there was something she had to say. "As if they really hang around in the woods. As if they exist! Do you think if they were there, parents would still let their kids out on their own?"

"So, you think it's all a lie?" he asked, a little sceptically. There were a few people in the village who didn't believe in the wolf curse, but Ruby had never voiced her opinion out loud. Most of them already had an entrenched opinion, and she didn't need to put herself in the spotlight with her attitude towards the subject. Especially with all the secrets she had to keep. "Then what about the three families?" he continued. "Where did they suddenly go? And why didn't they fight back when they were accused of turning into wolves?"

"No lie," Ruby replied calmly. "But it really doesn't look like there are ten or twenty wolves out there eating everything in their path, does it?"

She couldn't quite make out his features in the darkness, but she had a feeling his steps were slowing. "True, but..."

"And what should the families have done when everyone turned against them? Stay here and be despised? They probably just looked for a new place to live and make money. Outside this village, somewhere where no one knows them." It was the theory Ruby had had before she had first crossed paths with the pack in the forest, and it was the story she told everyone who asked her whether she wasn't afraid to go into the forest alone. That was probably easier to believe for most people than that she was friends with the pack.

For a while they were both silent, and only their footsteps on the soft grass could be heard.

They took a shortcut through several gardens and were almost back to Ruby's house when Matteo stopped her.

"Maybe you don’t believe in this wolf curse, but you should still be careful out there," he urged her, glancing toward the forest.

"I am," she replied quietly, moving on after a moment. "Thanks for coming with me," she finally said as the two of them stood outside her front door. Normally she would still have invited him in, but by now it was really dark, and her mother surely wanted to sleep soon.

"Anytime." He turned to go, finally disappearing behind a row of houses as Ruby squeezed through the door. The light in the kitchen was still on, and she found Catherine sitting at the table with a cookie in her hand.

"Everything go okay?" the woman asked, pushing the cookie jar toward her daughter. Ruby lowered herself to the other chair and reached for the candy.

Nodding, she bit into her cookie. "Holly was still awake. I don't think she's sleeping too well. And Hannes and Greta were cooking again. How was it on your end?"

"Pretty good, Marietta's cold is better, and Karla's baby is doing well again." She cleared her throat and put her cookie aside. "Kids are missing once more, though."

Ruby paused mid-motion. She had been about to take another bite of her cookie, but now her hand hung useless in the air. "Oh no! Again? Who is it?" So many children disappeared lately and hardly any were found again.

"Evelyn's children: Zola and Zander. I really don't understand what happened to them. I guess they were just gone in the morning, no note, no message. They were just gone." Catherine ran her hands over her face, worried and tired, while the girl could only stare at her.

"This is just unbelievable," Ruby sighed. The siblings were older than Ruby; she couldn't imagine that the two of them had just been snatched away by something out there. Then again, that had happened so often lately with kids from the village that it was hard to believe there was no connection. Evil mouths even claimed that the wolves were to blame, seeking out easy prey. She would never tell the pack that, of course.

Catherine yawned loudly and looked at her watch. She grabbed the cookie she had bitten into and put the cookie jar in its rightful place. Then she said good night to her daughter and went to bed.

Ruby turned off the light shortly after and went to her room. Instead of being able to sleep, however, she sat on her bed for a while, snuggled deep in her blankets, reading a book. Or at least she tried to read a book. Her mind kept wandering away – to missing children, the mysteries of the forest, and a young princess somewhere out there – and it was hard to concentrate on the words on the paper. Finally, her eyes fell closed and shortly after she disappeared into the land of dreams.

FIVE

A Girl alone in the Woods

The next morning Ruby was awakened by the patter of rain outside her window. Like almost every morning. Even before she arrived in the kitchen, the sun was shining again.

Her mom was already awake and sitting at the breakfast table with a roll and her favorite tea. She had her reading glasses on, and the newspaper lying next to her.

Ruby didn't like newspapers. Aside from the fact that she knew everything that was going on in Fairy Town, there was always bad news in there. But her mom kind of swore by the fact that you could always find out news. Or she didn't like to admit that she liked to use the paper to wrap her food in. Today, though, Ruby wondered if there was news there about the missing princess. Or about the queen.

The girl grabbed a roll, and smeared it with Granny's jam. "Anything interesting in the paper today?" Ruby sat down at the table with her own cup of tea and smiled innocently at her mom.

In Catherine's gaze, she saw delighted astonishment at the sudden interest. She flipped back a page and began to summarize. "Miss Loraine has a new supplier. Her fabrics are supposed to be much softer now. Also, she has new shades of blue. Evelyn had a dress made right away for herself and a suit for her brother in town."

She went on with more, but Ruby tuned out. If there had been anything about the kingdom, her mom probably would have started with it. Now there were only less interesting articles about happenings in the village. Whereby happenings was probably an exaggeration.

It wasn't much later that Catherine had eaten the last bite, drunk her tea and sat up. The reading glasses were now finally on the table, and the woman packed herself a small lunch in her newspaper. Just as she always did.

She walked around the house in an organized way, taking everything she needed and putting things out for Ruby. Sometimes the girl wondered why her mom still carried everything after her. She was sixteen years old already and had enough experience with going to her grandmother's house, and the things she had to do in the morning. But she had learned that it wasn't up to her. That was just the way her mom was.

"Don't forget to knock on Granny's door," Catherine began her daily lecture. "And don't forget to help her, even if she doesn't ask for it. You know how stubborn she can be."

Yes, Ruby thought to herself quietly. As stubborn as her Granny could be sometimes, so was her mom.

"And definitely don't stray from the path!" Catherine looked at her with a serious expression. "Don't you run into another one of those wolves!" Once again, Ruby just nodded, silently thinking to herself that her mom wouldn't be too pleased if she knew where a little of the food disappeared to each day.

She put on her shoes and jacket, said goodbye, and let the front door slam behind her. From the kitchen window, Ruby watched her ride away on her bike.

Ruby remembered how one day she had followed her mom. She had been curious then, and had wanted to see where Catherine worked, and who her friends in town were. It had turned out that Catherine had more reasons to be on time than just work. And that day, Ruby had seen it.

A man.

A man she had never introduced to Ruby. The one she hadn't even mentioned to her daughter.

Could Ruby blame her?

No, not at all.

If Ruby was being honest, she wouldn't tell her mom about a boy either. And who knew if she and this man even had anything worth mentioning. Ruby had watched her mom give him a long kiss and then walk down the street talking to him, but that didn't have to mean they were still together. Maybe it was such a short thing that she hadn't told Ruby about it because it was over before it had even begun.

When the big clock in the kitchen read nine o'clock, Ruby straightened up, set her dishes aside, and looked around the room. Then she took the things her mom had set out for her, including flour and milk and other baking supplies, and put more food in her backpack with the bags. It was for her friends, the pack, who she knew were not welcome in any store.

She went out of the house, and saw some children on their way to school. The school in the village was not big, but big enough so that all the children could go. Ruby had gone to school there once, too, before Granny had needed her every day.

Greta waved to her excitedly, and Hannes inattentively pulled a cookie out of his pocket. A smile flitted across Ruby's lips, and she waved back happily. And promptly stepped into a small puddle. Normally she would have laughed at that, if she didn't have to walk a long way through the woods now.

So, half limping and half hopping, she walked further out of the village, to her Granny. After only a few steps, she was able to ignore the wet foot and continue walking normally. But while she tried to enjoy the silence for the first few minutes, she soon wished the pack would join her.

Although the sun slowly rose higher, and she put more and more of the path behind her, she spotted no one. Strange. Usually, they were already there when you could no longer see into the forest from the village. And normally it wasn't so terribly quiet.

Against her instincts, Ruby paused. It was no later than usual this time. Where were the others?

There was a noise! No, it was just a bird. She spun around once. They had to be somewhere! Yesterday they had said that they would see each other today!

It didn't help, Ruby realized. It didn't help to stand around waiting for people who weren't going to show up. She had to keep going. She wanted to keep going. To Granny's house, dry her foot, and get to work. Good, maybe she wanted to dry her foot for the most part.

A light breeze passed through the leaves of the forest and birds chirped. Why had she thought it was too quiet? It all sounded the same.

As she walked along, she sang to herself. A song her Granny had taught her when she had been very little.

Where have all the flowers gone?
Long time passing
Where have all the flowers gone?
Long time ago

And suddenly her friends appeared. So suddenly that she was surprised. Hopefully no one had noticed.

The younger ones were the first to come running towards her. "Little Red!" "Hello!" "Little Red!" shouted Corey, Mara, and Will. Further back was Leo, obviously keeping an eye on everything and everyone. He grinned at her when she was nearly knocked down by the three of them.

This time Ruby didn't make a spectacle of the food she'd brought, but merely took the full bag out of her backpack while walking and handed it to Nikki.

"Thanks," the latter said. "Mom wants to make some blueberry muffins. I'll bring you some tonight."

Ruby just smiled and stifled a comment that she still had pastries from her Granny. "Thanks, that's sweet of you," she replied instead.

Nikki beamed. She was happy to do something good for her friend for a change. The girl walked beside Ruby, engaging her in conversation. "How are the people in the village?" she asked.

Ruby realized she was only asking about one particular person. Yet she played along. "Pretty good ... well ... somehow Zola and Zander seem to have disappeared..."

"Oh damn, that's been happening a lot lately, hasn't it?" For a second, it seemed like Nikki wasn't actually looking for information about Greta. The disappearing kids were a problem in the village, and thanks to Ruby, Nikki knew about it too.

"Yeah, but I don't know if that has anything to do with it," Ruby pondered aloud. Zola and Zander's mother wasn't the nicest, and when they had gone to school together, Zola had talked about running away often. But Ruby didn't say this thought out loud.

"Well, actually, Ellie didn't run away. She went and got herself a prince. It's just that no one knew."

"Yes, and Marietta and Mary also just left to work and then came back, too," Ruby agreed. That's why the rumor about the wolves' guilt hadn't caught on.

"So, Zola and Zander are showing up again, too," Nikki concluded confidently.

"Yeah, probably." Ruby really hoped so. She didn't like to think about what might happen to them. Although the two of them were a little older than she was, they too had only ever known life in the village.

Nikki shifted the bag back to her other side. "How is Greta doing, by the way? And her family? Do they have enough food?" She spoke so softly that the others, jumping wildly through the forest, couldn't hear her. And Ruby almost overheard her too, but they were questions she was already used to from Nikki. When her family had lived in the village, Greta had been Nikki's best friend. She was always asking about her, and Ruby believed she sometimes secretly watched them from the outskirts of the village.

"Unchanged," Ruby pressed out.

"Do you think I can visit them?" asked Nikki hopefully.

Pressing her lips together, Ruby looked at her friend. "I don't think that's a good idea." Aside from the fact that some people in the village were taking this wolf thing quite seriously, Leo wouldn't be thrilled about Nikki sneaking into the village either. Involuntarily, her eyes fell on him. He would do anything to protect his pack.

Nikki tried to smile, but all that came out was a grimace. "I see." She cleared her throat and swapped the bag to her other shoulder. "What about the village festival? It'll be in a couple days, right?" she asked then, as if nothing had happened. But longing resonated in her voice.

A feeling of guilt swept over Ruby. Nikki had not been able to be at the festival last year either because they had been banished a few days earlier. If Ruby told her about the activities, she would certainly not feel any better. "Yes," she finally replied. "But I don't think there are any real plans yet. At least, I haven't heard anything yet." She raised her shoulders, making it seem as if it wasn't at all important to her.

Still, she immediately saw sadness appear on Nikki's face. "I'd like to be there," she admitted.

The annual village festival was an opportunity for all the villagers to forget their worries and problems for one evening and celebrate together. Everyone contributed something: Food, decorations or activities. Every year it was wonderful, and every year everyone looked forward to it. In fact, the village loved to have parties. Every occasion was taken advantage of, and the village festival was in the middle of summer, when Easter was long over and Christmas still a few months in the future.

"Maybe you could just put on a cap..." began Ruby, hearing for herself how silly that sounded.

Luckily for her, Nikki laughed. "Right, because no one can recognize me with a cap on."

Ruby joined in, pushing the thought out of her mind again. She should probably let the subject rest.

SIX

An Idea

It wasn't much later that they arrived at the three oak trees. The place where they always said goodbye. With a cheerful "Bye" Ruby moved away from everyone, and shortly after she reached the small clearing where Granny's house was, the pack had disappeared somewhere in the woods.

Only two minutes later she arrived at Granny's door. Even if her friends came with her all the way here, they would have less concern about getting caught than they would near the village. Although Granny wasn't thrilled with the idea of wolves running around in the woods, she kept emphasizing that she wasn't scared of anything in the forest.

At this time of day, she was usually busy preparing the coffee table for the meeting with her friend Lisette anyway, and wouldn't spot any of the wolves. After all, she didn't even look out the window to see if Ruby was coming, so the girl worried little about the old lady spotting her friends.

At the last second, Ruby remembered what her mother had said. *Knock, be polite.* With a sigh, she banged her fist on the door. "Grandmother! It's me!" Then, without waiting for a response, she entered. She always did. Because if she had Granny Annie jump to the door every time just so she could enter the house, she would complain even more than she already did.

"We're in the living room," chimed Granny's voice to Ruby's left. A moment later, she heard laughter. Ah, so Lisette was already there.

Before joining the two women, she put her backpack down in the kitchen. Then she said hello. "Hi Granny, hi Lisette. You're here so early? How are you?"

Granny was already looking at her with a big smile for a change. It was definitely Lisette's doing. "Fine, fine. I'm just awfully tired. I can tell you, my child: never grow old."

And the two laughed louder than before. Ruby had to stifle rolling her eyes. Even when Granny was in a good mood, she complained.

"I'll put things away in the kitchen," Ruby announced, and with a polite smile she slipped away into the other room. There, she turned on the radio and sang along to Elvis Presley and Taylor Swift while tying her hair into a tight braid. Instead of just putting away the groceries, she washed the used dishes and put on a cup of tea for herself.

When she finished her chores, she peeked into the next room. The two women were still happily and excitedly bantering, so Ruby didn't want, or need, to interfere. Instead, she went out the back door, which was at the other end of the kitchen, into the backyard and was greeted by the noise of excited chicken.

The rather large chicken coop had once housed at least fifteen chickens, but by now there were only two left. Granny Annie had run out of energy and time to take care of all the animals, and had to part with some a few years ago. Since Ruby was there every day, it had become her job to take care of the remaining two.

It was a nice change from the otherwise rather monotonous work in the garden. Because besides the chickens, there was a huge vegetable bed, some bushes full of berries, apple trees, a smaller vegetable patch, and big pots of herbs. So instead of going to school, Ruby took care of the garden. But she didn't mind. She had always done well in school, and this way she could choose books that she liked to read. From which she could learn something she actually wanted to learn.

"Hey Anna, hello Elsa," Ruby greeted the hens. Granny Annie liked to make fun of her for naming them, but she didn't care. It was fun to treat them like real pets. Giving them food, petting them. Unfortunately, cuddling chickens wasn't so easy because after a while they started picking at her when she tried.

Nevertheless, Ruby crouched down by them and stroked their soft feathers. Next to the coop door was a garbage can of leftover food, a scoopful of which she tossed to the chickens. She also filled the small water bowl in the rain barrel by the house.

While the chickens pecked for food, Ruby checked their nests for eggs. There were actually three, one of which was still warm. Carefully, the girl put them into a small basket that always dangled from the coop door and was there for just this purpose.

She went back to the two hens and stroked Elsa's light brown feathers before walking out of the coop with the basket. She left the door open so the animals could go into the outside enclosure while she worked in the garden, and made sure she locked their gate securely. It had happened a few times that she had to chase after Elsa or Anna because they had somehow gotten loose.

She put the basket with the eggs next to the back door of the house, grabbed the big watering can and took care of the plants next. Since she was here every day, she didn't always have to weed - a task she deeply detested - but she did have to keep checking that no insects or slugs had invaded the leaves.

By the time she had made her rounds, her back ached, and she went into the house. Her tea was cold by now, but that was the way she liked it best, and she drank the whole cup almost in one go. She probably should have made a pot right away.

Again, she heard laughter from the living room, and decided to continue passing the time outside. This time she filled up her teacup with cold water and took it into the garden. Her chores took her almost two more hours, and when she stepped back into the kitchen, her hair was sticking to the back of her neck.

After throwing some cold water in her face and making sure she didn't look completely messed-up, she went to Granny and Lisette, asking if they needed more tea.

The women grinned at her as if they had just discussed something terribly inappropriate, and Ruby could well imagine they really did. Absolutely didn't want to know about it, though.

Lisette was the first to catch herself. "I'd love some. That's sweet of you, Ruby."

"Rosehip, please," Granny Annie interjected when the girl had already turned her back on her.

"Okay," she called back weakly. Rosehip didn't smell that great, in her opinion. Whenever it bloomed in the garden, Ruby had to suppress a gag reflex. Likewise when she made the tea.

Before she stepped into the living room with the pot and a plate full of cookies, she put on her smile. Granny should have no reason to fall into a bad mood after all. "Do you need anything else?" she asked after setting them down.

Granny brushed a grey curl behind her ear and stretched her back. "Can you go ahead and get the dough for the bread ready and get the vegetables from the garden? I'm going to lie down right after."

"Sure thing." Sometimes the extra work bothered her because it was usually Granny's job to make the dough. But today all that wasn't so bad; after all, Granny could get pretty mean when something didn't go her way. And this way, Ruby had her peace.

When she got the eggs from outside and beat them into the bowl, Lisette went home. And as she floured the countertop, the bedroom door slammed shut behind Granny. Except for the soft music from the radio, everything around Ruby was silent, and she knew she only had about two hours before she was interrupted again. So she hurried.

When the dough was finally done, Ruby was too. She grabbed two books from her stack in the kitchen, and took a drink of water before heading back outside.

This time, she didn't stay in the garden. The rebel in her loved to do something Granny and her mom thought was too dangerous. (Loved it as long as they didn't know about it.) And in fact, it wasn't even a tiny bit dangerous; after all, she merely went into the woods for a few minutes to sit down, lean against the broad trunk of an old tree, and read her book.

The second book lay on the ground beside her until someone took it and sat down in its place.

"Hey Red," Leo's deep voice greeted her. His knee grazed her thigh as he stretched out his legs.

The girl put her finger where she had stopped reading and looked up with a smile. "Hi, I hope you had a more relaxed morning than I did," she replied, undoing the braid that was already half undone.

"That bad?" he asked with a laugh, and the sound and his presence relaxed her more than she had expected.

"Do you know Granny Annie?" Sarcasm. Of course he knew her. If only from Ruby's stories. "She doesn't care that it's 27 degrees out here and the sun is almost unbearable at noon, but woe betide me if I haven't taken care of the entire garden before she wakes up from her nap." Leo knew these tirades of hers. Knew that Granny's demands annoyed her. And always listened to her patiently. She took a deep breath, rested her head against the tree trunk behind her, and closed her eyes. "It probably could have been worse, but I just don't feel like doing this every day anymore."

She heard him take a deep breath. Then Ruby felt Leo gently nudge her with his shoulder. "Oh, come on, I'm not that bad."

For a moment she looked at him, confused. "Not you," she then laughed, bumping her shoulder against his. "All that work, and constantly just running back and forth between the village and Granny. Nothing to experience."

"You want to go on adventures again, like when we were little," Leo noted, and the thought brought a smile to her lips. Yes, that was exactly what she wanted. Back then they had had no worries, no problems. Ruby had gone to her neighbors' house and fought pirates and searched for enchanted items with Leo, Nikki, and Luke. Every day was different. And new. And exciting.

"What do you think about a costume party?" she asked suddenly.

His brow furrowed. "In general, or ...?"

"Nikki asked me about the village fair today," Ruby quickly began to explain. "She misses Greta really badly, and maybe that would be a way she - or all of you - could go to the village again. See people, play games. A bit like the old days."

"A costume party," he repeated, and there was doubt in his voice. She knew, after all, that he wasn't the most spontaneous person, but Ruby felt strongly that she could persuade him if she wanted to.

"Yeah, a costume party. You know, if everyone dressed up, then no one would recognize you. You could walk around the village, safe, without anyone suspecting anything. Everyone will be way too happy to have a party anyway, after all the bad news and stuff. And that wolf thing was so long ago that hardly anyone will even think about it, especially since no one assumes you're there. I think this could be really good. And Nikki and Greta could see each other again without being interrupted. I think if we don't do that, Nikki will go crazy." Her excitement almost got the better of her, so she didn't recognize his doubtful expression until he spoke up.

"Do you really think this is a good idea? It sounds dangerous as hell."

Inwardly, Ruby groaned. *Dangerous*. How often she heard that word! "Why dangerous? It's the same village you've all lived in for years." It didn't seem to be a convincing argument to him, so she quickly added "It'll be fine."

"Only not everyone in the village is as kind-hearted as you. If just one of them catches us..."

"That's not going to happen," she quickly interrupted him before he could jump into anything. On the other hand, he already had a point. Anything could happen in this village. Magic and all.

"What if one of us runs into Evelyn or Monsieur Frederique? Those two are still stirring up hatred against us, after all. It would just give them more reasons to distrust everything."

"Well, sort of, but..." began Ruby. "Wait, how do you know?" She was sure she had never mentioned anything like that around the pack. Not even when asked about it. In fact, she had always been careful *not* to mention names. How did Leo know about them?

While she stared at him impatiently, he pressed his lips together. She didn't like where this was going at all.

"Did you..." Ruby tried to hold back but couldn't. And Leo made no effort to come out with the truth on his own. "Have you been to the village?" she asked now, straightforwardly.

"It's not that..." He stopped himself. His face contorted into a grimace; he probably saw that there was no point in lying to her. "Yes. Yes, I was in the village."

His confession stunned the girl even more than the actual fact that he had really sneaked there. Why would he do it? He was the one who forbade everyone to go near the village. The one who forbade the pack to talk to old friends and acquaintances because it would risk their safety. And then he went and did it himself.

Shock must have been written all over her face because his features softened. "It was just that one time, okay?"

"When? And where?" stammered Ruby.

"A couple of weeks ago. At night. Your Granny was sick and I met up with Holly." Holly. Ruby breathed a sigh of relief before she even realized she'd been holding it in. Holly was good. She could be trusted. She wouldn't betray Leo.

Ruby remembered the day he was talking about. Granny Annie had had a cold and made a hell of a fuss. It had been terrible! Granny was even more exhausting than usual when she was sick.

"Our supplies were running low, and it occurred to me that Holly had always stressed before how she liked to share. So I kept her company for a while, and she gave me some food for my family."

"She's like that," Ruby nodded. Although she didn't know the story yet, it didn't strike her as particularly far-fetched that the old woman would take care of poor children. No matter how evil they were supposed to be.

SEVEN

When Granny was Sick
(Seven weeks ago)

It was a sunny day, but Ruby had hardly noticed it, the way she had been bounced around by her grandmother throughout. The soup was too cold, then too unsalted. Her tea was empty again, and where was the honey? Why didn't Ruby herself think of giving honey to a poor old woman when she was sick? Think for once, child!

Usually, when Granny Annie was sick, Ruby tried to bake or cook something herself to take back to the village and the pack. Even if it was nowhere near as good as what her grandmother could whip up. But she had hardly kneaded a dough together when Granny had called for her again. It had to be admitted: she'd had a bit of a fever, and her cough sounded bad, but it wasn't easy to administer medicine to a stubborn old woman. Instead of drinking her cough syrup and sleeping for a few hours, she called for tea, soup, and hot water bottles. She didn't believe in taking medicine until she had tried everything else. Which made it even more exhausting for Ruby.

Eventually the bread was in the oven, and when it began to smell burnt, Ruby was relieved to find that Granny Annie had a sniffle that was not to be underestimated. Scraping off the black bits, she reluctantly tucked it in with what little vegetables she had been able to gather today. Unfortunately, not everyone in the village who needed them would get any.

Ruby was glad when Granny was feeling reasonably better by evening. Or maybe she was just saying that. Probably, like Ruby, she had little desire for the girl to spend the night in her house. They both knew how that would end: with arguments and hurt feelings. Neither of them would get much sleep. Still, Ruby offered it.

"No, no. Go home," Granny Annie urged the girl, blowing her nose loudly. "I'll take my medicine and sleep all night. You should go, Catherine will worry if you don't." Silently Ruby wondered why she hadn't taken her medicine hours ago, but remarking on it now would not make Granny happy. She was stubborn, and if she sent Ruby home now, and took medicine, that was be fine with her. Or it should be.

"I told Mom last night that you were coming down with a cold. She won't be surprised if I don't come home." It had happened before when Granny was sick or hurt, Ruby had had to stay overnight to keep an eye on her. "She specifically told me to stay over if you got worse." Ruby didn't know why she was contradicting her grandmother. She wanted to go home, too. Still, it was hard for the girl to go when she had seen all day how bad Granny actually was.

"I'm feeling better already, child. Go home already and let an old woman sleep."

Ruby's eyebrows drew together. She realized that messing with her Granny wasn't helping anyone. "I'll go when you're asleep," she finally said. At least then she knew she would actually be asleep.

Granny also gave in to this compromise. It looked like she didn't have enough strength left to argue with her granddaughter.

"Would you like me to make you another cup of tea?" asked Ruby, when she had been standing next to Granny's bed for an uncomfortable amount of time. It was always strange for her to be in Granny's bedroom because she was never actually allowed to be in here. Usually the door was always closed; Granny was very particular about her privacy. Even now, Ruby didn't quite dare let her eyes wander for fear of upsetting her grandmother.

"Yes," the woman croaked. She was already having trouble keeping her eyes open and could only manage a near-sitting position more poorly than not. Before Ruby turned toward the door, she saw Granny taking her medicine with a big gulp.

By the time the girl returned to Granny's bedroom with the cup, she had dozed off and was snoring softly. She placed the tea next to a half-empty bottle of medicine on the nightstand and carefully left the room.

That evening, she was more than happy to have the pack with her. It distracted her from worrying about Granny. Of course, Nikki and Leo noticed immediately that something was wrong. The 14-year-old approached her about it, and Ruby told her friend about her day and her grandmother's sickness.

"If you want, we can watch her tonight," Nikki offered. Ruby gave her a doubtful look. "You know, from the woods. If she's coughing badly or needs help, we'll hear it, and we can check on her."

Ruby didn't know what to say to that. "Really? You ... you don't have to do that. I ... she's probably fine..." She heard the doubt in her voice herself and was pleased when Nikki and the others insisted.

After making her rounds of the village that evening, she fell into bed, exhausted. But instead of falling asleep immediately, she lay awake for a while, staring at the ceiling.

Leo watched from the shelter of the trees as the light in Ruby's house was one of the last to go out. Only when everything was in darkness did he dare make his way to Holly. In the meantime, Luke was taking charge of Granny Annie's house and the wolves that had stayed there. It was good to have a brother who could be trusted with such things. At least this way Leo didn't have to worry about it. He still worried, of course.

Holly didn't look startled to discover him at her front door at such a late hour. Instead, wonder showed in her expression, which quickly turned into a smile. "Leo! It's good to see you. Come in, come in. You must be cold."

He didn't explain to her that he hadn't really been cold since the whole wolf thing. But he stepped into the house behind Holly and let her pull him into a warm hug. "I haven't seen you in a while, Leo. How are your parents? Your siblings? Where are you living right now? Oh wait, better not tell me, so I can't accidentally blurt it out," she added before he could say anything.

With his friendliest smile, he sat down across from her at the kitchen table. "Everyone is doing quite well. But ... it's hard to always find enough food for everyone."

His conscience told him that it was deceitful to rely on her pity and take advantage of it. But what could he do? His family was hungry. And Holly had always been happy to help.

"Oh dear," she replied with a furrowed brow, just as he had suspected. "Does Ruby bring you anything to eat now and then, too? She hasn't been around at all today. Is she all right?"

"Yes, she's fine. But her Granny is sick, so she couldn't cook anything today." Leo paused. Maybe he shouldn't have let on that Ruby knew about them. It might put her in danger. Quickly, he shook off the thought. He really didn't have to worry about Holly.

"Oh dear, is she badly ill?"

"Just a cold," Leo assured her.

"Oh, it's just a cold at your age, but it can be bad at ours," Holly explained to him.

"Ruby would have stayed there if she hadn't gotten better that evening." Leo was sure of it. It might bug her to work for Granny all day, as she kept pointing out, but she wouldn't just leave her alone when she was really bad.

"Oh, I guess you're right. She really is a good girl."

"She is," Leo confirmed. He never knew anyone who cared about everyone else the way Ruby did.

Holly's wrinkled hand patted his. "And it reassures me that you're keeping an eye on her out there in the woods."

Leo smiled at the thought that Holly didn't see him as a danger, but as Ruby's protector. "Of course."

"You know, you should be careful coming into the village. Evelyn and Monsieur Frederique are still telling everyone that the wolves are kidnapping children."

"Kidnapping children?!" He was horrified. It wasn't news they were said to be evil. Leo knew that, and so did the rest of the pack. And Ruby, of course, had told them about the missing children. But he hadn't known that they blamed the pack for it.

Holly noticed his reaction and took a deep breath. "Of course, not many people believe them. Ruby's been telling everyone that there are no wolves running around in the woods, and she's the only one who's really out there."

Leo liked talking to Holly. Somehow, she always managed to put him at ease. "Yeah, Ruby knows what to tell people." His smile was interrupted by the grumbling of his stomach, and Holly looked at him sympathetically. For his part, he was embarrassed by the whole thing, and avoided her gaze.

"Maybe I can help you and your family out," Holly now announced, rising from her chair. She reached into various cupboards and shelves, pulling out food that was wrapped in bags and foil. Some looked like sandwiches that Ruby sometimes brought in. As Holly was wrapping all this up for him, he stepped up to her, and she gave him what felt like a week's worth of food. "Thank you, Holly," he said emphatically.

She soon let him go, and after making sure everything was alright at Granny Annie's house, he and his pack filled their growling stomachs.

EIGHT

In the Woods with Leo

"So Holly knows you're out here?" continued Ruby. Somehow, she was disappointed that she wasn't the only one who had been trusted with this secret. But she also knew that Holly would never betray the pack, and Leo had had no choice at that moment.

He lifted his shoulders apologetically. "I think so, she always suspected. Why else would she have just let me in?"

The girl frowned. That could have gone tremendously wrong. "It could, but ... sometimes she can't keep secrets. And now she knows for sure you're out here." She didn't know why she said that herself. Holly was one of her favorite people, and she would never intentionally hurt anyone.

A grin appeared on Leo's face. "You're worried about us," he teased.

Her face turned pink. "Of course, you're my friends!" Unfortunately, it had to look like there was something else behind it. And Leo knew exactly what it was.

She was grateful to him that he didn't respond and just kept grinning. "What was going to happen? Even if they find out there are wolves out here in the woods, they still don't know it's us. And even if they have a hunch, they still don't know exactly where we are. Think about it, we've been in this forest for a year, don't you think we know our way around better than the villagers?"

"The villagers," she repeated. Never before had she perceived the word as a bad thing. Until now. She was a villager. Not a wolf. Not a member of the pack. Leo had to notice her sudden mood change as well, but when he did, he said nothing. "Well, in that case, nothing stands in the way of a costume party," she switched the subject. "With the costumes, no one will recognize you."

He was obviously not thrilled with this conclusion, but at the same time he couldn't disagree with her. "If you get us all the costumes," he countered lightly, knowing it would be a huge task to take on.

Her eyebrows shot up in surprise. She hadn't expected him to give in so quickly. But his objection definitely made sense. Where would they get all those costumes? "Don't think that's going to stop me," she grinned at him, and he laughed.

"I didn't expect anything else." He got up to his feet, holding out his hand to her.

"It's not that late," she objected, looking in the direction from which she had come. Behind some bushes, you could still catch a glimpse of Granny's house.

Once again, he laughed, and continued to hold out his hand to her. "Come with me, I want to show you something."

And this time she let him pull her up. "What do you want to show me?" she asked him as he led her deeper into the forest. She wasn't exactly afraid, but Ruby did notice quite quickly that he didn't let go of her hand.

"You'll like it," was all he replied, and Ruby grew impatient.

"I don't like surprises." Part of her wanted to just stop, and demand he tell her what he was up to. But then she'd just look like a petulant little child, and she didn't want that.

"That's a lie," he laughed, turning to face her. His eyes sparkled and her heart did a little skip. "You love surprises."

He had stopped and suddenly his face was so close she could feel his breath on her skin. It was upsetting her. She was tempted to kiss him. And she could tell by looking at him that he was thinking about it too. But she let the moment pass and turned back to walking. "So, which way?" she asked, hating the slight tremor in her voice.

They were quiet for a moment, his hand still clasping hers, and Ruby wanted so badly to turn back to him. To see what he was thinking. What he was feeling. But then she probably wouldn't be able to keep it together. "That way," he finally replied, continuing straight ahead. He, too, avoided her gaze. But he did not let go of her hand either.

For a few minutes they walked side by side, not saying a single word. And Ruby almost forgot that this was Leo, one of her best friends and Nikki's brother. But not quite.

When they arrived at a very special tree, she forgot everything and stopped abruptly. "Wow!" she could feel Leo looking at her, but she was unable to tear her gaze away from this beautiful tree. "I haven't been here in ages!" As a little girl, Ruby had run through the woods a whole lot, declaring this tree her personal secret hideaway, but ever since she had an endless list of chores at Granny Annie's, and the wolves were doing whatever they were doing in the woods, she wasn't allowed to do that anymore.

"You know this tree?" asked Leo, perhaps a little disappointed that he wasn't the one who had discovered it for her, but Ruby was too busy marvelling. The trunk split into two trunks a foot or so above the ground, and wonderful trees grew from both.

"This used to be my hiding place," she told him absent-mindedly.

"Hiding place?"

Grinning, she nodded. Ruby knew something he didn't. "You can climb up there and no one will spot you among the leaves." Looking at him again, she wasn't quite as perplexed as before. Maybe that had just been a strange moment earlier.

Before it could happen again, she averted her eyes. Without letting him answer, she went to the trunk of the tree and climbed higher and higher until she could sit down on a strong branch. She pretended to admire the beauty of nature instead of staring at Leo. Eventually - it seemed like half an eternity - he sat down next to her.

"Isn't this great?" she asked, still avoiding looking directly at him. Her heart was pounding way too fast. And it certainly wasn't because of the tree's height.

"You're right, it is great." For a moment they both just looked straight ahead, where they had a good view of the surrounding trees through the dense foliage. Then, out of the corner of her eye, Ruby saw him turn toward her. Hell, without meaning to, her head did the same. He was sitting on the other side of the trunk, their two branches slightly facing each other, as if the tree had grown just so they could both sit up here and look at each other.

"Do you remember our pact?" he asked, a lightness in his voice that Ruby envied. She could hardly think about the pact without her heart beating faster.

"Of course." She tried not to think about it, but the fact that he was smiling at her now didn't make it any better.

"I was thinking about it earlier when..." He faltered, and this time it was he who couldn't meet her gaze. "I wanted to kiss you."

Even if Ruby had wanted to, she couldn't respond. Their pact was almost a year old. She hadn't thought anything would happen between them after all this time. His confession hit her completely unexpectedly.

His faithful brown eyes looked at her for a long time. Somehow, it catapulted her back a year. When they had really kissed. When the pact had been made.

How he had stroked her cheek, standing so close to him that she could barely breathe. How fast her heart had beaten, and how she had pressed her lips to his.

Leo looked at her as if he knew exactly what she was thinking about. And maybe he wasn't as cool as he was pretending to be right now either?

"The pact expires in three days." Ruby couldn't take her eyes off his. She wondered if he even heard what she was saying. She knew she was going to have a hard time concentrating on anything right now. "Until then, let's just act normal."

It looked like that brought him out of his trance. "That makes sense," he replied with a smile. "It's only three days away, after all."

Grinning, she raised her shoulders. "I don't know, a lot can happen in three days," she added jokingly, trying to make the awkwardness go away.

"I..." His branch cracked and his eyes widened for a moment.

"Maybe we should go back down." She had to stop a giggle to escape her throat as she remembered that Leo had once been afraid of heights. While she didn't know if that was still the case, she didn't want to laugh at him for it. He was back on the ground remarkably quickly, though.

They didn't discuss much more on the way back to Granny's house. Except that Leo wanted to be the one to tell the pack about the new plans. Ruby agreed. She was probably still way too confused to form coherent sentences anyway. And at least he agreed with her now!

"A ghost party!" she then exclaimed simply, eyes gleaming. Leo wasn't quite as excited as she was. "You know, instead of a costume party. So everyone, including the villagers, can easily turn a bedsheet or something into a costume and join in."

He laughed. "Yeah ... yeah that might actually work."

"Told you, it'll be fine." She had to look somewhere else to keep from tripping over her own feet, and then she saw the house a few feet away from them again.

Their goodbyes were strange. It wasn't until they were standing right in front of the fence that protected the garden from stray wild animals that Leo spoke again. In fact, he reached for her hand to stop her from going any further, and her heartbeat uncomfortably fast. "Hey Red..." Why was he so close again? Was he trying to show her that it made her nervous too? "Three days." Involuntarily, she gasped.

Smiling, he let go of her, and quietly she replied, "Three days, Leo."

NINE

Found Children

Later, on the way home, the mood was incredible. Leo barely got to finish the sentence before everyone was happily jumping around in a circle. A costume party they could all attend didn't happen every day.

Nikki didn't even ask her about Greta. It was nice to see everyone so happy, albeit loud as hell. When Ruby got home and plopped down on a chair in the kitchen, she was able to breathe again for the first time.

"Busy day?" asked Catherine, placing a sandwich and a glass of water in front of her.

"Mmm," Ruby replied as she took a big bite. She really wanted nothing more than to relax for a few minutes, but her mom was unusually energetic as she stood up and put her dishes in the sink.

Briskly, she turned to her daughter, and a strange smell hit Ruby. It was a mixture of the smells her mother always had on her: mint and strawberry, but there was something else. Something Ruby couldn't place. But she dismissed the thought as Catherine began to speak. "It's a good thing you're early today so we can do our rounds together. I was thinking, if it's still light out, we can..."

"Um, Mom?", Ruby interrupted her. Catherine immediately paused and smiled at her. "Do you think we could turn the village fair into a ghost party this year?"

"A ghost party?" she repeated, confused. It obviously wasn't what she had expected.

"Well, like a costume party, but with ghosts. So everyone can just use old bed sheets. It would be something different than usual."

She frowned, but her expression remained amused. "I can tell you've put some thought into this."

Ruby nervously wiped a few crumbs from her lips. "So, do you think the village would go along with it?"

Her mom took a few seconds before answering, settling back into her seat at the table. "I'm not very fond of costumes, but I think the kids would definitely enjoy it. And some of the others might, too. It can't hurt to bring up the idea."

Ruby was surprised by this statement. But also happy. "Then I'll tell everyone on the village walk today about it. You know, see what they think."

Catherine grinned. "Like anyone could refuse when you give them food."

Ruby giggled. In fact, it was very rare for anyone to refuse her anything. Did it have something to do with the food? She didn't think so. Most of the time she didn't have food with her when she asked people for something.

That evening, they walked together, first to Greta's house. She and her brother thought it was a terrific idea, but soon had to send Ruby and Catherine away because her stepmother had a headache. Matteo and his mother were also enthusiastic and offered to sew some costumes for the villagers.

Ruby was happy through and through. Everyone on her route wanted to make this year's festival a ghost party. She hadn't expected so much approval. Not so quickly, anyway.

Despite the joy, Ruby fell into bed that night more exhausted than usual. Her stomach grumbled, but she didn't want to get up and walk through the dark house again. As she closed her eyes, she remembered the moment with Leo that day. And the memories that came with it. Had the pact really started a year ago?

In her dreams, she found herself in the forest. Leo was walking in front of her, pulling her along by his hand. He turned to her. *You love surprises.* Looked at her with those beautiful brown eyes. She couldn't stop looking at him. *I wanted to kiss you.* He leaned forward and ...

Ruby woke up. It was still dark outside, but the rain was already hitting the roof. It had to be early in the morning. Ruby didn't usually wake up before sunrise. And suddenly she remembered what she had dreamed. She felt the blood rush to her cheeks. No, it didn't mean anything. Leo and she were just friends. For the next three days - no, now only two days - they were just friends. Her dream had absolutely nothing to do with what had happened yesterday. Nothing had happened! They had just made this plan. Talked about Holly. And about their pact ...

Ruby turned to her other side and tried to go back to sleep. Unfortunately, her mind was going crazy. In her half-asleep state, she dreamed of his hands on her skin, his closeness, his lips ...

She jerked her eyes open before she could imagine a kiss. No! She couldn't think about him like that! It would make everything terribly difficult! Their pact hadn't expired yet. They were still friends. Just friends. At least for the next two days.

It was only after half an hour that she had calmed down enough to close her eyes and yet again sink into a state of restless sleep. Her dreams, however, did not allow her to relax quite as much as she had hoped. When she woke up, she was still terribly tired. And incredibly confused.

"Good morning, Ruby." Unfortunately, Catherine looked up as her daughter entered the kitchen and discovered dark circles under Ruby's eyes. "Hey, are you getting sick?" She immediately got up from her seat and placed the back of her hand on Ruby's forehead.

"No, no," Ruby said quickly. "I just didn't sleep well." She felt her cheeks heat up and turned to walk to the refrigerator. "Is there any apple pie left?" Sugar was just what she needed right now. And Granny's apple pie was still the best apple pie in the village, even after two days.

She ignored her mom's raised eyebrows. "For breakfast?" she asked. "At least have some tea with it."

Ruby couldn't help herself. Her mom poured her a cup of peppermint tea, then sat back down in her seat. "You do realize Granny's going to tell you some things when she sees you with those dark circles under your eyes?" she said, taking a sip from her own cup.

"I know," Ruby nodded, annoyed. For some reason, dark circles reinforced Granny's view that teenagers were lazy. Ruby didn't understand the logic, but contradicting Granny didn't help either. It'd only make her bitchy again.

"Can you wake me up when you leave?" asked Ruby after a few moments. Fatigue threatened to overtake her, and she didn't want to visit her grandmother in this state.

Hopefully, she wouldn't dream about Leo again. Leo. She shook the name out of her head.

Yet again, her mom raised her eyebrows. "And you're sure you're not getting sick?"

Ruby acknowledged her mother's furrowed brow with a shake of her head, then went upstairs. She didn't bother undressing again but settled into bed with her clothes on for the day. She really didn't care what anyone would say about it. She was too tired.

At least this time a certain wolf did not disturb her dreams. Instead, she saw ghosts and spirits gathered in the village, and all of them had the voice of the old witch who had told them about the curse of the wolves a year ago. It was really creepy. When she awoke, Ruby wondered whether a night of ghosts was really such a good idea. What if no one but the wolves wore costumes? What if the pack gave themselves away, and someone started hunting them?

For better or worse, Ruby saw that there was more to this plan than just a party. And she saw that this little bit of dreaming could hardly replace a night of good sleep. And now it was too late anyway. She heard her mom's footsteps coming up the stairs.

"Ruby?" She knocked gently on the open door. "I've got to go. Are you sure you're okay?"

"Yeah," Ruby croaked, scowling and pushing the covers aside. Her mouth was dry, and her eyelids felt like weights were hanging from them.

Catherine didn't seem entirely convinced. But she just sighed and began her daily lecture. "Okay ... Please remember to always be polite, and to knock. And always say please and thank you."

After Catherine left the house, Ruby ran downstairs to the kitchen. She drank her still-warm tea quickly, glad she didn't burn her tongue on it, and took a piece of apple pie with her on the way.

By the time Ruby arrived in the woods, there was only one bite of the pastry left. The pack showed up and Ruby fortunately didn't choke. But she had to be careful that none of the children stole the food from her hand.

"Hi," she greeted the pack, careful not to look Leo in the eye. She didn't know how her face would react if she did.

"Is that pie?", Shawn asked her, getting dangerously close to her breakfast.

"Yes," Ruby grinned. The boy was always hungry. Always. His eyes were wide and fixed on the pastry in her hand. But if she gave anything, she'd have to give everyone something. And she certainly didn't have enough on her for that.

"Cherry or apple?"

"Apple."

She watched as he nearly tripped over his own feet to stay further from the food. "Apple. Mmm ... apple pie is my favorite!"

"Shawn, stop trying to talk Ruby out of her breakfast!" shouted Leo. Startled, Ruby winced. How had he overheard everything? Why was he so close?

In an inattentive moment, she turned her head in his direction, catching his gaze. Damn. This time she almost tripped over her own feet herself. She had to tear herself away with everything she had and get her thoughts in order. *Don't think about the dreams!*

Or about the pact!

Damn it.

"But I'm hungry!" said Shawn, pulling Ruby out of her head. She laughed with the others, trying to remember what had happened before. And to not look at Leo.

Relieved, Ruby realized that for now the focus was on the conversation between the two boys. And that Leo was definitely not looking at her anymore. So, she could stuff the last piece of apple pie into her mouth and watch her feet do their job pretty well.

Nikki came up to her, and luckily the first thing she said didn't have anything to do with her strange behavior. And surprisingly, not with Greta either. "Isn't it cool that we can go to the ghost party?"

"Yeah," Ruby replied in surprise. "Well, I haven't told everyone in the village yet, but most of them really like the idea."

Nikki grinned. "Of course! It's a *great* idea, why wouldn't they like it?"

"Yeah ... Matteo even suggested to sew some costumes. I could bring some ... Or do you think your parents can handle it? With the costumes for all of you? Do they think it's too dangerous for you to go?"

"I don't know," she admitted. "Honestly, Leo didn't want us to tell them. He wants to do it. And if you ask me, it's better that way. The guys don't necessarily have the greatest talent for breaking news." She looked at Shawn, Corey and Will, the youngest of the group, who were climbing trees and hanging onto branches at a breathtaking pace. Ruby was surprised that those three had been able to keep it a secret until now.

"Yeah, I'll take your word for it," Ruby muttered.

Nikki tossed her hair back, glancing at a person behind the boys who was talking non-stop with Philippa. "You know, Mike said this morning that we should just - how did he put it? - *make use of the freedom of the forest and not go to a* - and I quote - *childish festival.* In his opinion, we can only do no wrong if we stay where we're allowed too." Ruby looked at her friend in shock. Mike didn't know her very well, although he, like Leo, had been in some of her classes at school. That he held these views as a wolf himself was not something she would have expected. She would not have expected that anyone held those views

Her gaze also wandered over to Mike. "Well, I don't think it's a bad idea if it doesn't hurt anyone, and ... Wait a minute..." Looking over more closely, Ruby spotted Leo and also recognized who was walking next to him. Surprised, she stopped. "Zola?" She had been so intent on not looking at Leo that she almost didn't notice the slender, dark-skinned girl surrounded by the group.

Nikki also paused, looking around for the girl who had recently disappeared from the village. "Oh yes, she and Zander joined us last night. The two of them got lost on the way out of the woods and then luckily showed up at our houses."

"On their way out of the woods?" Ruby repeated, confused. Slowly starting to walk again. "I thought they had been kidnapped! They suddenly disappeared."

Nikki looked at her reassuringly, and at that moment Ruby discovered the dark circles under her eyes. "Believe me, it was a surprise to all of us. We also thought they had been snatched and then we were awakened by them at night. It turns out they ran away from home."

By now Leo and Zola had realised that they were being talked about, and they caught up to the two girls. Ruby couldn't take her eyes off them but was determined to look past Leo.

"Little Red!" the petite girl with the tight corkscrew curls exclaimed when they were only a few feet away. Surprisingly, Zola hugged her and held her close for a moment longer than necessary. Ruby hadn't noticed how worried she actually was about the siblings until she was in that hug. And all this despite the fact that the two had never been particularly good friends. True, Zola had been in Leo's class and gone out with him for a while, but these days Catherine usually took over her part of the village round.

They exchanged a few pleasantries, though nothing Ruby didn't already know. About Zola doing well now she and her brother were no longer wandering in the woods. About Ruby being glad she was better now and would definitely tell Catherine. About Zola being sorry she hadn't been able to tell her she was running away before it happened, and about them always appreciating her Granny's food.

Eventually Leo and Zola moved away again, and as they walked the girl put her arm around him. And Ruby had to force herself not to stare at them.

TEN

A Secret

Granny Annie was in a good mood. When Ruby arrived, Lisette wasn't there yet, but Granny was already preparing a big pot of tea, and a plate of cookies was already draped on the living room table. Ruby stole one for herself after shaking out the sofa cushions.

"Well, does it taste good?" Her Granny stood in the doorway, hands on hips, but the wrinkles around her eyes showed she meant no harm.

It was nice that there was no harm in her taking cookies and doing unwanted things today, because she was hungry and tired. And at the same time too exhilarated by her recent discovery to focus only on that. "Hmm," she replied with her mouth full. "Do you have any bread left? I'm really hungry today." She'd rather not mention that she hadn't eaten a lot for breakfast.

"In the kitchen, where it always is," Granny replied. That sounded more like her grandmother. The old woman frowned, and Ruby was expecting some comment about the bags under her eyes or her big appetite, but there was none of that.

"Thank you!" Granted, she was also quick to take the teapot from her Granny's hand, and hurry to the kitchen. So, if Granny were to make a comment, it would probably even be appropriate.

Normally her Granny hated it when Ruby took things out of her hand, but today she maybe even saw it as a sign of her good parenting. Or she was in too good a mood for it to bother her. Ruby didn't hear her mumbling to herself even once, and when she poked her head into the living room again, her grandmother actually smiled. It was tiny, but it was there.

"Do you need anything else? Anything else you want me to get?", Ruby wanted to know, letting her gaze glide around the room.

"I don't think so." Just then, there was a knock on the door. Granny's expression brightened considerably once again. "Oh, can you answer it? It's Lisette!"

Lisette was similarly excited, but she always was. She pulled Ruby into a hug without asking, then strode confidently down the hall to the living room with her long legs and fluttering dress. Ruby could hear the two women greeting each other and retreated to the kitchen.

There weren't many dishes from the evening that needed cleaning, and she had quickly washed her own cup of tea as well. So, Ruby decided to take things a little more relaxed that day and relax outside in the sun.

Well, as she was about to do that, she heard Anna and Elsa begging for food, and had to take care of them for a moment, or she would have felt guilty. But as the two pecked happily in the sun, Ruby was able to sit back. It wasn't too long before she dozed off.

In her dream, ghosts were again roaming the village, but this time it wasn't spooky. She heard familiar voices behind some of the costumes, but she couldn't make them all out. Nikki was there, talking to another ghost. Her mom was wearing an old bed sheet along with her favorite brown boots. And Greta was walking around as usual with her little brother in her arms. Even the baby was wearing a white cape.

Suddenly Ruby bumped into a person, but before she could make out who it was, he took her hands in his. They were soft and warm, and without hearing his voice, she knew immediately who it was.

"Hey," Leo said.

"Hi," she replied.

"Our pact expires in two days," he reminded her. "Do you know what you're going to do yet?"

If he could have seen her face in this costume, he would know that she was biting her lip, unsure what to say. "Leo..." She hadn't thought about it yet. In fact, she believed she would know somehow when the time came. After all, nothing should come between them now. Not until two days from now.

She didn't see his face, but she knew he was looking at her curiously. "Red?"

When she awoke, the chickens were still clucking happily in the run, and Granny and Lisette in the living room. No one had paid any attention to what she was doing. Or noticed that she had fallen asleep.

Sighing, she turned to her tasks, for sleep was obviously no longer her friend. The dreams were getting more and more confusing and she didn't want to think about what they might mean.

The vegetables were happy to be watered, as dry as the earth was underneath. And in the apple trees hung some beautiful red fruit that would make wonderful strudels.

When Ruby finally put everything in the kitchen, her wet hair clung to her forehead. The work could be exhausting, but fortunately it also distracted her from her thoughts. As she drank some water, her stomach grumbled. She still hadn't had a proper meal.

The girl grabbed a plate, a knife, and a piece of bread. In addition, there was some cheese, which she had brought from the village a few days ago, and a jar of jam, of which there was always enough of. Then she went outside again.

By now, the sun was at its peak. It looked as if Ruby had slept longer than she had intended. Soon it would be time for Granny Annie's nap, but Ruby hoped she was in such a good mood today that she put it off a little longer, and instead spent the time laughing with Lisette. She took a big bite of the bread, enjoying the sun on her skin.

The next few hours passed, and nothing happened. Granny didn't check on her or call out, Ruby only heard the occasional laugh from the two women. When Lisette left, she once again pulled the girl into a tight hug. She, too, was in a better mood than usual.

Granny still had enough energy to prepare her own dough and let Ruby eat an apple. "Look, and if you want the dough to be extra soft and moist, you need one thing: butter."

Granny was in such a good mood that Ruby didn't call her out on the fact that she had learned this from her when she was seven. Back then, they had baked a lot together and eaten even more. Today, they shared chores and gave most of the food away.

"Sleep tight, Granny," Ruby said as the old woman went to her room.

As usual, Ruby grabbed two books and headed off into the woods. Today, she wasn't so sure whether she actually wanted to go there. Or, well, whether she wanted to run into Leo. After everything that had happened yesterday, and what she had dreamed, she would rather keep her distance for a while. But wouldn't that be strange? After all, they were still friends!

Arriving at her usual tree, she considered going straight to the split tree. There was a good possibility he wouldn't check on her there and she would have her peace, but that would somehow be even meaner than not showing up at all.

So instead, she sank down on the grass, leaned her back against the wide trunk, and opened her book. The words blurred before her eyes. She had to concentrate to keep from falling asleep. Maybe she should just get comfortable? Allow herself a little nap?

No, then she would probably have strange dreams again. And she didn't want that.

She waited and waited, and just as her eyes were getting used to reading the lines and not just staring at them, he appeared. "Hi, little forest fairy," he greeted her, settling down beside her. Fortunately, if he noticed her holding her breath, he didn't say anything.

When his arm brushed hers, she involuntarily gasped. "You have terrible timing," she explained to him, trying to sound as composed as ever. "When I least expect you, you show up."

Grinning, she looked at him. Convincing enough! She almost believed herself.

Leo absently ran a hand through his tangled hair. "Sorry, I would have been here sooner, but there was a problem in the pack."

For a moment, she managed to forget everything that had happened between them. That didn't sound good at all. "A problem? What's going on?"

"Oh, nothing much ... Corey fell out of a tree and must have sprained his ankle." It was obvious he had noticed her reaction and was trying to calm her down. A sprained foot didn't really sound like nothing. But maybe in the pack with all those crazy kids, it wasn't as big a deal as it was in Ruby's world.

"Oh..." It was difficult to not look away. At least when she didn't want to let her mind wander.

Leo must have noticed that she wasn't convinced yet, because his voice took on an even more reassuring tone. "He's fine. He was just fooling around with Shawn again, jumping over rocks, hiding in bushes and climbing trees. That's just what happens sometimes." Immediately, Ruby had the image of this morning in her mind: the three boys hanging from a tree.

"It's almost funny that nothing ever happened before," she countered.

"Absolutely." Leo scratched the back of his head. "I've told him so many times to get a grip. To not fool around so much..."

Suddenly Ruby had to laugh. She didn't even really know why. "Well, but he's seven!" she interjected. "Weren't you like that when you were seven?"

"Not really." A definite lie. They had gone to the same school then, and Ruby could remember it like it was yesterday.

She raised her eyebrows. "Well, I remember when you used to get in real trouble during recess because you were always fighting with Toni and Bruno ... Only to make up with them the next day."

"That was different," he laughed.

"What was so different about it?" she teased him. It was business as usual again, no nervousness. "Instead of falling out of trees, you were fighting. It's just childish behavior in my eyes, too."

"Well Ellie thought it was good," he replied, as if it were a killer argument. He knew it would get a reaction out of Ruby.

"Well, of course she liked it! She liked everything you did. She was totally into you." That hadn't been a secret. At least among the girls. But Ellie had actually just always adored him.

"I know." He sounded almost shy. But it didn't surprise Ruby one bit. He and Ellie had dated secretly for a while. When they were older, of course. It was when they were thirteen, Nikki had caught them making out once and told Ruby about it.

"I just mean there's still hope for Corey to become charming and sensible someday, too," she returned to the initial topic.

"So, you think I'm charming and sensible?" he replied, smiling. Oh no! She hadn't meant it that way.

"I didn't say that..." Her cheeks grew warm, and she turned away, pretending to look around for something.

After all, he was gentleman enough not to dwell on it. After a few moments, the silence became almost unbearable. Ruby cleared her throat. "Let's walk a bit," she suggested. Walking would help her. Calm her nerves.

She scrambled to her feet before Leo could offer her his hand. Then they started walking slowly. "So ... Zola has joined you," she began a new conversation.

It was good that he got right into it. "And Zander," Leo added. Zander was Zola's 'little' brother, though he was not so little anymore. He was sixteen or eighteen. Ruby wasn't so sure about that, but he was tall and thin like his sister. Even a few inches taller.

Ruby found it a little harder than usual to concentrate on their conversation. Leo was so close. So close that she could feel his warmth. But she wasn't going to let that distract her. "Where was he? I didn't see him at all this morning."

Leo's expression was matter-of-fact, but she still wondered if he was having such trouble staying with it, too. "In the village." It took Ruby a moment to understand that he meant the wolf village, not her village. "Asleep. Mom thinks he stayed awake the night before to protect Zola and was completely wiped out because of it."

Ruby nodded; it made sense. But something was still weird about the whole thing. "I still don't understand what actually happened. Do you know why they ran away? From Fairy Town, I mean."

His eyes narrowed. It seemed he didn't know what to say. Or whether he was allowed to. How much had Zola and he talked in the last few hours? How many secrets had been exchanged? "I don't think anything really happened at all. But their stepmother has never treated them particularly well, and now that they're both old enough, they've just decided they're not going to put up with it anymore."

Nothing new. Evelyn had never been particularly kind to children. Not even to her own. But Leo's wording didn't please Ruby at all. "What do you mean *never treated them particularly well*?" The dread was audible in her voice. She almost tripped over a big root.

He cleared his throat. "It ... it's not my place to tell you."

It wasn't like her, but she ignored what he'd said. "She didn't hit them, did she?" Ruby squeezed out incredulously.

The look on his face told her she was right. And the slight shake of his head that she wasn't supposed to know. "Red..."

His voice was low. Still, she was abruptly reminded of her dream, and almost winced. She had to look away to keep from losing her composure. At least she spotted a squirrel that she could focus on for a few seconds. That helped.

"You can't tell anyone, Red," he said seriously. It really did seem like a secret. "No one."

She nodded quickly. "I won't." Suddenly she felt so much less jealousy of Zola, and so much more compassion. "Is there anything I can do?" The need to help was great, and she even forgot for a moment what had happened between Leo and her.

"I don't know," he answered honestly. "It's probably best if you don't let on that you know."

Ruby didn't realize they had arrived at the split tree until they were standing right in front of it. "Oh," she let out. It was as stunning as ever, so beautiful that Ruby didn't want to think about what had happened here yesterday. What she still had to deal with.

"That's actually one of the reasons I wanted to talk to you," Leo began. He seemed composed, but Ruby tried to convince herself that he was a little nervous, too.

"That? The ... tree?" she stammered, though of course she knew it definitely wasn't about the tree. But she was stunned. And speechless.

"Uh ... no." A nervous laugh. She tried to join in, but they both sounded miserable. At some point, Leo managed to compose himself. "Listen ... I think I should tell you ... Zola and I are ..."

"Leo," she interjected quickly. She didn't want to hear what he had to say. Well, she wanted to hear it, but she didn't want to at the same time. Because if he said it, then she would know. And if she knew, then it would change things between them. "What's between you and Zola is none of my business. Our pact doesn't expire for two days," she reminded him. "And until then, we're friends. Just friends."

He swallowed. "Friends," he repeated, nodding.

Ruby had to avert her eyes and looked at the tree instead. Her beautiful split tree. The one that had never let her down before. And when she dared to look in its direction again, Leo was on his way there. With elegant movements he climbed up, sat where they had sat yesterday. Sat where Ruby had sat as a child.

He smiled, this time it looked real.

And she followed him.

Neither Ruby nor Leo said a word as she climbed the tree as well. But his hand reached for hers when she was almost there, and though she didn't need his help, she let him pull her up the last bit.

Once again, they sat side by side on their split tree.

And let it work its magic.

Ruby took a deep breath. "Do you think it will ever be alright?" she asked. And she didn't just mean the thing with Zola and Zander and their violent stepmother. But also the wolves being banished from the village, the poverty of the villagers, and so much more that they had no influence over. That they could not change.

It surprised her when Leo reached for her hand, however, she did not pull it away. Instead, she allowed their fingers to intertwine. His gaze was piercing as he looked at her, and his tone was determined. "We'll get our happy ending someday," he assured her.

She couldn't help herself. She had to believe him.

ELEVEN

Swans and other Teases

In the evening, Zander had joined the pack and greeted Ruby with a polite smile. It was good that he was there, because the pack had someone other than Ruby to rally around.

Fortunately, Leo stayed at the back of the group, and made no move to approach Ruby. While she wanted to continue to be friends with him, after everything that had happened in the last few days, she didn't really know how to look at him. This was exactly what was not supposed to happen. This was exactly what they had created the pact for.

Nikki walked beside her, not noticing that today Ruby's mind was somewhere else. Even though she couldn't see Leo, she thought she could feel his eyes on her. If Nikki did wonder at some point about her current lack of conversational skills, Ruby planned to simply bring up a topic that the whole pack would want to deal with: The party in two days.

They were already halfway there when Nikki suddenly gave her a wry look. But instead of voicing what she was actually thinking, she nodded to the bags over Ruby's shoulder. "You don't have to carry all these by yourself. Come on, pass me some."

"Thanks." She didn't resist this time, which earned her another questioning look.

But unlike Ruby, Nikki knew how to mask her confusion. Or she believed it didn't matter. Instead, she slung a few bags over her shoulder with ease. "No problem," she announced loud enough for the others to hear. "Somebody's got to help you out when there are obviously no gentlemen around to make themselves useful."

Indeed, everyone was staring at Nikki, and as Ruby let her gaze slide over the whole pack with interest, it lingered on Leo for a brief moment. Who was also looking her in the eye.

Fortunately, Luke didn't take his sister's shameless allegation without objection. Although he, too, had walked a few feet away, his words reached them loud and clear. "Oh Nikki, you're always talking about being emancipated. But that also means you have to ask for my help when you need it." He and Mike laughed, and a couple of the younger ones joined in.

Nikki's eyebrows drew together suspiciously. "That's not what being emancipated means at all." And without any warning, Nikki grabbed a large, juicy mushroom that was growing by the side of the path, already nibbled on by some slugs, and threw it at Luke with incredible speed. It definitely would have hit him, too, if her brother hadn't ducked away swiftly.

Still, everyone laughed, and when Shawn, Will, and a limping Corey also threw mushrooms at each other, the initial topic was forgotten rather quickly.

Saying goodbye was harder than usual. Ruby didn't remember how she usually did it. Say goodbye? Just walk away? Waving?

That day she mumbled a goodbye and tried to make her face look relaxed while keeping herself from looking at Leo. She couldn't make out what he was doing on his part, but when she looked back once more after a few seconds, she saw him and Zola walking at the end of the group again, engaged in deep conversation.

Her mom wasn't home yet when she arrived at the house. It was a little unusual. Ruby was rarely alone.

Did it have something to do with this man? The man she had kissed in town? Was Catherine late because of him?

Ruby quickly dismissed the thought. Although curiosity urged her to confront her mom, she knew she wasn't supposed to know anything. If her mom wanted to keep it a secret, it should probably stay one. In the end, Ruby didn't want Catherine digging around in her secrets either.

So, Ruby decided to act like she always did. Making her mom feel like something was different would probably not make her trust her daughter more. She placed her bags on the table and divided up the food for all the families. Then she treated herself to an evening snack.

Today, she had slipped the pack a little more food - and taken it from her own ration, so she bit into a dry piece of bread from three days ago. After all, the wolves now had two more mouths to feed.

Ruby heard a noise from the door, and quickly closed the cupboard where she had taken the food from. A moment later, her mother stepped through the door.

Resting her hands on her hips, Ruby stood up. "You're late, young lady," she commented in mock anger as Catherine entered the kitchen. This moment, when she could have some fun with her mom, was the perfect opportunity to forget the day's events and carry on as if nothing had happened.

The familiar look appeared on her mom's face: raised eyebrows, pursed lips. "Excuse me?" she asked, "It's not that late." She glanced at her imaginary wristwatch. "Only half past you-have-lost-your-mind."

"Your watch must be broken," Ruby replied, furrowing her brow as Catherine sometimes did. Then she looked at her free wrist herself. "It's already after your-hair-stands-up-to-all-sides o'clock," she then added.

A loud laugh escaped Catherine, then she undid the knot at the back of her head and retied it. "Let's get something to eat. Are you hungry?"

Nodding, Ruby dropped into a chair while her mom made herself some tea. "Very. Will you come and do the village walk later?" she asked Catherine then relaxed again. The girl knew full well that her mom's feet must hurt. And her knees, as she repeated whenever asked. But at the same time, she wouldn't openly admit it, and was eager to spend time with her daughter, which she declared even more often.

"Yes, I'll come with you," Catherine said quickly. "Just let me get something to eat." She reached into the bag that, as always, was meant for her, and pulled out a roll. "Mmmh, Granny's been productive again," she commented on the abundance of bags as she lowered herself into her seat. Apparently, she hadn't yet noticed that her own wasn't quite as full as the others that day.

"Yeah, she was in a good mood when I arrived," Ruby replied innocently, helping herself to a cookie.

"Oh yeah, what did you do today?" she started a conversation that passed for *quality time* between her and Ruby.

"Nothing much." Ruby almost blushed as she thought about her afternoon in the woods. But she forced herself to smile and instead talked about her book, which she hadn't read in a while. "It's about a girl trapped in another world. Really interesting!"

"What I would do to be young again and have time to read!" affirmed Catherine. "There aren't enough hours in the day to do everything that wants to be done." Although she struck a cheerful tone, there was something wistful in her voice.

Ruby hadn't thought about the fact that her mom had dreams, too. Dreams she hadn't yet achieved and might never achieve. Because she wasn't young anymore and didn't have time for them. The girl had to stop herself from thinking about whether she would feel the same way later, and instead remembered Leo's words. *We'll get our happy ending someday.* It put a little smile on her face. But then she quickly caught herself again. "Um...how was your day?" she asked, seeing her mom being pulled out of her own thoughts.

"Oh, just work, and some annoying customers. But that's nothing new." It almost sounded like she wasn't telling Ruby everything either, but the girl didn't elaborate.

And after they had eaten and talked about this and that, they walked off to finish their village walk before it got too dark.

The common route, too, led them first to Greta and Hannes' house. Ruby knocked on the heavy wooden door as usual. When no one opened after a few seconds, she banged on it again, this time harder. More seconds passed, during which the two women stood impatiently in front of the house.

"Knock again," Catherine urged her. Ruby did as she was told. Her fist pounded against the wood, but nothing moved. After a few moments, Catherine made another attempt, but when nothing happened this time either, she simply turned around.

"Mom," Ruby stopped her. "We can't just leave! What if something happened to them?" It was fear that spoke from the girl. She had never known anyone not to open the door for her. Most of the time it was Greta, and sometimes Hannes, very rarely their mother, who then snapped at her and ordered her not to bother them any further. But there had never been a day when *no one* showed up.

"Don't worry about it. Just because they don't open the door for once, doesn't mean something has happened," Catherine tried to reassure her daughter.

But the girl in the red leather jacket would not settle for that. "But what if their stepmother sent them to bed without food? They barely get enough food as it is. We can't let that happen!"

"They probably just went to bed early. Made themselves some soup or ate leftovers from yesterday. It won't be anything bad." There was something gentle in her mother's voice, but at the same time it was firm. As much as she enjoyed running around the village to help her neighbors and friends, it was exhausting to be out all day.

Reluctantly, Ruby let herself be persuaded to keep going. But her mom was right when she said "Come on, the others are probably hungry already." Still, she looked back once more. Maybe she would spot some movement, a light, anything that could tell her what was going on in the house.

But nothing.

Matteo and his mother were already expecting them that evening. And as Catherine was putting their food away in the kitchen, like she always did when she was there, the boy came up to Ruby excitedly.

"Come, I want to show you something," he said, and led her into a part of the living room that was full of shoe parts, fabrics and leather. There, next to his old sewing machine, was a grey and white material. Only when Matteo lifted it to show her did she realize what it was.

"Costumes!" she exclaimed excitedly. They were ghost costumes, smaller pieces of fabric than sheets, with eyes and mouths cut out. If you wore it, you could probably see and talk, and walk, with no problem, since Ruby estimated they went to above the knee at most.

"Yes," he grinned delightedly. "After getting my chores done early today, I set to work on it. These two are already done, and this one just needs a decent hem."

Impressed, Ruby looked at him. She had known he was good, but this was far more than she had expected. Besides, she hadn't even thought he would sew a few costumes just like that. Not knowing who they were for or if it was even going to happen at the party. So, she told him that, too.

"As convinced as you were about it, I can't imagine it not happening." She stared at him, and he grinned. "You know Little Red, it's hard not to like you, and if you told the others on your route just as enthusiastically about the idea, half the village is on your side already anyway. You know what I mean?"

Embarrassed, she laughed. "I ... yeah, you're probably right."

"Ruby?" Her mom's polite voice rescued Ruby from this strange situation. She didn't have to speak up, because the house wasn't exactly huge, and the living room even less so. "Let's go on, it's getting late."

When Matteo's mom once again tried to give Catherine money for bringing them food - as she always did when Ruby's mom was around - Ruby turned to Matteo once again. "Hey, thanks for the costumes. I honestly wasn't expecting it."

"No problem at all, Little Red," he replied with a smile.

The next stops along their way were less exciting, but just as enjoyable. While Ruby and Catherine didn't talk about Leo or pacts or crazy dreams, they delivered food to everyone who opened their doors. At Zola and Zander's house, Ruby briefly wished she could tell her mom everything she knew. For example, that the pack was now taking care of them. That would have implied, however, that she could talk about the wolves and that Catherine saw no danger in them.

Instead, at this point, it was up to Ruby to reassure her mom when no one answered the door. "I'm sure they're fine."

In the darkness, she could see Catherine nodding mutely, and wished she could have told her more clearly. *They are fine. They're with friends.* But that wasn't an option.

When they arrived home some time later, Ruby yawned loudly. She had completely forgotten how tired she had been all day today. With everything that had happened, there hadn't been time for it.

That night she fell into her bed and fell asleep immediately. No dreams haunted her, and she felt good and refreshed when she made her way back to Granny's the next morning.

"Hi," she greeted the pack and Leo. His eyes were fixed on her, but no one noticed because their attention was on Ruby. Thinking of Shawn's hunger yesterday, she handed out cookies and pressed a few more into Zola's hand. With a nod, she pointed at Zander who didn't seem to want to take anything from her. She smiled gratefully at Ruby.

Shawn couldn't hide his happiness. "Thank you, Little Red!" he exclaimed loudly, hugging her so suddenly that she almost tripped over him. Everyone laughed.

"Here you go, Shawn. I'm glad you like it." She joined in the laughter as well, trying to relax.

"Take it easy, Shawn," Mike said, putting an arm around his little brother. "You won't go hungry forever."

"Are you speaking from experience there?" asked the small but smart Mara, which got her a few laughs. She looked up at the boy, who was almost three heads taller than her.

"Yeah," Corey now agreed. "As big as you are, I'm sure you've devoured a rhino at some point."

Amidst the general laughter, Ruby's gaze went to Leo. His posture was relaxed, and when Zola nudged him and whispered something in his ear, he laughed. It stung, but Ruby had brought it on herself. After all, she had insisted on keeping the pact yesterday. *Just one more day*, it flashed through her mind. Tomorrow everything would be allowed, but somehow, she wasn't sure if Leo even wanted that anymore.

For a moment, she wished she had let him finish yesterday. What had he wanted to say? *Zola and I are ...* what?

"How about you just practice for the ghost party already and make yourself invisible, Mara?" countered Mike now, starting a battle of mild insults amongst the group. Ruby deliberately stayed out of it and made fun of the undeniably stupid comments with Nikki.

It was almost all back to normal.

They even almost missed the space where they normally said goodbye, but luckily it could be prevented at the last moment. "Oh hey," Ruby broke through the banter. "I've got to get going. I'll see you tonight, okay?"

In a surprisingly good mood, the girl finally walked the last bit to her grandmother's house. She almost just walked in, but at the last second, she remembered her promise to always knock. "Grandmother! It's me!" she shouted into the hallway as she entered the house. With aching shoulders, she walked into the kitchen and put down the heavy backpack. That day she had brought milk, cheese, and empty jars of jam that her Granny could make better use of than anyone else in the village.

"Granny?" called Ruby again when she still didn't hear a response. She was usually in the living room, which was easy to hear from the kitchen. Ruby poked her head into the next room but didn't spot Granny behind the couch searching for her perpetually lost glasses nor in her favorite chair.

Strange.

Was she still asleep, perhaps? No, she couldn't have been. Granny Annie was always upset that the youth of today would sleep too late. Would miss the day. She wouldn't stay in bed until ten o'clock.

A peek into her bedroom confirmed Ruby's assumption. No sign of her grandmother.

The girl knocked on the bathroom door, heard nothing, and ultimately went back to the kitchen. That's when she saw it: the open back door. In the garden, her Granny was bending over the vegetable patch.

"Granny!" she called, and saw the woman flinch. Deliberately, she struck a friendly tone. "I've been looking all over for you! What are you doing out here?" Ruby ran to her as her grandmother slowly stood up.

"Don't scare me like that," she grumbled, "Can't I take care of my own garden?" The girl could tell that her back was hurting, but she certainly wouldn't address that. Not when Granny was in a bad mood.

"I was just looking for you. Do you want me to help you? Do you want to get the cauliflower?" The vegetables next to her still looked a little too green, except for one or two, but Ruby obviously couldn't afford to question her Granny today.

"No," snapped the woman. "They're not good at all yet. I had to check to make sure the birds hadn't eaten them. Can you believe that? Birds! In my backyard! And this morning I actually saw some swans. Swans! Here! What? You think I'm crazy? The critters trampled all over my tomato plantlings."

Ruby must have looked a little confused, because when she looked at the patch her Granny was talking about, she could hardly believe her eyes. "All trampled flat! You've got to be kidding!" she exclaimed in disbelief, thinking of how painstakingly tedious it had been to plant them a few days ago.

"What are you looking at me for? I certainly didn't do that! You have to look out for those animals today, so they don't come back, you understand me? Don't let them trample down anything else," Granny instructed her, and then began to walk back toward the house.

Great! If anything happened later, it would be Ruby's fault. No matter what, no matter how bad. And Granny was in such a bad mood that not even Lisette's presence would help.

When the other woman showed up, Ruby was yapped at to put on some tea and bring some pastries into the living room. And then again because it was the wrong pastry, and again because it wasn't arranged right. She was hardly surprised that Lisette took her leave after quite a short time. And instead of lying down immediately, Granny *also* sat down in the lawn chair to make sure the swans didn't come back, and to watch Ruby work.

Thanks to the bird attack, Ruby was once again allowed to tend to the planting of the vegetable bed. But before she could do that, she tried to save the young plants, or get them out of the ground.

Of course, with comments throughout from her grandmother. "There's another one over there! Be careful! Don't step on it! To your left. Left!"

Ruby had had enough. She stretched her back and was only cursed more. She already didn't dare say anything anymore.

When Granny finally left to take her nap, Ruby wished her a restful sleep, but in fact she was just glad to have a break from this bad mood for a few hours. She tended to her plants for a while longer, knowing that Granny would get really mean if nothing was done after the break. And she reminded herself to watch out for the swans. "Swans!" she grumbled to herself. "As if swans would fly here just to trample her plants!" It had probably just been white birds, or other animals entirely. "Why would swans be hanging around?"

She was warm and sweaty. She got a drink and stood indecisively in front of the garden. Could she afford to leave the garden against Granny's clear instructions? Granny wouldn't notice if no swans appeared in the meantime. And how likely was that to happen?

Since Ruby came to visit Granny every day, she couldn't relax sitting in the garden anymore. The thought and visual reminder of all the hard work was driving her crazy. And as much as she loved Anna and Elsa, their clucking eventually got on her nerves.

So, she set off with a book to her usual spot in the forest. Only when she had sat down, leaned her back against the tree and closed her eyes for a moment, did she remember that this was usually the time when Leo appeared.

Would he come today? Would they talk as usual? Somehow, she doubted it.

Ruby took a deep breath and kept her eyes closed. Even if he wouldn't come here, this was a well-deserved break. A break she had to enjoy. After a few quiet moments, she turned to her book. And read. For the first time in ages. At least that's how it felt.

She heard his quick footsteps before he could announce himself. Instead of lifting her head to greet him, she stayed as she was. Maybe then she would be able to keep her feelings under control.

"Hey Red." Involuntarily she looked up, his smile was just amazing. If she hadn't told him yesterday that they were just friends, she would have told him that too. Now, she had to pull herself together and greet him as if it was a day like any other.

Instead of sitting down next to her, he held out a hand. "Wanna go to the split tree?"

He probably expected her to say yes, but her gaze went in the direction she had just come from. "I don't think that's a good idea." Seeing his disappointed expression, she quickly added "Granny is having a bad day. In fact, I'm actually supposed to be in the garden right now..."

He thought it was an excuse.

"Long story," she laughed, and his features relaxed a little.

Now it was his turn to sit down in his usual space next to her. "You didn't even bring me a book today." He even sounded a little hurt when he said that and looked at her with wide eyes. Like there was really no reason why anything should have changed.

Ruby lifted her shoulders apologetically. "I wasn't sure you'd show up today."

A "Why?" was clearly on his lips, but he swallowed it down. "Well, it means you'll have to talk to me now," he grinned.

And just like that, things were back to normal. There were definitely topics she didn't want to bring up, and fortunately, she didn't have to. "Did you see any swans today?"

"Swans?" he replied, puzzled. The question actually seemed to catch him off-guard, and Ruby laughed.

"Yes, Granny Annie said she saw some this morning. They trampled her vegetable beds and nibbled on a few plants," she explained.

"So today I didn't see them, but there are some in the area." Surprised, Ruby looked at him. "Yeah," he laughed. "I wouldn't have believed it either, but I always see them sitting over by the lake or flying over the woods." He nodded upward and Ruby automatically looked to maybe catch a glimpse of white feathers. But all she saw were green leaves and blue sky.

"Wow, why haven't I seen them before?" It was more a question to herself than to Leo, but by saying it out loud, she was able to avoid the weird silence between them.

"They're not near the village, and they're not around here much, so it's not unusual you don't see them."

"Unless they destroy Granny's garden."

"Hmmm..." His brow furrowed. "I wonder about that, honestly. There's something so majestic and friendly about them. The fact that they trample flower beds just doesn't make sense." When she didn't reply, he tilted his head and looked at her. "Mara once swore they were humans, well, even princes, searching for their lost sister. She begged us for days to help them."

Once again, Ruby laughed out loud. Fairy Town was magical, but not *that* magical. "Let me guess: You finally gave in and went looking for those princes."

It was meant to be sarcasm, but Leo looked at her seriously. "We really did." Then he smiled sheepishly. "When all you do is run around in the woods all day, you can use a change of scenery every now and again."

Ruby tried to ignore the sting his statement gave her. She always complained that she was just running errands and doing chores for others, but constantly staying away from others, doing nothing, and not going crazy at the same time had to be exhausting too. "So?" she finally echoed. "Did you find them?"

Reluctantly, he shook his head. "They were just gone. Mara thought they realized they were being followed, and that we should probably leave them alone when they came back so they could be peaceful and safe in the forest."

"And you listened to her?" Ruby wanted to know and was met with a caught look.

"No." His pressed lips were a sign he didn't want to say anything else, but Ruby wouldn't let up.

"Then what happened?" She tried to suppress the mischievous grin but didn't quite manage it. Nevertheless, Leo continued, albeit a bit pained.

"When they came back, I followed them. Maybe I didn't seem like a threat because I was alone, or maybe they didn't notice me, but I followed them to the lake. However, nothing exciting happened, and when at some point they ran into a small cave, I left. I couldn't see them in there anyway."

Ruby's laugh turned into a frown. "Swans don't go into caves."

It was Leo's turn to laugh. "That's what bothers you about this story?"

She nodded seriously, and his eyebrows shot up. "Maybe they really are cursed princes." But shortly after she said it, she really became aware of what she'd said, and that it was very unlikely that these were the same swans that had gotten her into so much trouble today.

"Maybe I'm a cursed prince," Leo joked, completely distracting her of her theory.

"Turned into what?" she asked with a laugh.

"A wolf, of course." His words sounded as flippant as if it were the most normal thing in the world, but Ruby winced nonetheless.

When she didn't reply, there was silence. An uncomfortable silence. Of course Leo had noticed her reaction, and she could only hope that he didn't think she was afraid of him.

"Red..." His hand reached for hers, and she could feel him wanting to talk about it. But she couldn't let him ask her whether she was afraid of him. She wasn't. Of course she wasn't. She had to find another topic.

"What's it actually like? Living in the forest?" she asked quickly. For the entire last year, she had never asked that question, for fear it was too personal, even though she had always wanted to know. And now was probably the best time to ask it.

He pressed his lips together briefly, then he answered her. "Well, it's quite normal I'd say." His gaze wandered into the distance, and she could see him trying to remember back. "It was difficult in the beginning. We couldn't live in the village anymore, but we also didn't have enough money to move to another village. Not to mention that there were already rumors there as well. And mom was afraid that we would get caught there too, and that they would try to hurt us. Then we found these old cabins in the woods, and we made one habitable. For a while we slept on the forest floor, because that was more comfortable than on the boards in the house, but by now it's quite cozy.

When Mike's family was kicked out too, we helped them get settled. And then we had to start taking care of food and other things that were needed. And even though the forest gives a lot, we had to ... had to steal some stuff." He cast a sidelong glance at Ruby, obviously embarrassed by the fact that he had stolen something. But her look told him that she didn't judge him for it. When it came right down to it, she had also stolen food from her Granny all the time so she could give it to the pack. Relieved, Leo went on. "Blankets and brooms and pots and stuff. And then Mara's family came along, too, and now we kind of have our own little village. So ... It's not so different from before. A little smaller and lonelier, but all in all not so bad."

Although Leo had talked about the village they lived in a few times before, never had he done it in so much detail. Perhaps that was a sign that she could ask him one more question that had been on her mind for a while. "What about the wolf curse? How ... What is it like?"

This time she saw him hesitate, and worried he was going to pull away the hand that was still on hers. She should have known this was going too far. But he didn’t move. Nor did he say anything.

"You don't have to answer that if you don't want to," she added quickly. "I just wanted to know..."

"It's okay," he assured her, squeezing her hand - probably subconsciously. "I just don't quite know how to explain it. I've never told anyone about this before. I mean, outside the pack."

She nodded, giving him time to find the right words.

TWELVE

Curse of the Wolves

(One year ago)

A year ago, when it all began, no one knew that such a thing as a curse of the wolves *even existed. It was only when an old witch traveling through Fairy Town told them about it. Many didn't believe what she said – or at least didn't want to believe it – until it finally happened.*

It was pitch dark outside when Leo was woken up. His sister Nikki was standing next to his bed, shaking him. "Leo? Leo! Leo!" she kept repeating in panic until he opened his eyes. Sheer terror was written all over her face.

Suddenly he was wide awake. "What's wrong?" he asked her, sitting up.

"Shhh." She held her index finger in front of her lips, then nervously glanced behind her toward the half-open door. "There are people downstairs," she whispered nervously. "Mom and Dad are talking to them, but they ... they're convinced that we're ... that we're wolves."

Upset, Leo threw back the covers and wanted to jump up. After the last few days, he was tired of listening to these conversations. They had no proof that anyone was a shapeshifter. "This is crazy! They can't just accuse everyone of being a wolf! They can't always..."

Nikki held him back. She was stronger than she looked, but her hands were shaking. "You don't understand, Leo. They're not just talking, they're threatening Mom and Dad that..."

"All the more reason to show them that we won't just let them accuse us of something so ridiculous. They can't just call us wolves and then..."

He tried to pry her hands away, but she tightened her grip. "Leo!" She was so obviously scared that Leo had to go downstairs to these people to protect her. But despite his intensified attempts, she held him back. "Right," Nikki whispered so softly he barely understood.

"What?" He paused. Was sure he must have misheard.

"They are right," the girl repeated. "That there is a wolf living here. I am the wolf, Leo. I don't know why or how, but ... It's all so terrible!"

Though it was dark, Leo saw the tears covering her cheeks. He wrapped his 13-year-old sister in his arms. "Don't you worry, it's going to be okay. Mom and Dad will work it out somehow."

The girl sat down in bed with him, her feet cold from the icy wooden floor. "Tell me what happened," he gently urged Nikki. It was still pitch black, but neither felt the need to turn on a light. Instead, Leo heard Nikki's sobs all the more clearly and put his arm around her shoulders soothingly.

"I don't know what happened. One day everything was normal, and the next I woke up in the woods. It was really weird." She ran her hand over her damp cheeks. "No one saw me, I swear. It was still dark outside, and I just went home, washed up and went to bed."

"When was that?" a voice asked from the direction of the door, and Leo felt Nikki wince beside him. But it was only Luke, her brother.

"Five days ago," she answered, pulling her legs up so he could sit down, too. "That's probably why they didn't see me, because they would have come right over, right?" Seeking agreement, she looked back and forth between the two boys. She didn't want to be the reason her family was threatened.

Leo nodded, but Luke stared at her with a blank expression. It took a moment before he could bring himself to speak. "It happened to me two days ago."

Wide-eyed, Nikki looked at him. "What?"

"The exact same thing?" added Leo.

Luke nodded. "Except it seems someone saw me," he added dryly.

Again, tears streamed down Nikki's face. She reached for Luke's hand and squeezed it. "It's not your fault," she assured him, but whether he believed her, she didn't know.

The cursing downstairs grew louder, and the three of them winced in equal measure. Nikki could tell the two boys wanted to jump up and run downstairs, even though Luke was definitely afraid of the consequences. She knew because she felt the same way.

Still, it took a few seconds before Leo actually moved. "I'm going to go see if everything's okay. You two stay here," he instructed them. Even then, he had been adept at taking the leadership role when necessary. He went down the stairs, pretending he had no idea what it all was about.

Cold air rushed toward him, and he recognized his parents standing in the doorway with their backs to him, arguing with some people - he couldn't see how many - outside the house. As he pushed his way between them, he wrapped his arms around himself. Sleeping, he wore only a shirt and shorts, which was definitely too cold for the night air. "What's going on?" he asked around the room. Even though he was sixteen, and towered over them a good bit, his mom immediately tried to push him back. For a moment, everyone fell silent.

"Honey, go back to sleep, we'll work this out," his mom began, but someone outside the house shouted something in between.

"He probably is one, too! We're not safe from anyone here! They have to leave! All of them! Go on, get out of here!" If Leo hadn't already known what it was about, none of this would have made any sense. But unfortunately, he did know, and the accusations hit him even though he knew it was true.

What disturbed him more than the words, however, was who they came from. Miss Evelyn had been shouting all this. She lived only a few away, and while she wasn't necessarily the friendliest person, Leo wouldn't have believed that she would be the first to try to drive him away.

His mom was finally able to push him behind herself, and he was so distracted that he didn't fight back. They all cursed at each other some more. Leo tried to push through again, but like his sister, his mom was stronger than she looked.

For a while he stood behind his parents, listening to the people outside ragging on each other, antagonizing the family. As beasts, monsters, monstrosities. And every word made Leo angrier. How could all these people - neighbors, acquaintances, friends - betray them like this? How could they be so terrible? To utter such words just because some witch had told them about a curse!

Hot, merciless rage rose in Leo. The ball in his chest grew and grew until it finally swallowed the boy.

And then it happened.

A tingling sensation spread across his skin. "Mom?" he tried to get her attention. No response. And given all the people, maybe it was better that way.

The tingling grew stronger, and Leo raced up the stairs to his room. Where his siblings still sat. Fortunately.

"Is everything okay?" Nikki asked, wanting to slide aside to make room for him in his own bed again. But he was pacing the room, too worried to sit down.

"How does it feel?" he asked. His voice intense, but no louder than the screaming from downstairs. Confused, the other two looked at him.

"How does what feel?" Luke finally replied. He had a suspicion, but he didn't dare believe it.

Nikki drew in a sharp breath. "Oh no, Leo, not you too!" She jumped up and carefully approached her brother, who was standing in the middle of the room. "Are you hot? Cold? Do you feel tingling in your hands?"

At the word tingling, Leo nodded vigorously. That was exactly what it was! Now did that mean it was going to happen to him, too?

Nikki turned to Luke with wide eyes. "We've got to get him out of here."

"How are we going to do that?" Luke had now joined the two. "There's a bunch of people

downstairs. If they see us sneaking out, they'll distrust us even more."

"What if they see him here in the house? Would that be any better?"

His siblings' voices became strangely muffled for a moment, barely intelligible to Leo, and everything around him blurred. He told himself he had to stay sane. Keep his composure. He didn't want to be the one to get his family in trouble. As Leo drew attention to himself, they both realized again how serious the situation was.

Beads of sweat formed on Leo's face. "Nikki's right. I have to get out of here."

The other two looked at him with concern. Nikki was the first to regain her composure. "Through the window," she said. It was quite high, but it led directly to the forest, and was just on the opposite side from the front door, where all those people were raging.

Luke tore open the window and looked down. A normal person might break something in that jump, but he didn't think that would happen to him. Before any of the others could stop him, he jumped out, and fortunately landed safely on the grass.

"Come on," Nikki urged Leo. She was already at the window. "You'll soon be a wolf, which means you won't hurt yourself as quickly as a human. The distance to the ground is absolutely no problem." At least, that's what she hoped. When he didn't move, she tugged on his arm. "If you don't hurry, they'll find us."

Then she watched as he climbed over the window frame and took the plunge. She was more than relieved when, to all appearances, he was alright. Then she leaped after him.

The three of them ran from the light of the village into the darkness of the forest. The screams grew quieter, and it didn't sound like anyone was following them. Even though Leo was the oldest of them, he was having trouble keeping up. His breathing was rapid, and sweat was running down his face, burning.

"This way," Luke shouted without slowing down, and they continued to run. Only when all light was gone, and not a single voice could be heard, did they slow down. When his siblings stopped, Leo sank to the ground, breathing heavily. Nikki was immediately beside him.

"It's going to hurt, and you're going to want to scream," she explained in an urgent tone. She didn't know how much longer he would be able to understand her. "Don't. We're quite a distance from the village, but they might still hear us."

As if on cue, a biting pain ran through him, making him howl. Nikki didn't know what else she could do, and looked up at Luke, who was nervously running his hands through his hair. "Do you know anything else we could do?"

He shook his head. "Do you know how to turn?"

"No," she replied, "I just did it that one time."

"So did I," he said.

"Do you think it would help if we also...?" Nikki was unsure how it would make anything better. Especially since she had no idea how to control it.

Luke, too, just raised his shoulders. "Let's do it," he then said. "It's worth a try."

Leo cried out again, writhing on the floor. Slowly, his bones had to be bending, and it was time to make a decision.

Nikki could no longer watch her brother's pain take over. With a quick decision, she nodded to

Luke. "Let's do it," she sighed, and stood. It was hard to concentrate. Hard not to think about the screams and the dangers, but to try to turn into a wolf. She had no idea how. She had no idea if it even worked.

Then she felt it. A spark. A spark inside her. Her hands tightened. Her back arched.

It was different from the last time. Everything was clearer. Instead of pure pain, she felt something else. Power. Strength. She heard more than usual, saw more clearly than usual, and when Luke approached her in his wolf form, she perceived him to be slower than he actually had to be.

Although the grey-eyed wolf next to her couldn't actually smile, she knew he was happy about the successful transformation. Then they heard Leo again.

He hadn't fully transformed yet, but his body didn't look quite human anymore either. Nikki knew that part was painful, but also that he wouldn't remember it for a while. At least, that's how it had been with her.

With her enhanced hearing, Nikki at least knew that no humans were around. A few birds maybe and foxes, possibly other animals of the forest. But no humans.

When Leo had completely transformed, Luke and she boxed him in from both sides, so that at worst he could get a few feet, but do no real damage. And it worked! It actually worked!

They were all the more surprised when the next day at school someone claimed to have seen the three of them outside. And it didn't stop at silly school rumors. Soon the whole village was talking about it. In the evening they besieged their house again, and the next day the siblings were not allowed to go to school. Until their parents finally decided to leave.

THIRTEEN

Everything goes down the Drain

"So being a wolf in itself isn't bad at all," Leo summarized. "But it's not nice that it happened."

Ruby nodded in understanding. He was still holding her hand in his, and she, in turn, was definitely not going to let go now. "Thank you for telling me about it." True, her voice was low, but she was sure he had heard her anyway.

His smile wanted to capture her, but she wouldn't let it, quickly averting her gaze. The chirping of the birds reminded her of the swans, and thus of Granny's garden, and thus of Granny herself. "I have to go. If Granny notices I'm not there..." She left the rest unspoken and straightened up. Though she wanted to let go, her fingers remained intertwined when he stood up as well.

"Don't worry about it. Granny Annie won't lynch you," he assured her with a smile. But then again, he had no idea how she could react if anything didn't go according to plan. And today she was in such a bad mood already!

Ruby remembered what he had told her. "Can you ... can you hear her?" she asked then.

"No," he admitted. "But we're too far away, too. When I'm not a wolf, I don't hear that well."

She nodded, but her thoughts were already elsewhere. "I should be on my way anyway."

When she tried to let go of his hand, he stopped her. "I'll come with you."

A queasy feeling spread through her. Yes, she liked holding his hand and being near him. Did that make it the right thing to do though? After all, they wouldn't make their decision on all this until tomorrow. End the pact at last.

What if this was just being friendly for him? What if he actually started something with Zola again? Was that what he had wanted to tell her?

Although her instinct was to get to Granny's as quickly as possible, she forced herself to walk slowly, hand in hand with Leo. And to act as if everything was normal.

"Hey," Leo said eventually into the silence, and she looked up. "Why did you think I wouldn't come by today? I always do."

Ruby shook her head slightly. Did she really have to say it out loud? And hold his hand while doing so?

His gaze remained expectant, and she realized that he was indeed anticipating an answer. "That thing that happened yesterday," she reminded him. "I mean, it's weird between us, you have to admit. After all, when we're out with the pack, you don't even talk to me anymore."

He paused, and without thinking about it, she did the same. Amazed, he looked at her, and this time his hand disengaged from hers. However, it was only to push away the strands of hair that had come loose from her braid and fallen into her face. "I'm sorry if it's weird. Zola's brand new to the pack and I don't want her to feel like an outsider."

His answer was sincere, even if it didn't sit well with Ruby. Why did he have to bring Zola into it? That was probably why she couldn't quite keep the irony out of her response. "Well, you're doing a pretty good job of it."

Unable to look at him any further, she turned away and continued walking toward Granny's house. Why couldn't she keep it together? After all, what he did with Zola was his business. And if he told her tomorrow that he preferred to be with Zola ... She would have to put up with that.

His footsteps were barely audible, but Ruby still knew he was following her. Of course he did. Friends didn't let friends just leave in a huff. Even if they didn't know what it was about.

The thing was, just a moment ago he'd been holding her hand, touching her, and then talking about Zola as if it were the most natural thing in the world. It seemed holding her hand was just nothing special to him.

"Red, hey!" He reached for her arm, but she immediately shook it off. She didn't turn to him either, but waited until he was standing in front of her. He was completely clueless. "There's nothing wrong between us, is there? We can still be friends, even if it's weird right now, right?"

She was about to answer him, even though she had no idea what she was going to say yet, when something behind his shoulder caught her attention. "Damn," she cursed softly. There Granny Annie was, and when she saw her, anger was written large and clear across her face. Somehow, she and Leo had run too far.

Desperately, she looked Leo in the eye. "Get out of here," she whispered.

"What?" He was about to turn his head to see what Ruby had seen, but she held his face with both hands.

"Go now," she ordered him insistently, and this time he didn't question it. He probably knew what was going on, even without looking around. Or maybe he trusted her without knowing anything...

Leo was gone when Ruby turned to look for him again. And that was good, because Granny probably hadn't recognized him.

Hesitantly she walked to the fence, while her grandmother didn't move. Just stood there, eyes narrowed to slits and hands braced on her hips.

"What do you think you're doing?" she blasted out as soon as Ruby had climbed over the fence. "Sneaking into the woods while I'm asleep? I gave you one job; you were supposed to watch my garden! Now look what happened!"

The girl barely had time to examine at the pitted vegetables before the woman continued her rant.

"I get up unsuspecting, and what do I have to see? My garden - destroyed! And just when I think it can't get any worse, my granddaughter struts in with a boy! What were you thinking, Ruby? Have you completely lost your mind?"

Ruby thought a lot. Thought to herself how unfair it was to be yelled at like that when she had worked all day for her grandmother. Had worked for her grandmother *every day*. That it wasn't her fault if Granny's garden was destroyed, and that she was damn well entitled to a break! But she didn't speak up about any of this. Instead, she ran to Granny, who was now holding her chest and breathing heavily. The last thing she wanted right now was for Granny to get worse.

"Come sit down," Ruby urged her. One hand on her back, the other on her elbow. But even though the woman could barely breathe, her pride kept the upper hand.

"You ... you..." she gasped, unable to get a sentence out.

Ruby toyed with the idea of just leaving her standing there. Obviously, she didn't want her help. She was far too upset and stubborn to let anybody help her now. For although Ruby tried to urge her toward the chair, the woman didn't move a bit.

"Granny, you need to rest." Slowly, she was running out of desire – and nerve – to be nice. Her jaw tightened uncomfortably as Granny took a swing with her elbow to get rid of her granddaughter's hand – accidentally hitting her in the face.

She didn't even seem to notice. And if she did notice, she didn't care. But Ruby's cheek hurt, and she tasted blood in her mouth. Not a lot, just where the edges of her teeth had pressed into her flesh thanks to the impact. Still, she had a feeling it was about to swell.

"You...", Granny started again. By now she didn't sound so bad, and Ruby felt no need to hold her any longer. That's why she also let go of her back and took a few steps back. "You can't just leave when I'm asleep! Meet a boy! That's irresponsible!"

Ruby clenched her teeth tighter. She would have loved to scream, but that wouldn't help the matter.

"It's bad enough they're hanging around here at all, but for you to go see them!" And suddenly Granny's voice quieted, but that only made her sound more dangerous. "You will not meet this boy again; do you understand me? When you are here, you will not leave the property. When you go home, you don't stop and you don't get off the path, and when you come here, you hurry the hell up. Every day you are here at a different time. That's not acceptable. If I catch you doing something that stupid one more time, then..."

She didn't have to finish the sentence, and she couldn't. Ruby interrupted her before she had the chance. "Stupid? *Stupid?!* I come here, every day. I'm always here, helping you, and what do I get in return? Nothing! Once. Once a day I want to go outside and just be alone - once! - and that's too much? I am sixteen. I'm not a kid anymore. You can't deny me everything just ... just because you feel like it!" She screamed, and she hated that she was screaming. It made all of this seem like she was just a toddler having a tantrum.

And Granny looked at her like she was just a toddler having a tantrum. "Pff! That's just outrageous! Take care of the garden now, and then go home. And ... and tomorrow you don't have to come back!"

She stomped back into the house, and Ruby would have loved to shout something after her, but she knew it wouldn't help. She heard a noise from the woods, and when she turned around, there he was. Leo. Had he been listening to everything?

He opened his mouth, but she wouldn't let him speak. Tears burned hot in her eyes, and she just wanted to be alone. "Go," she ordered, and her voice sounded harder than she wanted. He didn't even hesitate. Just left. Disappeared into the woods. Ruby couldn't hold back the tears any longer. How could her Granny do this to her?

It was Anna and Elsa, after all, that comforted her. The two hens clucked excitedly as she joined them in the coop, stroking their feathers. They had probably heard all the screaming and wouldn’t lay any more eggs for a while. Served Granny right! She didn't deserve such great hens at all.

"Ruby!" the girl heard Granny call, and immediately her jaw tightened again. With the basket of eggs in her hand, she went back to the garden, and saw Granny Annie standing at the front door, looking sullen. What had she expected? That she had run off into the woods to her boy?

With a little too much force, the girl pushed the basket into her hands, and then bent over the vegetable patch again. Hearing nothing more, she assumed that Granny had gone back into the house, but it wasn't until a few minutes later that she dared to actually take a look.

No one was standing there anymore. And a glance toward the woods proofed that this time she really was alone.

An hour later, she angrily trudged out of the house. Granny had not given up. Had mercilessly let her fix up her garden, and then actually sent her home. And what could Ruby have done?

Complain to stay there longer? To keep getting yelled at?

However, it bothered her that she now had no food for the villagers. And that the pack didn't know she was going home early. And that she had to go home alone.

In her mind, all the mean words Granny had berated her with today gathered, and anger filled her. As if that wasn't bad enough, the walk through the forest also seemed a lot longer than usual. Probably because she was alone. Damn.

"Hello," said someone from behind a tree. Ruby froze. She didn't recognize the voice. Her heart raced, partly because she was still so angry with Granny, and a little because here she was walking home all alone. Well, not all alone apparently.

Despite her doubts, she turned around.

"Don't be afraid," the man said. Was he a man? He could be fifteen like Luke, or twenty like Matteo, she didn't know. His light hair contrasted his tanned skin, and his blue eyes shone so unusually bright that Ruby immediately felt a little safer.

"Who are you?" she blurted out.

"Oh sorry, I should introduce myself. How silly of me." He cleared his throat, slowly coming closer, and Ruby realized that he was quite tall, his hair almost golden and his teeth almost unnaturally white. And he had to be strong, judging from the muscly arms.

When he stopped a reasonable distance in front of her, he cleared his throat again. "I'm Benedict, but my friends call me Ben." He held out his hand to her, and she paused for a moment before taking it.

"Ruby," she replied. That was all she could say right then. Her brain still seemed to be deciding whether she liked him or should feel threatened by him.

Benedict smiled, showing gleaming white teeth. "I'm passing through ... *was* passing through," he explained. "I'm getting tired of traveling. It's lonely, and exhausting. It gets cold at night, and your feet hurt from all the walking."

"I get that," she responded, forcing herself to keep walking. "I'm on my feet all day, too. It can get pretty tiring."

Without hesitation, he matched her pace. "Hey, a fellow sufferer!" he laughed. "Why do you have to walk so much?"

Surprised, Ruby smiled. Someone who understood how exhausting it could be, and didn't judge her for complaining! "During the day I take care of my Granny and her garden, and at night I go back to the village and ... help my mom." Even if she was proud of her village walks, she didn't have to brag about people's poverty.

"Where are you going now? To the village?" he echoed. Ruby noticed that he was only carrying a half-empty backpack; he obviously didn't have very much food with him anymore.

"Yes," she answered, "My Granny ... let me leave earlier today." She bit her lip. Why had she said that? Why did she have to lie even to a stranger?

"That's nice of her."

"Mmm." She couldn't bring herself to confess what had actually happened. But then, he didn't need to know that. She should probably try to forget about this whole thing with her Granny.

Especially if it was only going to hurt herself anyway.

Out of the corner of her eye, Ruby saw him give her an interested look, but she pretended not to notice. "I'm looking for Bertram and Luisa. They live in the village, don't they?"

He must have noticed that the names meant something to her. Bertram and Luisa were Mara, Philippa, Corey, and Will's parents. How much could she tell him without compromising the identity of her friends?

"No," she answered reluctantly. She couldn't lie any more today. Not argue with any more people. "They don't live in the village anymore."

"Oh, really? Where then?" There was genuine surprise in his voice, and Ruby wondered how she could help him without putting the pack in danger.

"I don't know." That was the truth. All she knew was that they lived in the forest in a small village with the other wolves. But she had never known exactly where it was. "How do you know them?"

"Oh, Bertram used to be my neighbor. In the city where I grew up."

If he knew Bertram, she could trust him. Bertram and Luisa had come to the village back then, and had had a place for every child. Once, when Ruby had been really sick, the two of them had taken care of her so her mother could go about her work in town. She trusted them both. And if they trusted Benedict, she probably did, too.

Ahead of her, the trees would soon open up to uncover the village right behind. Time to say goodbye. "I'm sorry I can't help you. But I have to go home now."

Fortunately, he took her hint and stopped. "Well then," he began. Ruby positioned herself a few steps away from him. "It was nice to have made your acquaintance." He raised an imaginary hat, grinning at her.

"Yes, likewise," she replied with a smile. "And good luck." Then she turned away and walked toward the village. He didn't follow her, instead she heard his footsteps moving away.

FOURTEEN

At Home in the Village

Like the other day, her mom wasn't home when Ruby arrived there. This time, however, it was not particularly unusual, after all, it wasn't late at all.

Unlike yesterday, she now had a lot of time to do nothing. So, Ruby made herself comfortable in the barely used living room. When she closed her eyes, however, the desired relaxation did not come over her. Instead, she remembered the argument with Granny. How she had yelled at Ruby. How easy it had been for her to send her away.

And she thought of Leo, whom she had had to send away. To whom she had not even been able to explain what had happened. Somehow, she wished she could have gone home with the pack again today. At the same time, she didn't want to be pestered by everyone about what had happened.

When she still couldn't relax after a while, she went to the kitchen. It hadn't even occurred to her that she was hungry until she was sitting in front of her bowl of soup. Within a few minutes she had eaten up, pushing the dish away from her. It was rare, having so much time on her hands. And even rarer that she didn't know what to do with it.

She should probably do something productive. Maybe clean her room or sort supplies. Instead, Ruby went out for some fresh air. Tried to just enjoy it for a few minutes. What else could she do? She didn't have enough food at home to cook for the villagers who didn't have enough themselves. And without Granny's pastries, tonight's route wouldn't make sense either.

She sighed and wandered aimlessly.

"Hey Little Red!" She had to look around to see who it was coming from.

Matteo waved her over. "Hey, what are you doing here? Shouldn't you still be hanging out at Granny Annie's?"

That's exactly what she didn't want to do. Talk about her fight with Granny. "Shouldn't you be working?" she distracted him.

"Touché," he laughed.

Instantly, she didn't feel so lonely.

"I'm just on my way to Miss Loraine's for some fabric. You wouldn't happen to be heading that way, too?" he asked.

"You're in luck. I don't have anything else to do right now."

"Cool." For a few seconds they just walked side by side, and Ruby saw how the village moved when it was daytime. And that it hadn't changed in the years she'd spent at Granny's during the day. Matteo cleared his throat. "But seriously, why are you here already? Don't you usually come back when it's already dark?"

"Not when it's dark!" she immediately objected. "I'm just always here with you just before dusk. My mom would kill me if I didn't get back until dark." She was quite aware that she hadn't answered his question, and from the way he was looking at her - with his eyebrows drawn together and a look that made her wonder if it was okay to ask - he knew it.

He was her friend, right? She could confide in him without the whole village knowing about it tomorrow. And without him asking about it unnecessarily. "I had a fight with Granny," she finally admitted. "It was bad. I mean, really bad. She sent me home. And she was so mad." Only now did she realize how much it hurt her that Granny Annie had been angry with her.

"Oh man," Matteo retorted, sounding just as upset as she felt. "That must be awful. Are you okay?"

She nodded, but her face claimed otherwise. She couldn't tell him what else had happened. She just couldn't. "What fabrics are you getting today? From Miss Loraine?" she asked instead, trying to change the subject.

The two continued to talk for quite a while. At least until Ruby spotted a face she hadn't expected. "Hey Greta!" she called out. Then she turned to Matteo. "Excuse me."

She ran over, somehow afraid it might just be a hallucination. But it was definitely the 13-year-old standing in front of her. A bundle of clothes in her hand, obviously on her way to wash them. She looked a little more tired than usual, but she was real. "How are you? I didn't catch you at all last night." Ruby walked with her in her direction, knowing how angry her stepmother could get if she took too long to do her chores.

"Oh, you were there? Sorry, we were already ... um ... asleep." She stared at the floor in front of her, and Ruby had an uneasy feeling that something was wrong.

"Are you sure you're alright?" she asked in a lowered voice. "I can help you, just tell me if anything's wrong."

"Everything's fine," she assured her a little too quickly and with a forced smile. "I was just really tired yesterday." She yawned. "And still am."

All this time, Ruby couldn't figure out if Greta was telling her the truth. And if she was honest, she didn't even try too long. Greta would show her if she needed help.

As the two of them made their way back, talking about this and that, another thing occurred to Ruby. "You guys are going to the ghost party, right?"

This time Ruby spotted a genuine smile on Greta's face. "Yeah, I'm really looking forward to it. Mom's not thrilled, but Dad said we could. Does everyone have to wear ghost costumes?" Her face suddenly wrinkled. "I mean, I want to, but I don't think we can use Mom's sheets."

Ruby was pleased at how open Greta suddenly was again. "No, you don't have to, but Matteo has a few costumes left. If you ask him, I'm sure you'll get some."

Her eyes grew huge. "Really? It would be amazing!"

Ruby was almost back home when she saw her mom get off her bike. Heck, she hadn't actually meant to run into her out here.

She waited until Catherine was inside, then followed her.

"Oh Ruby, what are you doing here already? I just got home too. Do you want something to eat?"

"Um ... I'm not hungry." Somehow, she was dreading telling her mom the truth. She didn't know which side she'd be on.

"Did you eat at Granny's?" Catherine asked still distracted from emptying her work bag, putting everything in its rightful place.

"No."

Her mom looked up in wonder. Then she glanced around the kitchen. "Where are the bags? And your backpack?"

By now, she must have gotten suspicious. They both knew Ruby never forgot the bags. But she didn't dare tell the truth.

"Ruby?"

She couldn't meet her mom's eyes. "I had a fight with Granny," she said guiltily.

"What do you mean, *a fight*?" Catherine was quiet, but she knew full well what was coming.

"We argued, that's what." That wasn't enough. Of course it wasn't. "She was in a terrible mood, and just yelled at me the whole time. And then she sent me home." Ruby could only look at her hands. "She didn't bake anything today."

"Oh, Ruby. You know how Granny can be. If she's in a bad mood, just let her be. Why would you still argue with her?"

Sighing, Catherine sat down at the kitchen table.

Ruby focussed on a spot on the table. "She told me not to come back."

When she looked up, her mother was staring at her in disbelief. "I'm sure she didn't mean that. I'm sure she'll be fine tomorrow, and even glad to see you."

Ruby nodded mutely and finally sat down across from her mom.

"But of course it's up to you to decide if you want to go tomorrow," she added soothingly.

And while Ruby was grateful to her mother for leaving the decision up to her, she knew there was a right and a wrong in this matter. And right would not be easy.

It felt strange to not walk around the village in the evening and hand out food. And Ruby felt guilty. After all, it was kind of her fault that there was no food.

She secretly wondered if anyone would have opened up at Greta and Hannes' house tonight. And somehow she wanted to know how many more costumes Matteo had made, and if they looked as cool as the ones from yesterday. But just walking there without having anything with her seemed absurd.

So after having a snack, she went to bed and tried to sleep. Sleep. It had been so easy for her before. Today it was torture. No wonder! It was still light outside. But she couldn't concentrate on reading, either. Instead, she wondered if going back to Granny's tomorrow was a good idea, even if it was the right decision. Or if it would worsen their argument even more. What if Granny wanted to tell Mom what had happened? Ruby wasn't sure how she would go about that, and with Granny's stubbornness, it wasn't too far-fetched.

She watched as it grew darker and darker outside. The village was preparing for nightfall. Outside her window, she could only see the forest, but she could hear the voices of her neighbors and friends.

She must have fallen asleep briefly, because when her mom suddenly stood in her room and wished her a good night, it was already pitch-black outside. However, while Ruby turned back over to go back to sleep, she didn't quite want to.

Her own house was silent now, too, but her head was not. She turned on her light, and grabbed one of her books. It was about time she read again, and right now she felt able to concentrate on it.

A noise made her look up. It had come from outside. But it was so dark by now that no one was supposed to be there. Was she just imagining it? Was her head merely playing tricks on her?

Ruby turned back to the text in front of her, read a few words, and...

There it was again! It was definitely not her imagination!

On her tiptoes, she sneaked to the window. The floor was extremely cold, and she couldn't imagine how icy it must have been outside.

Her eyes weren't used to the dark, and it took her a few seconds to recognise anything. What was she seeing down there? *Who* did she see down there?

And then she recognized Leo. He made a movement that she couldn't quite interpret at first. Should she open the window? She did. Then he motioned her to step back. She didn't know what he was up to, but she did it anyway.

The icy air hit her, and she wrapped her arms around herself.

And then he was there. Suddenly standing right in front of her.

"How did you do that?" she whispered excitedly. Her mom was in the next room. Probably asleep by now. Hopefully asleep by now.

He closed the window. "Magic," he replied sarcastically. She rolled her eyes. But smiled. She took it he wasn't mad at her for sending him away at noon.

"What are you doing here?" It was hard to keep her voice from sounding excited.

"I wanted to make sure you were okay. You know ... after what happened today."

Although she smiled, a bad feeling came over her. "I don't want my mom to catch you," Ruby then said even more quietly, nervously looking at her bedroom door. If she tried to, she could almost see her mother in front of her. *Ruby! What's a boy doing in your room?!* That would be the icing on the cake for this incredibly awful day. But other than Leo's breathing and her own heartbeat, she heard nothing.

Without looking back at him, she slipped back into her bed. Under the covers, which were still warm. Not that it helped her freezing feet.

Somehow, she was glad when Leo merely sat down at the end of her bed. And at the same time, she was hoping to snuggle up to him. But given what had happened between them in the last few days, that would probably be rather inappropriate. Or confusing. Or both.

"You weren't around later," he began far too loudly for Ruby's liking.

"Shh," she warned him. "Mom might hear you."

"You weren't around later," he whispered again. "On the way back. I had a lot of confused faces in front of me, and I couldn't exactly tell them I heard your argument. You're probably going to have a lot of questions to answer tomorrow." He tried to sound light-hearted, almost teasing, but the worry in his voice was unmistakable.

"If I go tomorrow, I do," she slipped out.

"What do you mean?" he asked, shocked. And she knew exactly why: for the twelve months the pack had been living in the forest, she had gone to see her grandmother every day. No matter what. Whether she was in a good mood or a bad one. Whether she was sick or healthy. She had always gone, and to now suggest that she wouldn't anymore was strange indeed. But worse was that it took away any chance she had of seeing Leo.

"Oh, I just mean ... we were just arguing," Ruby tried to play it down. She didn't want to not see Leo anymore. And he couldn't sneak into her room every night, after all. "She sent me away. I mean, she was in a really bad mood today, too. But, when she saw you..."

"She saw me?" he repeated.

"Yeah ... Yeah, but I don't think she recognized you. I mean ... she didn't say anything," Ruby quickly clarified.

Still, he looked horrified. "Do you know what it could mean? If she recognized me?"

"She didn't recognize you," Ruby reassured him.

Even when Leo had lived in the village, Granny had hardly ever seen him. She had, after all, very rarely been to the village in the last ten years. And he had changed since then.

"What's going to happen now?" he asked. And he didn't have to add what it was about. It was unspoken in the air between them. *To us.* And she wasn't quite sure if it was just about their friendship or about everything else, too.

"Nothing," Ruby decided. "Nothing's happening. She'll forget about it in a few days, and it's not like I'm talking about never going back. Just maybe not tomorrow. Then she can calm down, maybe even miss me a little, because who's going to do all the work if I'm not there?" She realized she sounded bitter, but she didn't mind. She really did feel like Granny never realized how much she did for her. And yet it was quite a lot. Even just the daily walk she took just to help her.

Going out on a limp, Ruby reached for Leo's hand. It was surprisingly warm, even though he was only wearing a thin sweater, and had been outside a few minutes earlier. "Don't worry about it. And Granny freaking out like that today wasn't your fault either. She was just in a bad mood." *And it was the first time she'd seen me with a boy,* Ruby added in her head. Even if it hadn't meant anything - or shouldn't have meant anything - it must have been a shock to her grandmother.

"Damn," he whispered suddenly, and Ruby pulled her hand back, startled. In the blink of an eye, he had torn open the window and jumped out. Ruby could only stare after him. What had happened now?

And then the answer came through her bedroom door. "Ruby?" whispered Mom sleepily, but alertly. "Is everything okay?" Puzzled, she looked around the lit room, her gaze lingering at the open window.

"Yes," Ruby whispered, hoping Catherine couldn't see her lie.

"Why is your window open?" The woman wrapped her own arms around the middle of her body. "It's freezing in here."

"I was warm," Ruby quickly explained, quickly moving to the window to close it. Then she slipped back under her covers. Catherine didn't say anything, and Ruby didn't know if she was suspicious or just tired.

"Good night, Mom." That would hopefully end the conversation.

"Good night, Ruby," she replied, but stayed in the room for a second too long, looking around before going back to her own bed.

Ruby felt bad about lying to her. At the same time, she was relieved that it had worked. And now she couldn't help but stare out, wondering where Leo was right now.

FIFTEEN

The Banishment

(One year ago)

The last time Ruby had felt like this - that longing, fear for her friends - it had been just as difficult a day as this. Probably even harder. It was the day she hadn't been able to say goodbye to her friends. The day of their banishment from the village.

A week before, everything had been peaceful. No one had called each other names, accused one another, or believed evil of each other. Ruby could not have named a more beautiful place than Fairy Town.

In fact, it had even been easier to go to her Granny's every day and put up with her moods when she could sit and talk with her neighbors in the evenings. Admittedly, Nikki had been hanging out with Greta more and more lately than with her, but there was always Leo and Luke. Most evenings she would run into at least one of them in their adjoining backyards. They were no longer young enough to play pirates and forget themselves in other worlds, but secretly eating cookies and hiding from their parents was still fun.

Everything changed when a witch named Casmira traveled through their village. She wasn't exactly the friendliest witch Ruby had ever met, but she wasn't the most terrifying either. After all, she didn't cast spells on anyone herself. Or at least she didn't show it publicly. No one knew exactly where the wolf curse had suddenly come from, but it was there after Casmira had told them about it.

At first the witch was only going to stay a night or two, but in the end, it had almost been a week when she had visited everyone in the village once. That evening she came to visit Ruby and her mother. The seldomly used living room was made up so that the old woman could sleep in it, and when Ruby came home from her grandmother's, she found half the neighborhood in her house.

It wasn't every day that someone new came to the village, and the joy of seeing an unfamiliar face showed even in the faces of the teenagers next door. Leo and Luke sat on the floor next to the bookshelf, the witch in the armchair Granny Annie had always sat in when she used to come to the village, and Nikki, Catherine, and another mother sat on the sofa, each with a child on her lap. A few stood near the door and behind those seated, and Ruby sneaked unobtrusively behind her mother while everyone listened fascinated to Casmira.

Ruby had seen her once or twice since the old lady had come to the village. But never this close and never in her house. She leaned against the back of the sofa and propped her arms up next to her mother's head. Then the old woman looked her straight in the eye. "And that's why," she said promisingly, "you should never mess with a witch. All you have to do is upset a witch a little, and she can put a curse on you. With a curse that you can't get rid of so easily. Some may try, but hardly anyone actually succeeds."

"What does it take to undo a curse?" a girl asked.

"It depends on the curse," Casmira answered. "And on the witch who cast it. There are many things to consider. But it is never easy to resist a curse. I knew a witch who used sauerkraut extract all the time, which can only be neutralized with strawberry blossoms." She laughed softly, but the mood in the room didn't relax. "You don't have to worry about that, though, as long as you don't annoy any witches," she added with a smile.

A few days later - the witch had already set off again - the curse began to spread in Fairy Town. And no one knew why. Leo's family was the first to be banished. Then the others followed. Soon there were fifteen people less in Fairy Town.

SIXTEEN

Surprises

When Ruby woke up the next morning, she stayed in bed longer than usual. Meanwhile, she heard her mother get ready for the day, but she herself couldn't get up yet.

Although she had told Leo that evening that she might not go to Grandma's today, that wasn't really an option. The longer she put it off, the harder it would be to go back. Besides, the people in the village needed food, and Ruby couldn't let them down twice.

So, she got up as usual, ate breakfast as usual, said goodbye to Catherine as usual, and started her way to Granny's.

"Hey Little Red!"

She hadn’t even stepped foot into the woods yet, when the familiar voices reached her. And she was happy to hear from them. Hannes and Greta. The two waved at her excitedly and she walked over to them.

"Hi," she greeted them both. "Are you guys on your way to school?" It was obvious, and with backpacks full of books, paper and pencils, the two reminded her of a younger version of herself.

Both kids nodded, but whether they were happy about it, Ruby couldn't tell from their faces. She thought she saw hunger. No wonder!

After all, she hadn't brought them anything yesterday.

"Wait a minute, I brought something..." Ruby rummaged in her backpack for a few seconds, and finally pulled out a box of jam sandwiches. Greta's eyes widened as she handed her the box.

"Are you sure?"

"Of course," Ruby answered immediately, smiling at her. This morning, just before she ran out of the house, she had thought of the kids, and grabbed the freshest bread from her stash. The smiles on their faces were more than worth it.

Even though it was the wrong direction, Ruby walked with them toward the school.

"Yesterday at lunch," Hannes began, "everyone was talking about the ghost party. They said there would be real ghosts. Is that true?"

Ruby laughed. "I don't think so." She thought about it for a moment. "But who knows what the ghosts have come up with."

Greta gave her a shocked look. She probably wasn't too thrilled about lying to her brother. However, the boy didn't seem afraid of the idea that ghosts actually existed.

"And do you think I can talk to them, or will they just try to scare me?" Hannes continued.

"Well, you won't be able to get scared if you already know that's what they're up to," she winked. "But I've never met a ghost before either. Maybe they're more talkative than we know."

Ruby was quite amused to see his eyes widen even more. Greta apparently did not. "Don't listen to her," she said, turning to her brother. "Ghosts aren't real."

"Of course ghosts are real," Hannes contradicted her, "Right, Little Red?"

She choked on her laughter. "Um..." Now, she couldn't tell him they were real and contradict Greta. Or say they weren't real and contradict herself. "I've got to get going. Have a great day at school."

"Bye!" they both said in unison and Ruby breathed a sigh of relief.

Off to the woods she went. It was time.

For the first few minutes she was all alone, and the silence seemed to devour her. Normally, she felt comfortable in the woods. And free. Today she was plagued by not knowing what would happen to Granny later. Was she still angry? Would she be happy to see Ruby? Or shout at her? Would she send her away again?

Fortunately, the pack soon appeared and made her worries disappear. Mara fell around her neck, and Corey limped joyfully toward her. "Hi Little Red! Where were you last night?" Mara asked, running up beside her.

"Yeah, we were waiting for you. We waited and waited until it was almost dark," Shawn butted in, joining her on her other side. He probably thought she had food for everyone again.

"I ... um..." Ruby knew she should have come up with an excuse before, but now she had to improvise. "I went back early to ... um ... organize a few more things for the ghost party."

She was glad it made sense and distracted everyone for now. "The party! Right!"

"It's today already," someone said behind her. Puzzled, Ruby listened up. Today already? She hadn't thought about it anymore at all. But Nikki was right. The party was already that night. And

Ruby hadn't prepared nearly as much as she should have.

"Can we help?" Shawn asked, and others joined in. "Oh yeah, we could..."

"How about you leave that to Red," Leo interjected. Ruby had been far too busy racking her brains over Granny and coming up with excuses to think about him. She smiled at him, and he smiled back. Somehow relieved, she realized that Zola didn't have her arm wrapped around him this time. She wasn't even near him. It looked as if she and Zander weren't even there that morning.

That's when Mara next to her squeaked loudly. "Little Red, Little Red! This is Ben over there. He's staying with us now." The girl pointed further behind where Leo had been before, and where Luke and Ben were now walking.

Ruby turned to face him. "Hi," she said shyly, not quite sure if she should bring up yesterday's conversation.

Ben smiled. And took the decision from her. "Hello *Little Red*, nice to see you again."

"See you again?" Leo repeated, looking back and forth between the two. The others seemed confused as well. "You've know each other?"

"We met briefly yesterday," Ruby admitted, "He kept me company on the way home."

She couldn't interpret Leo's look, but there was too much happening around them anyway to focus only on him. Ben came closer, Nikki grinned for some inexplicable reason, and Mara was almost jumping up and down with excitement.

Then the young girl interfered again. "Isn't it cool that he's one of us too?"

Ruby gave Mara a puzzled look. Had she missed something? *One of us*? What was that supposed to mean now?

Ben interrupted and at the same time answered her thoughts. "Actually, she didn't know that yet," he said to Mara in an overfriendly, almost arrogant tone, and then turned back to Ruby. He flashed his white teeth at her. "Well, yes, I'm a wolf, too. But don't worry, I won't bite."

"A wolf?" she replied, perplexed. She hadn't expected that. "How?"

"A witch," he replied, completely relaxed. "I messed with a witch, and she cursed me. In fact, that's also why I travel around. I couldn't stay in my town, and it's hard to find a place where they don't send you away again."

"The same thing happened to us," Luke interrupted. "None of us can show our faces in the village anymore. Yet we've never done anything to anyone."

Ben nodded in agreement. "But you still have each other, thankfully. There were a few others in my town, but they disappeared into thin air pretty quickly."

"Oh man." Ruby was speechless.

"But enough about me. I hear you're on your way to your Granny's?" By now Ben had taken Shawn's place beside her.

"Yes, I visit her every day," she replied. Today was not a good day to talk about her grandmother. Fortunately, the pack took care of this topic for her.

"Granny Annie is really sweet, she bakes for us every day," Mara said excitedly.

"Oh yeah, and she makes the best apple pie in the village," Shawn added.

"But she's been living in a house all by herself in the woods for ages," Corey, who was having his share of trouble keeping up because of his sprained ankle, now exclaimed. "And whenever Little Red goes to visit her, we come along."

"And sometimes we check on her when she's sick," Shawn said, although that had happened maybe three times in the entire last year.

Ben took the floor again, not letting his eyes stray from Ruby. "Pretty cool that you visit her every day."

Ruby raised her shoulders. Today she was quite uncomfortable being made to look like she was an angel for dragging herself to see her grandmother when the old woman didn't even want her there. "Somebody's got to do it. She can't take care of the whole house by herself."

But he didn't leave it at that. "No, it really is great. I don't think there are many people our age who take care of their grandparents. I just know I've never done that."

Smiling, she ran a hand through her tangled hair. Hardly anyone took what she did as work. "Well, I don't really have a choice."

"Oh," he objected. "You always have the option to resist the system." And with that sentence, he winked at her, and Ruby felt the blood creep into her cheeks.

It was surprising to see Leo interrupt. "Hey Red, the ghost party's working out, right? Everyone's wearing costumes?"

She turned to him as he appeared next to Mara, momentarily confused by the abrupt change of subject. "Yes, I'm pretty sure everything's set," she replied.

"Good." He smiled at her, and she smiled back. And wished he would continue the conversation. In fact, he was already opening his mouth, but then...

"You sew costumes?" Ben asked, surprised.

"No, a friend of mine does," she replied. Actually, she turned her head to look where Leo had disappeared to, but instead only Nikki caught her eye and walked toward her.

"But you organize everything?" continued Ben. "A whole village festival and working for your grandmother, that sounds pretty exhausting."

"You could say that."

"You could say that?" Nikki's voice rang out. "She takes care of everything, and she's damn good at it." Grinning, she squeezed between him and Ruby. "Excuse us for a moment." Nikki pulled Ruby with her until they were a couple steps away from the others. Far enough that they wouldn't necessarily hear the two of them.

"What's going on?" Ruby inquired.

"What's going on with you? Ben's obviously making a pass at you, and you're totally blocking him." Nikki was more excited about this than about him being a wolf. But if she knew who Ruby was actually interested in, she probably wouldn't be talking to her about it.

"Oh really?" Ruby pretended she had no idea, because quite honestly, she didn't. She hadn't even noticed Ben flirting with her. At most, he was a little too friendly.

"Really!" Nikki replied with a little too much volume, looking around for a moment. The pack could eavesdrop on the two of them, of course, if they wanted to. But it was hardly interesting to them what the two girls were discussing. Except, perhaps, for Leo. Ruby gazed in his direction, but he seemed preoccupied with Luke and Benedict right now.

"I didn't notice," Ruby commented.

"So ... you don't like him?" Nikki asked, dropping her shoulders.

Ruby had to suppress a giggle. It was a little like they were back in school. "Why do you care so much?"

Nikki hesitated. "I don't," she defended herself, but didn't do it very believably. "I just think," she then began defiantly, "if someone's already interested in you, you should take advantage of it! ... I don't mean that no one would be interested in you. I just mean..."

Ruby laughed. "I know what you mean," she assured her, "but maybe I just don't want to meet anyone right now. Maybe with everything that's going on, I just don't have time for that." She felt bad lying to Nikki like that. Although, quite theoretically, it wasn't a lie; after all, she hadn't even made a decision about the pact yet.

"I get that," Nikki said then, though she was obviously hoping for a different answer. "But let's face it," she continued, "he's really hot."

Involuntarily, Ruby's gaze fell on Benedict. She was right, he was extraordinarily good looking. But neither Nikki nor she had any good comparisons. They had already known the boys from the village when they were missing teeth and before they've had one growth spurt after another. How were they supposed to be unbiased?

Unexpectedly, Ben looked to her and gave her a knowing grin. Which forced Ruby to avert her eyes. "Maybe you're right," she admitted. More to Nikki than to herself. "But I hardly know him."

"Well, you can change that," Nikki replied casually. "Just talk to him a little."

"Wait a minute, Nikki," Ruby stopped her. The way the girl kept looking around at Ben, Ruby suspected she was about to call him over. "Let me do it myself, okay?" she begged her, "I think it's going to come out weird if you play matchmaker." Somehow, she was afraid of what Nikki would do if she didn't stop her. Something over the top. Or embarrassing.

And then a thought occurred to her: Nikki usually never wanted to talk about guys and being in love. Was this maybe Nikki's way of telling her she was in love with someone and didn't know how to handle it? Was she trying to figure out how Ruby would handle it so she knew what to do herself? Ruby decided it wasn't a good time to ask. Not when everyone in the pack plus Ben could hear her. "Let's talk later ... at the ghost party," she suggested, and Nikki's eyes lit up. Did she think Ruby would talk about Ben then? About how she actually liked him?

The rest of the way, Ruby stayed extra close to Nikki, not letting Ben pull her into another conversation. She didn't like not being able to tell Nikki why she didn't want anything from Ben, but at least she could show her that she indeed wasn't interested.

For a while, she even forgot to worry about what was going to happen with her Granny. Well, at least until she got to the place where the pack usually said goodbye.

When everyone had already left, and Ruby was still thinking hard about whether she actually wanted to go in, she spotted Leo still loitering nearby. Involuntarily, a smile crept onto her lips. "Shouldn't you be with your pack?" she said loud enough so possible overhearers wouldn't suspect anything, and maybe even come out of hiding.

But there was silence surrounding the two. "Shouldn't you be at Granny Annie's house by now?" he replied with a grin, moving closer to her. "I just wanted to make sure you were fine," he then added more seriously.

"Fine? Of course I'm fine." She was definitely not fine. Her stomach fluttered. And her smile disappeared. "What if she's still mad at me?" She heard her own uncertainty in her voice.

"And what if she's already forgiven you? Believe me, your Granny loves you. There's no reason not to go today." He was about to take her hand, but before he reached her, he changed his mind and just stroked her arm briefly. Leaving behind a trail of goosebumps. "It's going to be okay."

"You don't know her like I do," Ruby objected. "Granny's good at being mad at me and letting me feel it." Before she could get any more upset, she bit her lip. "But thanks for trying."

And then Leo did something she hadn't expected: he drew her into a hug. Although it was unusual, it made her feel very safe. "It's going to be okay," he repeated, and Ruby could feel his chest vibrating in unison with his words. "It's going to be okay." And somehow that made it all better. For a few seconds, she enjoyed the silence, the warmth of his embrace, and the tingle it caused on her skin.

Then she pulled away from him. "It's time," she announced quietly, and he looked into her eyes. Her thinking abilities were greatly reduced, but at some point she was able to have a clear thought.

"Do you want to come back over later?" For one thing, she hoped he'd say yes; for another, he had plenty of reasons not to.

"I was going to," he grinned.

"Better not."

Her words surprised him. Obviously. They surprised Ruby, too. She wanted to spend time with him. She really did. But she couldn't let Granny catch them again.

A slow nod showed he understood. But when she tried to turn away, he stopped her. "I thought we could talk ... about the pact."

He didn't have to finish the thought. She knew what he was going to say.

The pact had expired. Today they made their decision.

"We'll talk tonight," she promised, feeling his hand let go of her.

"Tonight," he repeated, nodding. And then he was gone.

SEVENTEEN

Observations

Ruby forced herself to knock. Her fist pounded against the door as usual, and her voice trembled far less than she had expected. "Grandmother, it's me!" she called as she stepped through the door.

She received no answer, but she rarely on normal days either.

It was only in the living room that Granny made herself known. Tea and pastries were dished up on the coffee table, and Granny in front of it with her hands on her hips. "Didn't I tell you to stay home?"

It was hard not to turn around right then. Granny looked angry. She definitely meant what she said, but at the same time Ruby knew what would happen if she really did leave. "Granny, listen," she begged, taking a deep breath. "I didn't mean to fight with you yesterday. I'm sorry I just left, but sometimes I need some time to myself, and the forest really isn't dangerous. I didn't think you'd mind if I went for a short walk. I'm sorry, I should have told you this yesterday, but when you yelled at me, I couldn't talk anymore." Most of what she said was true, and it wasn't easy to admit all that. But when Granny answered her, Ruby realized it wasn't enough.

"If you think I'm going to believe you about going for a walk, you're in way over your head. You're lying to me. You were out with a boy, and anytime there's a boy involved, it doesn't end well. Ask your mother."

"I'm sorry ... I don't know." Although she couldn't disagree with Granny that there was a boy, she couldn't confirm it either. It would have been just stupid. Instead, she had to start a diversion. Otherwise, things would never be right with Granny. "Yesterday, I just needed a break and went for a walk. Somehow, I was just terribly tired and to keep myself awake and be able to continue working later, I strolled through the woods for a while. You know that split tree further back in the woods? I used to hang out there, and yesterday I discovered it again." With that, she had her grandmother. Of course she knew the split tree. It had been she who had rescued her from it all that time ago, when Ruby didn't dare climb down on her own.

"The split tree, yes," Granny replied reverently, and her expression changed immediately. "You were there again?"

She nodded. "I didn't even know where I was running to, and then suddenly I saw it and remembered how I played there back when I was a child." The lies came much easier from her lips than before, and it was good. But it also scared her.

"Oh yeah, I know ... you must have been five years old and running through the woods. Back then, all you ever wanted to do was pretend to be a pirate or a detective, and when you found the tree, you climbed right up. It took me forever to find you. Got really worried. And then a giggle came out of that tree. That's when I realized that my Little Red was probably sitting up there. I was trying to bribe you with cookies. And with cake. I promised you all the candy so you'd come down, but you just wouldn't. And then, it must have been hours later, you were too scared to come down by yourself. So I even had to climb up to you. Do you remember that? So I – an old lady – climbed up that tree, almost broke my leg, just to get that little girl down there. You probably could have just jumped into my arms, I would have caught you, but you didn't want to. You've always been stubborn."

Ruby laughed in relief. If Granny started with a story from her childhood, the argument was over. Even though maybe it was only over right now because she had forgotten there might be a boy. If Granny knew there was a whole pack running around out there, what would she do?

Uncertain, Ruby tucked one of her reddish-blonde strands behind her ear. "So ... do you need anything else? Otherwise, I'll take care of the chickens right away."

The rest of the morning was fairly relaxed. When Lisette arrived, Ruby was still in the kitchen unpacking the morning's backpack. Unlike usual, her Granny was with her, telling stories of the old days. And even though that was nice, Ruby's guilty conscience kept surfacing. The fact that her grandmother was finally only concerned with Lisette calmed Ruby down.

In the garden everything looked as usual. Apparently, no swans had taken up residence that morning. Ruby smiled with relief. One less thing for Granny to be upset about.

When it was time for Granny's nap, Ruby set aside her work tools. She washed her hands and face, had a snack, and went back outside. Only when she was in the garden did she look back at the house. Granny was asleep. She had announced it a long enough time ago and pulled the bedroom door closed behind her. But Ruby couldn't handle getting caught again.

Instead of sneaking off into the woods, she actually stayed in the garden this time, but it wasn't relaxing at all. The thought of her angry grandmother made her anxious, and although she had a book in her hands, she didn't even bother to look inside.

How had she forgotten that the pact expired today? That she and Leo could actually be something like a couple by tomorrow? Her skin tingled at the memory of his embrace that morning, and she almost wished she hadn't stopped him from coming to see her. But then what would have happened? Granny might have caught her again, and then there would be no distraction for her to use. She couldn’t bring up a childhood memory a second time.

And this way, at least she had a little more time to think about what she was going to say to him. How did one even begin such a conversation? And was tonight really the right time to talk about it? Between all the hustle and bustle of the party? Between all the people?

A while later, which seemed far too short to Ruby, she straightened up. For a moment, she paused before entering the kitchen. A strange feeling came over her, as if something terrible was about to happen. She half expected her grandmother to be standing there, hands on hips and grim-faced. Instead, her bedroom door was still closed, and Ruby was able to relax for a few more minutes.

Because she wanted to make a good impression on her Granny, she spent that time in the kitchen. She checked on the previously mixed dough that had risen quite a bit since Granny had set it aside, put on some tea, and washed and cut some of the fresh vegetables from the garden to take back to the village later. Still no sign of Granny.

When there was nothing left to do, she sat outside again, reading her book and watching out for swans. She couldn't see any birds, but at least she was able to read a few pages again.

It must have been half an hour later when she finally heard a noise from inside, and Granny poked her head through the door. "There you are," she said, half surprised. "I was beginning to think you'd slipped out again."

It was nice to see that she was still in a good mood. And Ruby wanted to keep that up as long as possible. Hastily, she rose from her seat, and walked over to her grandmother. "I was out here watching to make sure no swans came by. Yesterday they must have just made a stop on their journey to some other place," Ruby tried to distract her. If she was mad at the swans instead of Ruby, the girl had a better chance of having a somewhat relaxed day. And just in case that didn't work, "Did you sleep well?"

"Yes I did," Granny smiled and stepped aside. "Come on, we have some baking to do today." The two walked into the kitchen and refocused on their work.

For the first time in ages, Ruby felt like she didn't know what her grandmother was thinking. Did she believe her? Or did she suspect Ruby was plotting something?

Usually, Granny wasn't so kind when there was something for her to worry about. Or if there was something she could be angry about. But for the next few hours, she acted as if nothing had happened. She baked bread and pastries and gave Ruby instructions as usual. But this time, without yelling at her or making insinuations. Very strange.

When Granny Annie finally yelled at Ruby for "cutting the good cauliflower wrong" she was almost relieved to know that some things truly never changed. And when she finally made her way home, she had taken some more criticism, but it fortunately hadn't been about walks, yesterday's fight, or boys.

Granny Annie's house disappeared behind the trees, and a moment later Ruby spotted the pack that had been waiting for her. Ben was with them again. Zola and Zander, however, were not. Ruby suppressed the urge to walk straight up to Leo or stare at him, and instead let Nikki chatter away.

Far too distracted with not looking at Leo and shutting out the thoughts in her head, Ruby barely listened. As far as she understood, Nikki was talking about her day, and how excited she was to go back to the village tonight. "... But I talk too much. How was your day?"

"Um... good," she answered, and this time she couldn't stop herself from looking at Leo. She quickly averted her eyes again and felt her cheeks heat up. "Except when Granny yelled at me for nothing." She rolled her eyes in annoyance, even though the morning's nervousness had definitely been ten times as bad as the yelling today. Then she lifted her shoulders and pretended to push the bad mood aside. "But she did a lot of baking and some cooking again." With a smile that on another day would have been a broad grin, she gestured to the bags she carried over her shoulder. "Speaking of..." She had to look inside the bags to see which one she had intended for the pack. Then she handed the appropriate ones to Nikki beside her.

"Thanks," the latter called out delightedly, followed by an echo from the others.

"Hey, do you need help carrying your bags? Can I take something off your hands?" Ben had beaten Nikki to it today, and was already extending his arm. Nikki gave her a knowing look.

But Ruby faltered. Her mom, and Granny Annie too, had taught her that you had to be even more polite to strangers than you were to friends. Because they might be witches.

Well, Ben certainly wasn't a witch, but he wasn't her friend yet either.

"Please, let me help you," he insisted, and finally she let him take some bags.

Ben took it as a chance to stay close to Ruby, and tried to engage her in conversation. But in the midst of the pack it wasn't always possible to talk without being disturbed. Someone was constantly interfering. And finally Ruby brought up the party, which they could all talk about together.

"Oh, that reminds me, do you guys know how late you're going to get to the village?" she asked at one point when Ben didn't say anything for a moment. It was a good reason to look at Leo. His look was not particularly warm. But then again, they were among people.

"The party starts at seven, right? I'd say half an hour later, so everyone is already distracted and in a good mood," Nikki replied.

Reluctantly, Ruby turned away from Leo. "Maybe at eight instead? It'll be getting dark by then," she objected.

"Eight?" exclaimed Shawn. "That's ages away!"

The other younger ones grumbled as well, but Leo silenced them all with a look. "Red's right. We have to be careful. Even if we're all disguised, we might be recognized."

Ruby flinched as Ben butted in again. His voice way too loud and unexpected, right next to her. "What kind of party is this anyway?"

Nikki explained, but Ruby thought she recognized him looking at her again and again. He was probably hoping Ruby would say something.

"I'd like to come with you," he commented when Nikki finished. It wasn't even a question. He probably didn't even think that it might hurt them all if he were there.

Ruby gave Leo a quick glance, which Ben noticed.

"That's not a problem, is it?" he asked when no one said anything.

"No," Mara called out, as if it was up to her to make that decision. She squeezed herself between him and Ruby and looked at the young man with her big eyes. "You're welcome to come. It'll be fun."

It bothered Ruby that Leo agreed. Though not quite as euphoric as the little girl. But Ruby had to admit that the new guy probably didn't pose as much of a risk of getting caught as some of the others. Especially since no one in the village knew him, and he could quite easily pass off as passing through.

Since no one said anything against it, Ruby bit her tongue and refrained from commenting. Maybe she could change the subject? "Do you all have costumes, or do I still have to smuggle some out of the village?"

She was almost embarrassed that it only occurred to her now. With all the hustle and bustle of the last few days, she had really let the planning of the ghost party slide. If she were more organized, she would have gotten the dresses from Matteo yesterday and brought them this morning. Now it was a little late for something so low-key.

"Our parents took care of it," Nikki replied before Ruby could get lost in her new plan. "They were surprisingly happy to get rid of all of us for an evening." Nikki grinned, and Ruby had a feeling that they probably hadn't told them the whole truth. Their parents would hardly be happy hearing they'd smuggle themselves into the village they'd been banished from a year ago. Involuntarily, she wondered what the pack had told them.

"Oh," Ruby brought out in surprise. "Cool. And do you guys need anything else?"

"No, everything's under control." Nikki grinned broadly at her, and Ruby almost forgot what she should be worrying about right now.

"Great." Close to a panic, she searched for a new topic that would keep everyone, especially herself, busy. But all she could think of was that she wanted to talk to Leo.

A few minutes later, after the majority had turned back to their own conversations and Ben had claimed Ruby again, they finally reached the point where they parted ways. Ruby smiled politely at Benedict and took back her bags before saying goodbye to everyone. She wished she could talk to Leo again for a moment, but with the party later, they probably both had things to do.

Apparently, it would have to wait until evening.

EIGHTEEN

Night of Ghosts, Part 1

By seven o'clock, most of the villagers were already dressed in their costumes. Ruby still had to coax her mom to throw on a sheet as well, and finally managed it with a comment about not wanting to be late. That always worked. And as Ruby packed the food into bowls and cans, she heard her mom's nervous *Cha, Cha-cha, Cha, Cha-cha* as she came down the stairs.

Walking outside and heading to the marketplace, she was surprised to find that the majority of people were indeed dressed up. Although some only wore white dresses that did not hide their faces, there were also a good amount of people who were completely covered. To all appearances, even some adults.

Ruby and Catherine placed some of Granny's pastries on one of the two tables that had been set up. There were already a few drinks and some bowls of apples, nuts and cherries. Ruby was pleased to see everything work so well, even if she felt strangely exposed without her red leather jacket.

As the two stood in the square, the girl grew more and more nervous. With the previous stress she had been able to ignore it, but now there was enough time to think about what could go wrong.

And what she still had to discuss with Leo today. And to count the minutes until the wolves would show up.

The mayor spoke a few words, and everyone listened intently. This man didn't even live in the village anymore, but in the city on the other side of the forest. However, he had held this role for decades, and the village and its people were extremely important to him. Besides, no one else had ever seriously run for mayor.

The final words were just reminders of mutual consideration and the wish that everyone would enjoy this extraordinary celebration. After a good round of applause, everyone turned to their own conversations.

Catherine attempted to talk to her daughter, but she didn't get very far, instead turning to the neighbors who had interrupted their conversation. "Little Red!" Even if she hadn't recognized his voice, the cut of his costume was a good indicator of who was underneath. Matteo approached her and congratulated her on being named in this year's address. The mayor had expressed how a costume party had been a good idea and thanked Ruby. Of course, she was blushing under her costume at that point. "I'm sure you'll make a good mayor someday," Matteo commented.

"Oh no," she laughed, "I don't want that at all. Just imagine if you had to take an interest in every fight that goes on around here. It would be terribly exhausting! And depressing."

"I don't know, I've actually always thought you'd make a great leader. And you're good at settling arguments." If Matteo knew that she avoided fights in her own life by spinning a big web of lies around her, what would he say about her then?

"No, I'm happy to leave that to you," she replied, noting how he eyed her.

"You're wearing a bed sheet," he stated out of the blue. "You could have said something and I would have brought you a real costume."

"Oh, that's all right." She waved it off, but also noted how she must look pretty shabby next to him. "I was going to leave that for those who didn't have one."

"And it went really well," he explained excitedly. "I think I got ten costumes to people. But if you want ... I have another one at home."

Her eyes widened, which he probably couldn't see. "Really?"

"Sure, come on."

She briefly considered telling her mom where she was going, but then decided against it. Tonight they would probably both be everywhere. If she started letting her know where she was headed now, there would be no end to it.

"Here," Matteo finally said as they stood in the sparsely lit room, handing her a lone costume that lay in its near corner. It was remarkably tidy today, as was the rest of the room.

"Thank you."

He helped her out of her sheets, and Ruby brushed her tangled hair out of her face. Maybe she should have tied it back?

His dress was a lot nicer than hers. As he helped her into it, she noted that while the fabric seemed to be the same, the cut was quite special. She could see much better through the eyes, and her legs didn't tangle as she walked.

Matteo took her hand and pulled her toward a mirror. "You look great," he told her, and she nodded.

"Thank you," she repeated, immediately feeling much more comfortable. Even without her leather jacket.

"How did you get ten of these done in such a short time?" she asked admiringly. Even if she didn't know anything about sewing, this pattern didn't look too simple. And Matteo didn't seem to have that much free time per se to take extra care of it either.

"So if you count those two," he pointed to his own costume, and the one she was now wearing, "that makes twelve." Pride could clearly be heard in his voice, and Ruby couldn't blame him. He was really good at what he did, and probably didn't hear that very often. "But it was really quite easy. Once I figured out the pattern, it was the same work over and over again."

Ruby nodded in agreement, as though she knew enough about needlework to know such a thing. "I think it's great," she told him. "Come on, let's get back out there. Do you know what activities have been prepared?"

She looked at him curiously, because with all the hustle and bustle of the last few days, she hadn't heard anything at all. While she thought she knew what was going on in the village, she now found that it wasn't quite that simple. Not when she spent a majority of the day at Granny's house and in the forest.

Apparently Matteo was better informed than she. "At Pauletta's house I saw a soccer competition and Owen turned his garden into a creepy maze. I can't tell you any more than that."

There was definitely more, though. Outside his door they saw lots of kids running around and screaming with joy, some parents running after them, and others who had already given up on it. A part of Ruby wondered if the pack was already there, because there seemed to be so many people.

With Matteo by her side, she strolled through the village, trying to spot all the activities. "Hey, what time is it anyway?" she asked him at one point.

"Quarter to eight," he replied, glancing at his watch. Then he looked up at her, and she could guess a grin. "Are you bored already? We can do something too, if you want."

"No, was just curious. Time goes by fast." She hadn't believed it was that late already. And then it struck her that she didn't even know where the pack would be coming from. So how did she know they were there? That everything had gone well?

Well, she had to think of something. And get rid of Matteo.

"I'm starving," she said then. "I'm going to get some of that food in the town square." It was a lie. Ruby was far too nervous to even think about eating. But Matteo didn't question it. After all, he had no idea what else she had planned.

"Sounds good, I'll come with you."

Ruby faltered. Damn. What was she supposed to do now?

She tried to stay calm, but her mind was working at full speed. It wasn't a long way to the town square, and Matteo seemed genuinely hungry. He reached for some of the pastries while Ruby half-heartedly took one of the apples.

"Tastes good," he munched,

Ruby smiled absently, unable to stop herself from looking towards the forest again and again. To the place where she usually entered the forest and where she would later meet the pack. She should stop doing that. No one was supposed to know something was going on.

She tried to concentrate on Matteo. But at the same time, she was calculating in her head. How long had it taken them to get there? It must have been almost eight o'clock. Or even later? Ruby doubted she could estimate the time right, and she couldn't ask Matteo again.

Would the pack even be on time? Were they perhaps already here? Involuntarily, she looked around again. But she couldn't make out any faces. Only ghosts. At least the plan was working so far.

She hadn't listened that closely when he had spoken, but a name came up that interested her.

"Greta?" she asked excitedly. "Have you seen Greta and Hannes?"

"No, but I thought they were here for sure. Well, I can't be too sure, after all, they're all wearing costumes. Anyway, I don't think I've seen them yet tonight. Have you? Is that them up ahead?" He pointed in a direction where two children about the same size as Greta and Hannes were walking around.

"Maybe," Ruby finally answered uncertainly.

"There's only one way to find out," Matteo then commented. "Hannes? Greta? Is that you?" he called out to the two figures. They turned around, but it was still not clear to Ruby if it was the children they were looking for. With big steps he approached the two and she followed him.

"Hi," Matteo said, and she tried not to let on that she was still doubtful as she greeted them as well.

"Little Red? Matteo?" the familiar girl's voice asked. It was indeed Greta!

Ruby sighed with relief. "Where are you going?" she asked, "Have you picked anything yet?"

The two looked at each other. Ruby could see that they had also been outfitted by Matteo. "Great costumes," she commented.

"Thanks, you guys too," Greta replied.

Ruby smiled, but of course no one could see that.

"So, we were going to cherry pit spitting," Greta then said. "Are you guys coming?"

"I was going to meet someone else here," Ruby said quickly. "My mom," she added as they met questioning looks. "You guys go ahead." And thankfully they did. Now she just had to find the pack. Or at least Leo.

If her friends knew she wasn't looking for her mother, but for wolves, what would they think? Would they think her crazy to be allied with such dangerous creatures? Would they perhaps understand?

Ruby wasn't sure, and she didn't want to ask them. Or hear their answers. Aimlessly, she walked in one direction, hoping to run into anyone she knew. And finally, there was someone in her way. Ben. And he recognized her, despite her costume.

"Hey Little Red," he greeted her confidently. He was wearing his normal clothes. Jeans and a baby blue t-shirt, complementing his eyes. It surprised her a little.

"Hi." His appearance completely caught her off-guard. "What are you doing here?"

"I wanted to see this magical village everyone keeps raving about."

She laughed. "It's probably not that magical if you didn't grow up here. And even then..."

He interrupted her with a wide grin. "Can't you feel it? The magic? It's in the air like no other place."

Unsure if he was just joking, Ruby raised her shoulders and smiled politely. "It's probably because I've never been anywhere else, but I don't feel magic."

She didn't hear his reply, because out of nowhere her mom appeared. "Ruby, honey, I thought you were out with your friends?"

"How did you recognize me?" The girl laughed.

Catherine joined in as well. "Your shoes. Red like your leather jacket." Her eyes fell on Ben. Tall. Handsome. Unknown.

And her laughter died out.

"And who's that?"

"Ben ... Benedict," Ruby answered quickly. "He's passing through."

"Benedict," her mom repeated, "I'm Catherine."

When he was able to behave appropriately for the situation, politely shaking her mother's hand, Ruby quietly let out a sigh of relief. "It's nice to meet you. In fact, I was thinking of staying a few days." He threw Ruby a wry smile, but she was far too surprised to respond. He was going to stay? In Fairy Town?

Her mom, however, had no problem responding. Ruby could picture the deep crease between her eyebrows, though of course she couldn't see it. "Do you know where you're staying yet? When did you get here?"

"Actually, I camped in the woods last night, and then I ran into Ruby, who told me about Fairy Town. But I would just do the same thing again. I don't want to be a burden to anyone."

Ruby wasn't sure he wanted Catherine to react the way she did. "Oh no, no. Don't do that. There are some dangerous wolves out there. I'm sure someone here has a bed available for you." She looked around, searching, but Catherine spotted only ghosts as well. "Oh you know what? It's getting late, and before you go back to sleeping alone in the woods later, you can spend the night on our couch."

Wow. She definitely wouldn't have offered that to just anyone, and Ruby realized that pretty quickly. Because when he said, "There's no need. I'll be fine," her mom hesitated for a few seconds before disagreeing.

"No, you stay here. Come on, I'll show you where to go later, then you can enjoy the party a little more afterwards." Her gaze went to Ruby. "Do you want to come?"

"Uh ... no." It must have been eight o'clock already. "I'm meeting some friends in a little while."

Catherine just nodded it off without questioning it. Then she turned back to Ben. "How old are you, Benedict?"

"I just turned eighteen a few weeks ago..." That was the last Ruby heard from either of them before they were too far gone. In that moment, a group a little off caught her eye. There weren't enough people to be the whole pack, but hadn't Leo talked about splitting the group?

She walked up to them. "Hi," she said, catching the attention of two people, from the rather restless troop. Briefly she considered how to address them as unobtrusively as possible. "I'm Ruby. Who's hiding with you?"

"Well what do you think?" It was Nikki, her voice as crystal clear as ever. "Have you seen her?" she asked immediately, and Ruby knew who she meant, of course.

"She just went cherry pit spitting with her brother and Matteo." Although she couldn't see their eyes very well, she strongly suspected they were shining with excitement. This was the closest Nikki had come to talking to her best friend in a long time. At least as far as Ruby knew.

"I actually have to watch the kids," she said, "but would you mind if..."

Ruby didn't really want to. Actually, she did want to talk to Leo. "Who are they specifically?"

"I'm not supposed to say names so no one recognizes us," she countered, but Ruby could hear an eye roll. "We've divided it up so that there are no more than two exhausting ones in a group," she whispered to her anyway.

"Hey, maybe we can take them that way, there are more games set up, surely you can hang out there for a while. Or do you have instructions to only keep them in a certain part of the village?"

"No, I don't. Although that might have been a good idea ... Hey kids!" It was legitimate for Nikki to say that. As one of the tallest in the group, she looked like a chaperone even in costume. "Who's up for some cherry pit spitting?"

"Yay!" some yelled, and Ruby could hear Corey and Mara. Possibly Philippa was among them, too.

As they headed off, letting the kids run ahead, Ruby and Nikki chatted a bit until Ruby thought of something. "Hey, we were going to talk about ... you know what." She didn't want to say his name, because she didn't want to talk about Ben. Even if Nikki probably thought it was about him.

"Oh, yeah," she exclaimed delightedly, but then deliberately lowered her voice. "You like him, don't you? How could you not like him? He's nice, he's damn good looking, and..."

"Nikki," Ruby interrupted her, "I didn't want to talk about him."

"Oh." She actually seemed disappointed. Like she'd pinned all her hopes on this possible romance. "Then what do you want to talk about?"

Her hand wanted to run through her hair, until Ruby realized it wasn't possible with the costume. "I think I know why you're so interested," she began, leaving a brief pause for Nikki in case she wanted to say something. But she didn't. So Ruby continued. "Tell me, are you..." She lowered her voice, knowing that even though the kids were far enough away, they could still hear her. "Are you in love with someone?"

Her silence spoke volumes. "Yes ... No ... I ..." she faltered.

"You don't have to tell me who or since when...," Ruby quickly assured her. "It's just ... if you want to talk about it..."

Uncertainly, the girl nodded. At least, Ruby thought she saw a nod. It was actually quite hard to make out gestures under those robes.

"I can't tell anyone." She spoke so softly that Ruby barely understood her.

"Why not?"

"It's complicated." Ruby understood. It was complicated with her, too. It was probably always complicated. Especially in Nikki's situation, whether it was someone from the village or from the pack. It couldn't be simple.

It didn't seem like she wanted to keep talking. And Ruby didn't urge her to. After all, she had now learned that Nikki was in love. That her suspicions were indeed true. Perhaps she would learn more in the coming days, but for now this information was all she needed.

"Do you know where the others are hanging out?" she asked Nikki before they had arrived at the activities. She didn't want to have to get rid of Matteo again, and she also couldn't lie to him again.

"Luke's group should be around here somewhere. And Leo was going to Holly's house. Why, are you looking for someone in particular?" There she was again. The Nikki she knew and loved. Who was probably smirking at her right now.

"At most, to keep me away from him," Ruby joked.

They were getting dangerously close to cherry pit spitting, and Ruby was desperately looking for an excuse as to why she couldn't go there. Once she was among all her friends, it wouldn't be so easy to disappear. "Excuse me a moment," she began as she saw a couple of people who looked like Matteo, Greta and Hannes. "I have to go home for a minute. I forgot something."

"What is it?" inquired Nikki, fulfilling her greatest fear. She had no idea what.

"Uh ... girl stuff." Hopefully, that would shut her up.

While she fell silent – thankfully the kids hadn't been listening – Ruby took the opportunity to make a run for it. Her house really wasn't far away, but unfortunately in the opposite direction from Holly's. And Nikki knew her way around well enough to know that. It was only logical that Ruby walked until she was out of sight. Which eventually brought her to her house.

"Damn it," she cursed softly. All she really wanted to do was talk to Leo. Why was that so hard?

Now she stood at her own front door, wondering if she needed to go inside to make her story believable. When she heard a noise from inside, however, her curiosity took over.

"Mom?" she asked when she finally saw the woman clearly standing by the refrigerator. "What are you still doing here?" Ruby had expected her to be out by now, even after showing Ben around. Things like that didn't take that long, did they?

She turned and looked at her daughter in surprise. Her costume was on the kitchen table, and she was holding a piece of cheese. "I was hungry after I showed Benedict the living room and fixed up the couch for him. Besides, I could ask you the same thing."

Catherine had been open before about how she didn't think much of these village parties, and when it came out that she had to dress up, too, she had been even more reluctant.

"I ... uh..." She had best think of something very quickly. It probably wouldn't be a good idea to tell Catherine that she was avoiding her friends to find the boy she might like and talk about her future. "I was thirsty." To emphasize this, she went to the sink and took a glass of water. They both could have done that in the town square, but Ruby suspected that her mom didn't want to be out right now either. Briefly, she wanted to ask her about it, but stopped herself. Because then she would have to explain why she herself was there. "Where did Ben go?" Glass in hand, she leaned opposite her mom at the kitchen table.

"He said he wanted to go back to the festival. But I believe he wanted to see you." She took a sip from a cup next to the sink, and looked at Ruby with a smile. "He's a nice boy."

"Mom!" Blood rushed to her cheeks, but fortunately Catherine couldn't see it.

"What? He's polite, offered to help me fix up the couch right away, and asked me at least three times if he really wasn't being a bother here. The poor boy has been sleeping in the woods," she added, shaking her head. Then she looked at Ruby with a suddenly far too serious look. "He wouldn't happen to be the boy you met yesterday when Granny was taking her nap?"

Nearly choking on her water, Ruby stared wide-eyed at her mom. "Where ... How do you know about that?"

And out of nowhere, Catherine pulled out a folded piece of paper. It had to have been behind her the whole time. How had Ruby not noticed it? "The letter was in your backpack. From Granny. Why didn't you tell me about it?"

"I did," Ruby countered too quickly, remembering her strategy with Granny. "I told you I had a fight with Granny. She's a firm believer that I was out with a boy, but that's not what happened!"

"Why would Granny make something like that up?" retorted Catherine, frowning.

"You know her, she gets dramatic fast." Her mother wasn't quite as quick to buy the whole story as her grandmother, but Ruby saw uncertainty in her expression, and she could work with that. "Really mom, how was I supposed to meet Ben at Granny's house yesterday? It's pretty far from here, and if you don't know about it, you'll never find it. You can ask him! He probably doesn't know where it is."

And with that, she had Catherine on her side. Even though Ruby felt incredibly bad for lying again, she was proud that it worked out. Granny was one thing, but Mom was a whole new level.

Ruby had no reason to stand in the kitchen any longer. With the glass in her hand, she looked to her mother, who was absent-mindedly nibbling on her cheese. It clinked as she set her drink down, and her mom looked up. "I'm going back out," Ruby told her. "Are you coming too, or should I tell people you've already gone to bed?"

"Give me a few minutes, I'll catch up." Her eyes fell on the white fabric on the table. "No costume, though."

Ruby laughed with relief. While she didn't necessarily want to run around outside with her mom, it was hard to sneak into the house later than allowed when Catherine was there the whole time.

"Okay, see you later," she said and headed for the front door. There were a few kids loitering outside.

"Is there anything to eat here?" one asked innocently.

Ruby grinned under her cloak. So that was her reputation now. The one with the food. "There are some tables of food in the town square," she answered, smiling, watching them scurry off. Shortly after she started walking, though, she stopped again. Was Leo still with Holly? Would she just find him there and be able talk to him undisturbed? She had to at least try, didn't she? If not, when could she talk to him and just him today?

With a suddenly greater motivation than before, she took a detour to Holly, who was out of sight of her friends. Even though they couldn't ever be completely sure it was her in that costume, she didn't want to have to lie to them again.

When she finally arrived at the right house, she saw a light inside and knocked timidly. If Leo wasn't there, she would just tell Holly that she had come to check on her. It was believable because she would probably actually do that.

A costumed person opened for her. From the size, it could be Leo, but she shouldn't name him in front of outsiders. "Hi, I wanted to talk to Holly for a minute."

Wordlessly, the person stepped aside, and Ruby nervously walked into the living room where Holly was sitting in her chair. Was it not actually Leo? And who was it then?

"Hello Holly," she greeted her, and as Holly just stared at her, she realized that she too was still wearing a costume. She quickly slipped the fabric over her head, revealing her face. "It's me, Ruby."

Her eyes lit up. "Oh, hello my dear. Why aren't you outside with the others? You don't have to miss out on the fun because of an old lady like me."

Ruby laughed as if Holly wasn't absolutely serious. "I just wanted to see if you had enough food. And if you might want to come outside with me. There are some fun games."

"Oh no, I'd rather stay in here and read for a bit. But you should go back out and enjoy the feast. Both of you."

Only when she said it did Ruby's gaze wander around the room. The other person had leaned against a wall, seemingly listening to the two of them unobtrusively. They made no move to reveal their identity.

"Sure thing," Ruby replied, continuing to try to sound normal. "Is there anything you need before I go?"

"No, my child, go ahead."

And Ruby did so. The figure followed her. Nervously, she formed her ghost costume into a ball, and held it pressed against her stomach. What if this wasn't Leo after all? What if she searched for him all evening and wouldn't find him?

It wasn't until they were outside, and the door was closed behind them that she heard him speak. "That was sweet of you." It was definitely Leo's voice.

She almost let his name slip out until she remembered there was a plan. Instead, she just stared at him for a few seconds. "Hey," she finally said.

"Hi." They were still standing outside Holly's door, and Leo took her hand to pull her behind the house. Where there were no windows, no people, and the village bordered the forest. "I was afraid you wouldn't show up at all."

In reply, Ruby's eyes widened. "What do you mean? We weren't didn't agree on a place to meet." At least, she didn't remember ever discussing that with him.

"And yet somehow you found your way here." Neither of them dared to take another step toward each other, but somehow that desire was in the air.

"Well, because Nikki said ... Oh." It had been his plan. As soon as she ran into any of the pack, they would have told her Leo was here. It was a good plan, except ... "How did you know I was going to ask about you?"

"I had a hunch." When she didn't reply instantly, he added more seriously, "We still need to talk."

"Is this really the ideal time ... and place for that?" Involuntarily, she looked around to where children's screams were coming from and hugged the costume tighter.

"I had wondered the same thing."

It surprised her, and she looked up at him. How she would have loved to look into his eyes, but in the dark and with the costume, that was impossible. "I don't think we'll have another chance to be alone and talk tonight"

"Don't worry, I have a plan." His voice showed confidence, and that's exactly how Ruby wanted to feel.

"A plan?"

NINETEEN

Night of Ghosts, Part 2

An hour later they met at Ruby's house. In that time, she had gone with Matteo and all the others in their ghost costumes to the infamous ghost maze that was set up every year, and in which someone disappeared every year. Whether this was real or just an act, no one really knew. Although she wondered where Leo was, and if he would get out of there okay, she stopped herself from looking around every few minutes.

No one suspected a thing. If they noticed that Ruby was even more nervous than before, they didn't bring it up. And for that she was very grateful to them.

With a little excuse, Ruby snuck away, and was at her front door in time to open it for Leo. She offered him something to drink, though she was far too excited to manage a decent sentence.

She still hadn't made a decision for herself, and it was driving her crazy not knowing what was going to happen. What Leo would say. How they would go on.

For a while they stood in the kitchen, both with a glass of water in front of them, when Leo unexpectedly took off his costume, dropping it on a chair. Wide-eyed, Ruby stared at him. If the window wasn't facing the forest, someone might see him!

"Oh, now don't look at me like that," he said, running a hand through his forever messy hair. "Do you know how warm it gets under this thing? And I don't even have a mouth to breathe!"

"At least let us go upstairs," she begged. Somehow, with the extra steps between her and the front door, she felt a little safer. "You can take your glass, too."

But he drank it down in one go and put it in the sink. Then he grabbed his costume, her hand, and let her guide him to her room.

When they got upstairs, she turned on the small bedside lamp and pulled her costume over her head as well. Not because she had any ulterior motives, but because she didn't want any fabric on her face right now. And you probably shouldn't have a conversation like this wearing a ghost costume.

"So ... the pact," he finally began.

Nervously, she bit her lip. A year had passed. A whole year since she had met him again in the forest, after he and his family had been cast out. Even then she had thought she knew him well. And now she knew him even better.

But was that enough?

"Do you remember how all this started?" she asked uncertainly. Of course he remembered. If he felt anything like she did, he hadn't been able to forget a second of that day.

"Of course," he replied, taking a step toward her. "I'll always remember that."

TWENTY

The Pact

(One year ago)

Once again Ruby was on her way to her grandmother's house. Like she had been every morning for years. But something had changed. Today she was not cheerful or carefree. Since her friends were banished from the village a few days ago, nothing was the same. Even the walk through the forest was not. Every morning her mother warned her to be careful in case there really were wolves out there, and every morning Ruby assured her that she had never seen wolves on her way.

The forest was all she had left. After the village had driven away a total of 15 people, it had become much sadder. And her mom and Granny didn't talk about anything else either. But the forest ... the forest had remained the same. The same old trees with their low-hanging branches. The same lush green grass, punctuated by flowers and mushrooms. The same sounds, like the rustling of leaves and the singing of birds. The same smells of wood and grass. The same path she walked every day.

It was the only place that brought her peace when she needed it.

At least until she made out a figure on the side of the path some distance away. Not an animal. A human being. How? She never met people on her way!

Her steps slowed and her heart pounded faster. Ruby wished she could make out who it was, but even with narrowed eyes she was still too far away to make out the person's face.

And then, suddenly, she knew who was leaning there against the tree, and she stopped in her tracks, frozen. Was this a dream? Was she imagining it? It couldn't be him!

It couldn't be Leo.

And yet this boy looked exactly like Leo. Leo, who had been banned from his home, and whom she had not seen for almost two weeks now. Thirteen days, *she thought.* It's been exactly thirteen days since we last saw each other.

Maybe she was just imagining it. Why would she see him again now of all times?

Slow, careful steps carried her farther toward him, each step making it more definite. It was him. It was really him!

A few feet in front of him she stopped; he hadn't moved an inch. "Leo?" It sounded like a question, because she had to make sure her brain wasn't just playing a stupid trick on her.

"Hi Ruby." The familiar voice removed all doubt. His dark brown hair was a little longer than it had been back in the village, but the same brown eyes beamed at her.

When he continued not to move, she walked towards him with certain steps. Relieved, she fell around his neck, but Leo hardly moved. Only after a few moments did she feel him tentatively place his hands on her back, pressing her against him.

She heard him take a deep breath. "Aren't you afraid of me?" he asked softly.

Her own voice was as quiet and careful as his. "Why should I be?" Ruby couldn't even remember how long they had been friends. Why should she be afraid of him?

"I'm a wolf."

She winced at the word, but just a moment later she hugged him even tighter. She hadn't wanted to believe it. The whole village had blamed him and his family, but she had convinced everyone that it had to be a mistake. And to hear those words from him now? She had thought she would be afraid, but she wasn't. So many feelings, but no fear. "I missed you so much."

Even though it took a few moments, he returned her embrace with as much desire as she did. With her head pressed against his shoulder, she inhaled in his scent. There was no place more beautiful than this.

It wasn't until they broke apart that thoughts flooded back into Ruby's mind. Thoughts and questions. A worried expression made its way to her face. "Where have you been? And how are you doing? How's Nikki doing? And Luke? And the others?" Involuntarily, she scanned his skin for injuries.

Her behaviour made him laugh for the first time that day. "Slow down," he asked. "I'm not going to run away."

She raised her eyebrows with a grin. "Like you didn't run away from the village?" The joke was inappropriate. After all, he hadn't just "run away." But they could both laugh at it.

Leo pulled her into a hug again. "I missed you too," he whispered in her ear.

They stayed closely together for far too long for it to be considered just friendly. But Ruby didn't care so much at that moment. For far too long, she had thought she would never see him again. But this meant that they would see each other again after all. That she hadn't lost him forever.

His arms around her loosened, but he reached for her hands, making sure she wouldn't move too far away. And for a moment, she thought he was about to kiss her. But there were still too many questions. Too much she needed to know.

"Are you alright?" she finally brought out. Though she would have loved to use her lips for something else. But this was important. She needed to know.

He nodded. "Yeah ... I mean, now more than ever." He shot her a beautiful, crooked grin. "...but yeah. I ... we're all safe."

Ruby's heart dropped, and her mouth couldn't hide the smile. "Good." Her eyes lit up with happiness. Not only had she found one of her best friends again, he was fine. They were all fine.

His hands still held hers clasped, and so gradually they both became aware of it. Leo slowly lowered them. "I'm sorry, I'm sure you have to get going." His gaze followed the path Ruby had walked until she had spotted him.

Her response was merely a lift of her shoulders. "I'm late as it is," she waved it off, knowing full well that Granny Annie was only getting angrier the later she arrived. But she didn't care right now. "Feel free to hold me up for a few more minutes."

Carefully, Leo brushed a stubborn strand of hair out of her face. "With the greatest of pleasure, Little Red," he grinned.

"Oh no, not you too!" she laughed, "You know I hate when people call me that."

"Why though? Red is your colour, and everybody knows it's yours."

"Alright," she giggled, "but I'm not little." And contradicted herself by standing on her tiptoes in front of him, still unable to look him straight in the eye.

He grinned. "Dream on, little one."

He took a small step toward her, so that they were awfully close again. "Can I kiss you, Lady Red?"

Involuntarily, she gasped. Her heart was pounding too fast to get a clear thought. "Um ... yes."

And then there was barely any air between them. Leo's fingers brushed her cheek, sending goosebumps all over her body. His eyes seemed to shine through her, and Ruby had such a hard time breathing. It was she who finally closed the gap between them, pressing her lips gently to his. He held her tight, and she held him tight, and there was nothing around them. There was only the two of them. Here and now.

Although it lasted for what felt like an eternity, it was over all too soon. "Wow, I didn't expect that," she whispered.

Leo grinned, and slowly slid his hands up to her neck, over her shoulders, and down her arms until his fingers interlocked with hers. Ruby's whole body was electrified. "I agree."

Ruby took a moment to lose herself in his eyes before sighing and turning back to the path. "Granny's going to kill me," she laughed, gripping one of his hands tightly, pulling Leo along with her.

Relaxed and holding hands, they walked side by side until one of them broke the silence. It was Leo. "You know, the pack is just out in the woods all day. Maybe if you go to your Granny's, or home, or both, we can just tag along."

"Wait, the pack?"

Leo grinned at her. "Wolves ... live in packs."

Ruby giggled. "I see. Word play." She ran her hand through her long auburn hair, thinking about his question. But there wasn't much to think about. "Sure, the pack can come."

He squeezed her hand. "How's your mom? And Granny Annie?" His voice was still light-hearted; he had no idea of the mess the village was in because of him.

Ruby made a grimace. "They're not exactly thrilled about me walking through the woods every day when those dangerous wolves are out and about." With a quick glance in his direction, she assured herself that he knew she felt differently. "I'm sorry. Everyone's still pretty ... confused."

His steps slowed. "How would they feel about it if they knew what just happened?" With a nod of his head, he gestured backward, toward the tree beside which they had just exchanged shy kisses.

Ruby sighed. "They probably wouldn't be too happy," she admitted, staring at the ground, lost in thought. What would her mother say? And Granny? They definitely weren't thrilled about the whole wolf thing, and some days they really seemed to think the 'wolves' were dangerous. Yet they were still people! Still her friends. Ruby looked over at Leo and couldn't imagine him ever hurting her. That he would ever hurt anyone. "It's all still very new." It was a miserable attempt to cheer him up. Because obviously the villagers' opinions did matter to him somehow.

"I understand," he nodded. His steps slowed and his hand detached from hers. They stopped and he looked at her with a serious expression. "Maybe we should postpone the whole thing." His eyes told her that he didn't really want that. "At least until everything settles down a bit." He tried a smile, but it wasn't very convincing.

"You're right," Ruby brought out slowly, though she didn't really want that either. For a few minutes she had been so happy. But now, thinking of the repercussions it might have, she couldn't disagree with him.

"How long?" he asked, seeming to stop himself from reaching out for hers. "When do you think they'll get used to it?"

Unsure, Ruby raised her shoulders. "It's only been two weeks and it's still taking a toll on everyone." She couldn't voice what she was thinking. Didn't want to bring the words past her lips. But Leo looked at her expectantly. "One ... year?"

"One year," he repeated flatly. Ruby couldn't tell what he was thinking. His eyes narrowed, and then he looked directly at her again. "A year is doable," he smiled. And infected her with it.

"We should make a pact," she suggested excitedly.

"A pact that says in a year we'll see if you still want to kiss me."

"And you me." Ruby's cheeks warmed. "And until then, we'll be friends."

"That's right." He brushed a strand of hair from her face one last time, making Ruby's heart skip a beat before they finally headed to Granny Annie's.

TWENTY-ONE

Night of Ghosts, Part 3

The memory made them both smile. And Ruby absentmindedly reached for Leo's hand. He was still so close that she had to take a small step back before she could focus on him again. "Do you ever think we shouldn't have made a pact?"

"Do you regret kissing me back then?" he countered with a grin. He knew for a fact that she didn’t.

Sure, it was time to speak plainly, but she hadn't expected such a question from him right away. "No, I ... I just mean that it's difficult to make such a big decision at a moment’s notice." She thought of Zola, who definitely still liked Leo. And of Nikki, who wouldn't like anything going on between Ruby and her brother. And the rest of the pack, who would look at her funny. And of Granny and her mom, who thought wolves were terribly dangerous.

He laughed. Soft and dark. A beautiful sound. "We've been talking about this for a year."

He was right. However, they'd also told each other to stay friends during that time, and Ruby had taken it seriously. Mostly, she hadn't thought of him as more than a friend. It had been harder at first, but by now she was pretty good at keeping her feelings under control. Well, at least as long as Leo didn't make any moves on her. "Sometimes I think that was a mistake." Leo looked at her so disappointed that she quickly had to clarify. "My mom and Granny are still scared of the wolves, and now – after a year – I can't tell them I knew you guys all along. They'd be so mad. And I don't know how the pack will feel about it when they find out, either." Ruby thought she heard Shawn's voice from outside at that exact moment. Even though he was probably in a completely different part of the village right now.

"It won't bother them," Leo assured her, "They like you. There's no reason why that should change." He looked into her eyes. Looking for some sign that she believed him.

Ruby didn't like to admit that something else entirely bothered her. But when Leo looked at her like that, she couldn't lie to him. "You and Zola..." she began before she could stop herself. "You still like her."

He had just been about to brush a strand from her face, but now he paused in his movement. "I do like her. But not like I used to," he clarified, and Ruby didn't quite know why she immediately believed him. Maybe it was because of the way he looked at her while he said it. Or maybe it was because he was here, and not with her. The smile on her lips disappeared as quickly as it had come, though, when in his serious voice he added, "But you have a thing for Ben."

"What?" she groaned. Where had he gotten the idea?

"You think he's hot."

The conversation. The one with Nikki. He'd overheard them! "If you were as good at spying as you think you are, you'd know Nikki thinks he's hot." She took another step toward him. "And that I'm not interested in him."

That was all she needed to say. He believed her – so much so that he got close to her once more. "So, the pact," she stopped him again creating some distance between them. As much as she would have liked to kiss him, it probably wasn't getting them anywhere. After all, the pact was what they came here to talk about.

"Yes, the pact," he repeated. For some reason, he moved a little closer to her. And poof! She couldn't think straight anymore.

Did he feel the same way? Was he also not so sure anymore about them being friends? Whether it had been the right decision to make a pact like this?

Before she could make any conscious decision, her lips were on his, and her mind went blank for good. One of his hands settled on her back and pulled her closer, the other buried itself in her hair. Her body, too, was doing everything it could to be close to him. On her tiptoes, she didn't have quite as stable a footing, but she could lean into Leo and he'd hold her. And besides, she didn't care how stable she was right now, as long as he kissed her and she kissed him and they didn't let go of each other.

None of them heard the door open. Or someone coming up the stairs. A surprised "Ruby?!" had them stop in their tracks. The voice. Her mom.

Caught off guard, Ruby and Leo shot apart. But while the girl could only stand petrified, Leo reacted a lot faster. With a movement so quick that Ruby could barely see it, he turned his face away and ran to the window. Even Catherine couldn’t stop him from disappearing into the night.

"Ruby?! What...?" her mom started, and Ruby tried to intervene before she could get too worked up.

"Don't get mad, it wasn't anything bad." Because she didn't have time to think of a good excuse, what she said didn't make much sense either.

Catherine crossed her arms in front of her chest and tilted her head. Her furrowed eyebrows showed Ruby that she hadn't convinced her at all. "You'll have to explain this to me. What's going on here?"

"Um..." Her mother's calm made her even more nervous. While she was trying to think of a good half-truth, it occurred to her that she had been doing nothing but lying to her friends and family for days. First Granny with the whole Leo thing, then Holly, but also Matteo, Nikki and the pack. And her mom. Her mom especially. How much longer could she keep this up? Could she possibly tell her the truth?

No, she decided. But she couldn't lie to her anymore, either. "I kissed a boy," she admitted, earning a suppressed smile in return.

"I saw that." Catherine became serious again, and it scared Ruby. "But who was that?" She seemed to think of something, and her look didn't get any friendlier. "Granny's just being dramatic, huh? Was that the boy in the woods? Was that ... Ben?"

"What? No! It was ... I just ... I'm sorry." She meant it. But it wasn't enough.

Her mother took a deep breath. "Ruby, that's not how it works, and you know it. You can tell me if there's someone you like! But to find you here kissing and doing whatever else..."

"Mom!" she quickly interrupted. She didn't need to know what Catherine thought would have happened here if she hadn't interrupted her. "It was just a kiss." *Lie.* "It wasn't anything serious." *Lie.*

"Then why were you in your room? Is that what you do if it's not serious?" She could see how disappointed Catherine was in her, and the disappointment was even worse than her anger.

"No. I..." She couldn't keep lying to her. So, she fell silent. "I'm sorry," she repeated softly.

"Ruby, we don't have secrets in this house. I expect you to tell me the truth." It made Ruby instantly so mad. *No secrets?* Catherine herself had secrets! It wasn't fair! It wasn't fair for her to expect from Ruby what she couldn't keep herself!

"No secrets?" Her voice trembled. "What about the man you met in town? Isn't he *your* secret?"

"You're going too far," Catherine growled. A long pause followed. The two women stared at each other, neither making a sound. For a moment Catherine waited to see if her daughter would say anything else, and when she didn't, she turned and went into her own bedroom. Petrified, Ruby stood there, staring first at the spot where her mom had disappeared, then where Leo had taken off. *Damn.*

And then she started walking. Without thinking about it, she hurried down the stairs, through the door, and out the front yard. By the time she realized she'd left her costume in the house, she'd almost arrived at the outdoor bowling alley. Where she had left her friends alone. And Matteo had discovered her. But before he encouraged her to have fun, he nodded in a direction with a worried expression.

For a short time, Ruby's curiosity even outweighed her dejection about the argument, and she followed his hint without turning around again. She walked along the path between two houses that led to another game for children. Ruby had no idea why Matteo wanted her to see it. Until she saw something else.

Ben and Nikki. Kissing.

"Hey!" she snapped angrily. Nikki was like a little sister. And even though Nikki couldn't tell, Ruby knew she didn't feel that way about Ben. Whatever was going on wasn't meant to be, she was sure of that.

She was also sure that it was entirely Ben's fault. While Nikki visibly flinched, he merely took a slow, relaxed step away from Nikki.

Once Ruby had their attention, she stomped toward them. "Put on your costume," she ordered an unusually nervous Nikki before turning to Benedict. Though she was a lot shorter than him, she looked him straight in the eye. "And you better go."

"It was just a kiss." He lifted his shoulders as if to say that such a thing could happen to anyone after all. "If you ever want one too, all you have to do is say so."

His grin made her stomach turn. "Go!" she repeated angrily, until he finally moved away.

By now Nikki had slipped the white fabric back over her head and was looking at Ruby almost in fear. But the redhead was only concerned. "Are you all right?"

"Yeah... I..." She sounded the same as Ruby had before, but she couldn't think about that now. Not about the argument. Not about herself.

"Did he make you kiss him?"

"What, no! It was ... something else..." Somehow Ruby had her problems believing her. But maybe Nikki just wasn't able to express herself properly right now. Or to tell the truth. After all, Ruby had felt the same way just a few minutes ago.

"So, you like him?" Ruby asked, confused.

"No ... well, maybe. I don't really know. He's nice."

Ruby wondered if *nice* was enough to kiss someone, but stopped herself from saying it. She'd told her own mom that it wasn't serious with Leo, so maybe Nikki's answer wasn't quite true either. With a shake of her head, she banished the thought of her own problems. "So you're okay?" she asked again, waiting until the girl nodded hesitantly before hugging her. "I'm sorry I was so loud, I thought he had..." What *had* she thought? That he had forced himself on her? Was trying to talk her into more than just kisses?

"Thank you," Nikki replied softly.

It seemed their conversation ended there, though Ruby continued to give her friend concerned looks. Nikki walked, faster than usual out of the small side street, and the two of them headed back toward Matteo.

Only now did Nikki slow down again, looking at Ruby as she walked. "Have you seen Leo?"

"No." The lie came far too effortlessly from her lips. Another lie. Oh great. Seemed like this was becoming a habit now.

"He should be around," Nikki continued. "All right, we need to start getting the kids out of here in a few minutes. With or without him."

Nikki had regained her composure surprisingly quickly. Ruby couldn't tell if her friend actually hadn't taken the matter all that seriously, or just wanted to get out of there as quickly as possible.

In a very discreet manner, Nikki called the kids over, who then immediately formed a cluster around her. "Listen up," she said loud enough for the group to hear, but not so loud that the rest of the village did. "Ten more minutes, then it's back to work, okay?"

Some nodded, others didn't seem at all enthusiastic. "Really, only ten more minutes?" whined someone who sounded suspiciously like Corey. After Nikki shooed them all away and sent them to play on, Ruby saw that he was still limping. And she also saw one of the adults turning to look at him, noticing his struggles, and approaching the boy. The woman – Evelyn of all people – who had been on the witch's side in the whole wolf debacle, stopped Corey and bent down to him. "Did you hurt yourself playing?" she purred, just loud enough for Ruby to hear from a distance. Even though the concern was apparent in her voice, she knew this woman was up to no good. Besides, Ruby couldn't let anything get out. If none of the children had a similar injury tomorrow, wouldn't it be way too obvious?

The girl quickly walked over and stood next to Corey, who thankfully hadn't said anything yet. "He just twisted his ankle playing catch earlier. I'm sure it'll be fine tomorrow."

Evelyn straightened up. "Maybe someone should take a look at it. I just saw Dr. Stielzchen close by." Searching and with her chin up, Evelyn looked around the crowd.

"Oh, we don't have to bother her. I already looked at it," Ruby quickly replied, and without a costume, the woman could identify her too. "It's not swollen, it's not blue, and he can still walk." Glancing at the boy, she put a friendly smile on her lips. "Go back to playing," she told him, and he did his best to walk as normally as possible.

Evelyn, however, who always liked to know everything better, looked at her with her lips pressed together. "If you say so, Little Red. But I hope for your sake it's really nothing bad."

Was Ruby imagining it, or did she sound accusatory? *I hope for your sake, it's nothing bad. For your sake.* It sounded like Evelyn was blaming her, should it be serious after all. Luckily, Ruby knew that Corey was nowhere to be seen tomorrow, so no kid would be walking around with an injured foot.

"Who is that anyway?" asked Evelyn unexpectedly, and Ruby worried that she recognized her fear of that question in her expression.

At that moment, she heard her name. Thankfully. "Hey Little Red," Matteo called, and she automatically looked back at him. If she was smart about it, Evelyn wouldn't see the relief in her expression.

She turned back to the woman and gave her an apologetic smile that was, of course, completely fake. After everything Evelyn had said about the wolves, Ruby couldn't stand her one bit more. "Sorry, I have to go. But I'm sure he's fine." Then she went to Matteo without waiting for a reply, glad that Evelyn didn't hold her back for some reason.

Matteo smiled at her sympathetically, with a toy fishing rod in his hand. "First the thing with Nikki, and then Evelyn. You're not to be envied today."

"Yeah," Ruby replied, and was taken back a few minutes to when she'd caught the girl making out. "Already quite ... wait what? How do you know it's Nikki?"

"I didn't. It was just a guess," he admitted. Probably with a grin.

"Oh damn," Ruby groaned, realizing she had just given away her friend's identity. "You're not going to say anything, are you?" She looked at him hopeful.

"No, of course not," he quickly assured her. "Where did you find her? I mean, I haven't seen her in a year."

"Don't take offense, Matteo, but I can't tell you that."

He nodded in understanding, and Ruby immediately liked him a lot more for it. If she'd talked to anyone else about it, her mom, Holly, Greta, or Granny, they would have wanted an explanation right away. Including all the key data: When, how, where, who, what. But Matteo just accepted it and was happy to see an old friend. Ruby wasn't quite sure if he recognized the others as well, but if he did, he didn't say so. It was probably for the best, too. The fewer people hearing the pack members' names, the safer they were.

"You were gone quite a while," he then noted. But he didn't demand an explanation, instead holding out a second toy fishing rod to her. "You want to play a little? Push on this one, and hold that one until you cast," he explained, and without waiting for an answer, he thrust it into her hand. Ruby couldn't help but laugh and do exactly what he said. "Wow, looks good," he commented, and she smiled at him.

"It's fun," she agreed.

"If you'd stayed there, it would have been fun an hour ago," he teased her. She rolled her eyes, recognizing the attempt to figure out what she had done during that time. But she wouldn't tell him. She didn't want to think about all that had happened to her in the last hour herself.

The worst part was probably that now she wasn't wearing a costume anymore and people could see if she was having fun or not. So she tried to make the evening nicer, even though thoughts were circling in her head. What had happened to Hannes and Greta? Were they alright? Where was Leo? Why hadn't Nikki seen him again? Was he okay? What was the whole thing between Nikki and Ben? Was it what Nikki had called *complicated*?

She was able to distract herself, at least a little. But she still hoped she could talk to Leo one more time. To tell him about the drama surrounding Greta and Hannes and see if he was okay. If the thing with her mom hadn't completely disturbed him.

It was also this thing, that now made her much more afraid of being caught. By her mom, by her Granny, by all sorts of people in the village who seemed super interested in what was going on around them. Like Evelyn, who had chatted up Corey. If Ruby hadn't noticed, would he and the pack have been busted?

"Hey," Nikki interrupted her thoughts. "We're heading out." She spoke so softly that Matteo couldn't hear her, and when she pulled Ruby into a hug, she just whispered. "I'll see you tomorrow, okay?"

"Of course. And take care of yourself tonight." Ruby whispered, too.

The costumed girl nodded, then turned to the children. The plan had to involve going to a more secluded end of the village where no villagers would see them go into the woods. At least that's what Ruby deduced as they walked in the direction of Holly's house.

Ruby had to force herself not to stare after them. It would draw attention, and that wouldn't be good for the pack. But now that the kids and Nikki were gone, she was almost alone with Matteo.

"Did you enjoy tonight?" asked Ruby, realizing that it was really dark by now, and most of the parents were getting their kids ready to go home. Yet again, she cast out for the ducklings in her game, and immediately had one hooked. She put it back in the water and cast again.

Matteo next to her did the same. "Yeah, it was quite nice."

"Quite nice?" She looked at him with raised eyebrows. It didn't sound very convincing. But he grinned back at her.

"Well, it could have been great, but a bunch of weird stuff happened. First," he lowered his voice, "Nikki comes out of the woodwork and talks to Greta like it's life or death. Then this thing with the guy she pulled into a dark alley. And I swear, I've never seen him before." By now he was speaking at a normal volume again. "And then you just disappeared in between, and won't tell me what was going on. Oh, and by the way, I take the fact that you're not wearing my costume anymore personally." It was a joke. Of course he wasn't mad at her. Although he had plenty of reasons to be.

Ruby put her fishing rod aside. "I really can't tell you what happened," she said, although she already doubted it. Matteo was her friend, he would keep her secrets. And inside she knew that she couldn't not tell all this to anyone for much longer. At the same time, it wasn't her decision who was allowed to know from the pack. And she knew how angry Leo would get if she told anyone.

Matteo, for his part, looked at her dejectedly. It seemed like he had hoped to get some information out of her after all. Or that they were better friends that this and told each other everything. Ruby would have loved to tell him.

"Okay," she finally relented. "The reason I've been away, and why I'm not wearing your costume anymore: I went home for a minute, took the costume off to get some water..." She didn't want to lie to him. It was tormenting her. It wasn't supposed to be like this between them. "Okay, I was seeing someone." It took a load off her shoulders when she was able to say it without a negative reaction from him. Instead, he continued to look at her tensely. "Someone who shouldn't be here. I can't tell you who it is ... And then maybe we kissed when my mom walked in, and then mom and I had a fight, and I left the costume. And I couldn't go back, of course, because then she might not have let me leave again." It felt good to be able to tell him all that.

Although she was still afraid of what might happen next.

But Matteo looked more worried than anything else. "You guys had a fight? About what?" There was no doubt that he was serious. That he respected what she couldn't tell him.

"The kiss," she repeated.

He grinned at her, and she wondered what it was that could make him grin in this situation. "The kiss with the mystery man. Was he good at least?"

Relieved, Ruby laughed out loud, but a loud crackling noise kept her from actually saying anything about it. It seemed as if a branch had broken off a tree, but when they looked in that direction, nothing was visible.

"That," she said, setting aside her fishing rod, "is a story for another evening."

TWENTY-TWO

A Night like no Other

When Ruby entered the house, there was light coming from the living room. She had almost forgotten that her mom had offered Ben to spend the night here, and now a door was open that was usually closed. After their last encounter, Ruby really didn't feel like talking to Ben, but to get to the stairs and her room, she had to go past it. In all likelihood, he had heard her come through the door anyway. Maybe she could just say a quick hello, and then head upstairs.

Of course, that wasn't what happened. When Ruby reached the living room, Ben was sitting in the brown armchair across from the sofa her mom had added a pillow and blanket to a few hours ago. He had one of the books from the old shelf on his lap and raised his head when Ruby made herself known.

"Hey, I'm going to bed. Do you need anything else?" Actually, she just wanted to go to bed, but her manners – which sounded an awful lot like her mother's voice in her head – told her to check on her guest.

Ben slammed the book shut and smiled guardedly at Ruby. "Hey, can we talk for a minute?"

Oh no. Not today. "Sure." A little reluctant and a lot tired, she entered the room and sat down on the sofa. Somehow, she wanted to know what the kiss with Nikki was all about. And she hoped that was exactly what he would be trying to apologize for.

"About what happened earlier..." he began, but he seemed to be waiting for her to say it. And was already wearing an apologetic smile.

"You mean when you kissed Nikki in a dark alley?" Her words sounded angrier than she had intended, but also kind of appropriate. She didn't know what to make of Ben anymore, especially after he'd flirted with her and kissed her friend.

Nervously, he ran his hand through his still perfectly styled hair, "Yeah, just that." He didn't seem like the type who could easily face such a conversation, but it took him a few moments - during which Ruby merely stared at him judgmentally - to collect himself. "Look, it wasn't as it seemed. It didn't mean ... that."

Once again, he paused, and Ruby couldn't help herself. "How was it meant then?" she asked pointedly. If he had no good reason for all this, why had he done it?

Despite his obvious guilt, he held her gaze. Then even a small smile crept onto his lips. "Don't think I'm an idiot now, okay? She kissed me, and I know I shouldn't have let her, but ... there was nothing I could do at that moment, you know?"

Hesitantly, he put the book that had been on his lap on a small side table. Then he rose, came to the sofa, and sat down beside Ruby. "The last thing I wanted was for you to see it. I like you Ruby, and I need to know if you do too."

With his sudden closeness and this unexpected confession, Ruby was completely overwhelmed. "I ... no ... I ..." She didn't want to hurt his feelings. But at the same time, she had no interest in him.

The smile on his face looked a little too strained to be completely honest. But he kept it up as he brushed a strand of hair out of her face. "I'll just have to think of something else to convince you, then."

As Ruby made her way to her room, her mother's closed bedroom door proved that she really hadn't been out since their earlier argument. Ruby turned on the light and tossed her shirt on the floor. Outside her window, it was quiet. Partly because it was facing the forest, and partly because Matteo and Ruby had been two of the last ones out.

The girl sat down on the bed but did not manage to do anything else. Her eyes fell on the two forgotten costumes, and all the events of the evening played again in her mind. But above all, the thing that had happened in that room with Leo. *Leo.*

As much as she would like to curl up in her blankets and squeeze her eyes shut right now, she couldn't. There had to be a way to make it all better!

Of course, she had no choice. If she snuck out of the house again now and got caught, Catherine would never trust her again. She had to spend the night in her bed, and maybe she could forget everything that had happened after all, and just sleep for a while.

Well, the hope was there, only unfortunately her head was too full to actually sink into a decent sleep. Instead, she tossed and turned in her bed, and awoke in the wee hours of the morning.

When a noise sounded from outside in the woods, Ruby made her decision. She flung aside the covers, threw on some clothes, and crept down the stairs. Passing the now closed living room door extra quietly, she grabbed her red leather jacket from the coat hook.

No one ran into her as she circled the house and went to where that movement had caught her attention. She hoped it was Leo, and not just some bird. And she hoped he wouldn't send her right back home because it was too late and too dangerous for her out here.

Ruby approached the trees; it was darker than she had expected. Still, there was no danger emanating from the darkness, even though everyone liked to tell her that.

"Hello?" she whispered, hoping Leo would make himself known. With each step, she doubted her decision to set out completely alone and in the middle of the night.

Still nothing. Ruby seriously wondered if she should turn back. "Is there anyone here?" she asked again. Maybe she had imagined it all.

"Hello, Little Red."

It wasn't Leo. It was Nikki.

"What are you doing here?" asked Ruby, confused. Nikki didn't usually come this close to the village. And certainly not at this hour.

"I don't know what to do," she burst out. It was too dark to make out the expression on her face clearly, but her voice sounded more than a little desperate. "I can't talk to Leo and Luke about it, and the other girls are too young to understand what it's about, and I just didn't know where else to go..."

"It's okay." Ruby pulled her friend into a tight hug. "What happened?"

"Greta and I got into a fight. Earlier at the party. And then I haven't seen her since. And I don't know how much she hates me now. I need to know if she hates me now. And I need to know that she's okay. But I can't snea-" She interrupted herself. "Can you go check on her? Can you find out what she's thinking?"

This was one of those moments when you just had to promise a friend to do everything possible, even if you didn't understand everything. Like what the argument could have been about, if it had such consequences. Or why Ben didn't even seem to be an issue anymore. Apparently, the thing with Ben was impacting Ruby more than to anyone else.

"Don't worry," Ruby said quickly when she noticed Nikki giving her an expectant look. A cold drop of water landed on Ruby's forehead. The morning rain would soon start with full force. "I run into her and Hannes sometimes in the morning on the way to school and I can ask them. And worst case scenario, I see them in the evening."

The second drop landed on the back of her hand before Nikki responded. "Okay ... okay." It didn't sound okay. It sounded like Nikki had to convince herself that it was okay. That she could wait. And Ruby knew Nikki wasn't that good at sitting still. Trusting someone else to save the day. Especially when it came to Greta.

TWENTY-THREE

A Morning that's way too normal

The third drop hit Ruby on the cheek just as she slipped back inside. It was quiet. So incredibly quiet. Only Ruby's heart was beating disproportionately loud. Was it because of what Nikki had just told her? Was it because Ben was sleeping on her couch just a few steps away from her at that very moment? Or because she didn't want to run into her mother after last night while she was sneaking back into their house?

Quietly she went back to her room, and lay down in her bed, but she couldn't sleep. This day was going to be very nerve-wracking. Not only did she have to deal with her mom and Ben before breakfast, but the thing with Greta gave her no peace. She couldn't even begin to imagine how Nikki must have been feeling.

And then there was the thing with Leo! What could she say to him after everything that had happened last night?

Ruby was more than awake when the rain outside her window stopped and the sun came up. A rough plan had formed in her mind. There wasn't anything else she could've done. She could hardly let the thoughts race in her head and not do anything about it!

From the safety of her own bed, Ruby could hear her mom's door open. Then her walking down the stairs. A high-pitched voice and a low-pitched voice talking to each other. And at some point, the front door closed.

Ruby wanted nothing more than to make up with everyone again. It would be so much more relaxed. But getting there wasn't exactly pleasant, and today she didn't have the nerve for loud and emotional conversations.

When she finally dared to leave her room, it was actually time for her to get out of the house. But she had had to make sure that Catherine was indeed gone. And she would probably have to forgo her breakfast today. She didn't want to spend too much time downstairs anyway, in case Ben tried to talk to her again.

It turned out that her worries had been completely unfounded. The living room door was closed when she came downstairs, and it didn't open when Ruby got her bags and a piece of bread from the kitchen.

With the hope of still catching up with Greta and Hannes despite her own tardiness, Ruby finally ran head over heals outside. She saw a few schoolchildren, but try as she might, she couldn't spot the siblings.

Disappointed and suddenly very exhausted, she made her way into the forest. Today, no one startled her as she approached the pack. They had already been waiting.

"Little Red!" shouted Mara as if she first had to alert the others that the girl was there. Ruby put on a less than convincing smile and quickened her steps.

"You're late today," Luke noted, who was leaning against a tree, not too deep in his conversation with Zander.

A look around confirmed to Ruby that Zola was also back today. And, of course, she was standing next to Leo. Her stomach tightened. But instead of getting stuck with them, she turned back to Luke. "It's been a long evening," she replied tonelessly.

The wolves started moving almost simultaneously, and Ruby caught Nikki's questioning, almost urgent look. Words were not necessary. Ruby shook her head slightly, watching as Nikki turned away.

Neither she nor Leo made any effort to chat with her, and if there weren't the entire pack around them, Ruby wouldn't mind it. A little quiet like that did her a world of good today. However, Shawn always saw something like this as an invitation to annoy her.

"Did you bring cake again today?" he wanted to know, walking close beside her. Did he want to look in her backpack? Or was this a distraction for something else?

"No." She wanted to say it kindly, but it didn't come out that way. Fortunately, Shawn seemed too distracted to notice anything. Everyone seemed too distracted to see through her fake smile.

Nikki was surprisingly quiet and didn't even try to speak to Ruby. And Leo effortlessly ignored Ruby. He was engaged in a conversation with Zola. And although Ruby wouldn't have been able to handle him looking directly at her after last night anyway, she wasn't too fond of that either.

Ruby spent the walk to Granny's house mostly in silence. Shawn had quickly returned to more exciting things: showing his friends how fast he could climb trees, for example. And just when she thought she was almost done, Zola joined her.

For a few minutes they walked side by side in silence. Then Zola cleared her throat. "Was the party good yesterday? I always thought the village fair was a bit boring. I'm sure the ghost costume thing was fun."

"It was." Ruby had to stop herself from asking her why she hadn't been there. She had run away. She couldn't just sneak back in there just to go to a party.

Zola played with a strand of her hair. But she didn't sound the least bit distracted. "Leo was back pretty early. Do you know why?"

Of course she knew. He'd left his costume in her room, and after that he couldn't go back to the village. How had he explained that to the others? And what had he and Zola been doing all evening? While she had been arguing with her mom and caught Nikki and Ben making out, what had they been talking about? Had they been alone? Had they been *alone*?

No, she couldn't think like that. But was there maybe some truth to it? She looked at Zola, who was smiling at her. Oh yes, she had asked her a question. "Someone probably caught him." It surprised even her that she could still lie, with all the chaos in her head.

Zola, on the other hand, seemed calm as can be. "Yeah, that must have been it. Anyway, I didn't think it was so bad that he had a little more time for me." She giggled, and Ruby couldn't hold back the thoughts at that moment. The idea of Zola and Leo. Together. It was driving her crazy. What had he said to Zola after he escaped from Ruby's room? Had he looked at her like that, too? Kissed her like that, too?

It was a blessing when they reached the three oak trees. "Bye," Ruby croaked, throwing the group a half-hearted smile. "See you tonight!"

TWENTY-FOUR

Chewing Gum

The day dragged on like chewing gum. Granny Annie wasn't necessarily overly mean, but she wasn't particularly friendly either. Motivation to complete her task sank even lower when Ruby remembered that Granny had smuggled a note into her backpack the previous day to rat her out to her mother. She had to remember to check her backpack that evening.

"I'm going to lie down," the old woman called from the back door, just as Ruby was bending over the cauliflower. "Don't even think about leaving again today!"

Of course, the girl thought. Of course she had to plow and plow again, and not move five feet from the property. And today, in fact, she would not get away with a half-baked excuse.

Instead of cutting off the next cauliflower and putting it in her basket of ripe vegetables, Ruby dropped onto her bottom and wiped the sweat from her brow. She would not be able to keep this up much longer. For a considerable amount of time she wouldn't be able to tell half-truths and keep things secret. Or be able to choose between her family and her friends.

With a sigh, she let herself sink onto her back. If her day wasn't so awful, this would relax her. Eyes closed, sun on her skin, a few minutes to relax all her muscles.

Naturally, she wanted to get up, and go to the forest, where Leo would probably be waiting for her, but she knew she couldn't do that today. There was no way she would not get away with yet another unauthorized trip. So she had to stay in the garden, let time slip by, and not think about all the things she could do with her time instead.

When she finally took her leave in the early evening, she was much more exhausted than usual. And maybe that showed in her mood. And in Granny's. But she was too exhausted to notice.

What she did notice was Zola's absence. And Ben's presence.

"Hello Little Red," he greeted her before everyone else did. His white teeth flashed at her.

"Ben." She tried to make her smile seem genuine. It didn't work. "What are you doing here?"

"Oh, as nice as it was of your mom to let me spend the night with you, it did get a little boring today. Most of the villagers are working, and no one wants to deal with a stranger."

She nodded. "Yes, I'm afraid our couch isn't very comfortable, and there isn't much exciting in the house either." Hopefully someone would interrupt their conversation before revealing any more truths. Where was Nikki, anyway?

Glancing through the pack, she spotted the girl with Mike and Luke. She looked even more tired than she had in the morning. Ruby turned to the pack. "Did any of you actually see Greta and Hannes last night?" Oops, she must have interrupted Ben during one of his monologues without realizing it. Her mind was racing so fast she couldn't help it.

"Yes, they were at the cherry pit spitting," Mara answered.

Mike also chimed in. "Yeah, and Nikki spent half the evening chatting with Greta, leaving me alone with the monsters."

Ruby was able to interrupt the small commotion that followed by raising her voice. "I mean after that," she continued in a firm tone. "They weren't around later that evening, and I didn't see them anywhere this morning either."

"I saw them," Ben announced, his smile suddenly not quite so big. "Last night, I was near the woods, they came in with a nagging woman, she was yelling at them, you could tell. She dragged them with her towards the forest, talked at them, and disappeared with them between the trees. When I saw her again, she was alone."

"What?!" Nikki's voice probably echoed through the whole forest. "You saw that, and you're just telling us now? They're out there somewhere. Alone." Suddenly she was standing right in front of Ben. Her eyes were sparkling. Pure rage. "How can you just keep this to yourself? Two kids sent into the woods, that's not normal even in the kingdom."

Leo stepped up to her. His sister looked like she wanted to hit Ben. And it probably wouldn't take much. His deep voice sounded soothing through the surprisingly quiet forest. "We'll take care of it, Nikki. Those two will show up..."

Nikki ignored him, continuing to stare at Ben. "If anything happened to them, it's your fault."

Luckily for Ben, Nikki let her brother pull her away before he said anything back. The two of them had already put several feet between themselves and the other boy when he finally voiced his defense. "It's not like I knew what was going on."

Ruby recognized Leo's grip tightening around Nikki's arm, but the girl only quickened her steps.

The rest of the way to the village was very tense.

TWENTY-FIVE

New Plan

That night, Ruby couldn't sleep. Again. She crept out into the forest. Again. Being careful not to wake her mother or Ben from her footsteps. Again.

The cool night air filled her lungs, and her eyes strained to make out tall roots and low-hanging branches in the darkness. She was not yet deep into the forest when a strange feeling came over her. A feeling as if a someone was following her.

"Hello?" She didn't have to speak loudly; the night was silent.

Nothing happened for a few seconds, and Ruby was about to push aside the thought that someone else was there, but then a response sounded behind her. "Hello Little Red."

She shot around. It wasn't Nikki's voice. Or Leo's voice. His voice was deeper, but not threatening.

Wrapping her arms around herself, she took a step toward the silhouette. "Ben," she groaned in relief.

A soft laugh reached her ears. "Yes, it's me. Who were you expecting?"

"No one," she replied quickly. After all, it didn't need to be known that Leo had visited her in her room before. "What are you doing here?" Now that she knew there was someone she knew here, she wasn't so scared anymore. Even her anger toward him wasn't so great anymore.

"I wasn't sure whether I was welcome in your house anymore."

"My mom will worry if you're not there tomorrow." That she herself didn't need to know him in the same house was no longer a question, but thinking about having to explain Ben's disappearance to her mom somehow made her feel sick.

She saw him raise his shoulders. "I didn't mean to impose."

While his charms threatened to persuade her, she had to remind herself why she had come out here. To rescue Greta and Hannes. "You know where the pack lives, don't you?"

"I do," he agreed. Though she couldn't really see him, his expression had to show confusion at the sudden change of subject. No matter, Ruby had an idea.

"Can you take me there?"

It wasn't long before they were deep in the woods, and although Ruby was there every day, she didn't know her way around that particular part of the forest. It had never occurred to her that the pack lived so far off her daily path.

"Tell me something about yourself," Benedict asked when Ruby had been quiet for a while. "What do you like to do when you don't have anything to do for your Granny or your mom or the village?"

Maybe it was a good idea to talk. About normal stuff. It would make the trip shorter, and Ruby wouldn't have to deal with what to think about him. About what he had told her. "I like to read quite a bit," she began, "and listen to music, but I do that while I work, too."

"Reading is cool. What are you reading right now? And who's your favorite author?" It surprised Ruby again how easy it was to talk to Benedict.

"It's a book by a fairly unknown author ... and it's about two best friends. I'm not that far into the story yet, but I really like Chloe Rumi." She couldn't get much more together at the moment, unfortunately. When was the last time she had even opened the book? It seemed like an eternity to her.

"Oh, I like her books. Have you read *Big and Small Questions*? It's really good."

Surprised, she looked at him. "You read Chloe Rumi?"

"Of course. I may not look like it, but I like to educate myself."

If she was honest, she had not believed that he was the brightest. His expression was much too arrogant for that. "Big and Small Questions I haven't read yet," she then replied to his previous question. "My mom works in the city, but even the library there doesn't have it in stock." This was actually something she had been annoyed about just a few weeks ago. And it was only now that the urge to stick her nose in this book came back to her.

"I have it with me ... well, in the Wolves' Village. I'll bring it to you tomorrow," he said, without hesitation.

"Oh no, you don't have to do that. I'm not even through with my current book, and right now I don't have that much time to read it either." All the events of the last few days flashed through her mind. Her sneaking around, her lies, her feelings ... Not that much time was probably an appropriate euphemism.

"Don't we all?" he laughed, and Ruby became aware of her current situation. They were still walking through the forest in the darkness, and Ruby could not yet see their destination. Was Benedict with his wolf eyes able to? For her, there was nothing but trees. "I'll bring it to you, and you just give it back to me whenever you're done with it."

"Thanks, that's really sweet of you."

"That's just me."

Ruby didn't know how to respond. His confidence unsettled her a little. But then she spotted something he must have had seen a few yards ago. "Are those their houses over there?" she asked, glancing at the very well-hidden wooden huts between the trees in front of them. While there was only a little light coming from one, it was enough to let Ruby make out all four. They were no smaller than her own house, just not as tall.

"You've really never been here before?" Ben replied, surprised.

"No..." She spotted movement by one of the houses and three seconds later, several figures stood in front of her.

"Red?" This time it was Leo's voice. Next to him, she recognized Luke.

"Yes, it's me."

With quick steps he approached. "What are you doing here?"

"Have you talked to Nikki?" Her voice was insistent, because if she was honest, she was afraid the girl had just gone off on her own.

"Of course they did," said another figure standing by Luke. Nikki. "But everything seems more important than saving our friends."

"We need a plan first," Leo replied, and it sounded like he'd told her that a lot of times that night. Probably because he had.

"Well, let's go," Ruby interrupted. "That's why I'm here."

TWENTY-SIX

On the Look-Out

When Ruby stood next to Leo in the middle of the forest some time later, her eyes had already become much better accustomed to the darkness.

The walking and the cold night air helped combat the fatigue that threatened to rise in Ruby. Although Ruby noticed that the siblings were walking slower only because of her, she tried to keep her pace evenly fast. If she walked any faster, she would be running. And she couldn't keep that up for long.

On the way, the three explained to her that the rest of the pack needed their sleep. Ben had agreed to stay in the wolf village. Besides, he had no idea what was really going on. And Ruby had no desire for him to spill what he had told her in front of the others.

Nikki hoped she would find Greta and Hannes before anything happened to them. Those 36 hours head start the two of them had wouldn't matter.

They were splitting up, and while Ruby would have loved to go with Leo, it probably would have just distracted her. Besides, the two boys were already gone much faster than Ruby could have kept up.

"Come on, we'll go this way," Nikki whispered to her. From now on, they had to try to move through the forest as inconspicuously as possible.

Without any objections, she followed the younger girl. For a while the two walked side by side in silence, but eventually it became so dark and thick in the forest again that Ruby had to ask, "Where are you?" Whispering, of course.

Beside her, Nicki reached for her arm. "I'm here," she said softly, pulling Ruby with her. "Can you see anything?" she inquired.

"No," Ruby replied. Above them, the dense foliage shielded the moonlight so well that she couldn't see even the tree trunks until she was only a few steps away. "Can you see more than I can because of this wolf thing?" Leo had said something like that, but Ruby wasn't quite sure how that would work.

"I think so. Since then, I've been able to see better, hear better, smell better ... Which isn't quite as cool when you live with a bunch of boys."

They both chuckled softly. Ruby had no brothers, but Nikki had two. And then there were the other boys in the pack, who ran around in the woods all day and probably didn't like listening to their parents when they needed to take a bath either.

"Is it hard?" asked Ruby then. "Being a wolf?"

"No, I don't think it's bad at all. Most of the time it's quite fun to run around in the woods and not have any worries, except that someone might catch you. But let's face it, nobody's in the woods but you, and we're all good friends with you. Sometimes I wish I could go back to the village, especially because of Greta. I miss having friends outside the pack."

Without thinking, Ruby interrupted her. "Earlier you said you would sneak into Greta's house," she reminded Nikki, feeling her pause in surprise. "You don't have to lie to me, I won't tell on you." Why was she so offended that Nikki had been lying to her for the past few months? She herself was hardly doing anything else lately.

"Well, you're pretty good friends with Leo, too." And though Ruby couldn't see her very well, she could feel Nikki's gaze on her. Then, to cover the awkwardness of the situation, Nikki kept talking as if Ruby had never said anything. "So, being a wolf in itself isn't a bad thing. I can do so much more than before, not just smell and see. I can transform when I want, and the boys respect me because I'm a strong wolf. I can tell you this, if you can just turn into a wolf when you have a fight with your brother and beat him, it's the best feeling in the world."

Ruby nodded, though Nikki couldn't see that now that they were both moving on again. "Sometimes I wish I was strong, too. And to be able to run around in the woods all day. It's pretty boring every day just walking from Mom to Granny and back again, doing my chores and not really doing anything else."

Nikki's steps slowed. "I hadn't thought about that at all. I thought you liked it."

"It's not that it bothers me," Ruby clarified. "But when I think about what I want to do with my life, it's not necessarily part of it. At least not a huge part."

"That's how I feel, too. Before this whole thing happened, I actually wanted to be a healer. But where can I train now? No one in the village or the surrounding villages will take on a possible wolf."

"I don't know, Nikki. If you went far enough away from here, there would probably be some options already," Ruby pondered. She thought of the city or kingdom Ben had talked about.

"I want to stay with my family, though. And with my friends." Ruby had already thought of that. But of course, she didn't say anything about it. "Speaking of friends..." The pause was getting a little too long to be inconspicuous, and Ruby worried about what was coming next. "You and Leo are more than friends, aren't you? What's going on?"

The question hit Ruby completely unexpectedly. What made Nikki think that? Had she noticed something after all? "Um ... nothing."

Nikki paused so abruptly that Ruby almost stumbled. "Nothing?" she repeated in disbelief, and her grip on Ruby's hand tightened briefly. "The way you're looking at each other, talking, and him sneaking out to *watch the village...*" she emphasized the last part as if it was clearly an excuse. Which it probably was. "It's not nothing."

Though she couldn't really see it, Ruby thought she noticed Nikki's intense gaze. "So when does Leo watch the village?" Hadn't he ever told anyone that he was meeting her at noon?

When Nikki didn't respond, Ruby felt compelled to answer her previous question. "All right, not nothing," she admitted. "But maybe this isn't the best time to talk about it."

Of course. Of course, she was talking her way out of it. But honestly, they were stumbling through the woods looking for their friends. Was there a worse time to talk about it?

Was Nikki really laughing now? The noise sounded wrong in the dark and otherwise quiet forest. "When is a good time, then? Whenever we see each other, we're surrounded by the entire pack, and you can't really talk about personal stuff in Shawn and Luke's presence without everyone knowing afterwards or there being some stressful conversations."

"Did you know that Leo and Ben overheard us when we were..." She almost let the sentence hang in the air, because it had come back to her that she didn't want to talk about Ben. But Nikki wouldn't just let that go. "...when we were talking about Ben?"

"Of course," Nikki replied with a laugh, before she too noticed that it didn't seem to be the answer Ruby had been expecting.

"How?" asked Ruby immediately. And wished she could pull it back again, just to make it seem not quite so overzealous.

Yet again, Nikki laughed. "There are no secrets in the pack. Someone is always eavesdropping."

Wonderful. And she had honestly thought she could at least have a few personal conversations with Nikki without all of them knowing about it.

"Now, back to you," Nikki continued. "You and Leo?" She asked as if she already knew the answer, but that didn't make it any easier to answer.

"Shh," Ruby suddenly interjected. "Do you see that?" she whispered extra softly.

A light. A tiny light, in the middle of the dark forest. "Yes." Nikki sounded excited too, seemingly completely oblivious to their conversation so far. "It's still quite far away, though. Come on." Nikki started walking toward it, but Ruby stopped her.

"Shouldn't we make a plan? If we get caught - by whoever lives there - and Greta and Hannes are in there, then something bad could happen. Let's find the guys and make a plan."

The suggestion wasn't well received by Nikki. "There's no time for that, they could be at the other end of the forest by now. What if something happens to Greta and Hannes right now? What if we can help them now and not later?!" Real fear was in her voice and Ruby knew very well how she felt. But at the same time, she didn't want to just let her friend walk into a potentially dangerous situation.

She gripped Nikki's hand tighter as she felt she might sprint off at any moment. And then Ruby wouldn't be able to catch up with her. "Let you and me at least make a plan," she pleaded urgently. She didn't know why, but this house gave her the creeps. "I don't know about you, but I've never seen this house before, have you? And there's a light on in the middle of the night. Don't you think that's a little strange? I want to save Hannes and Greta too, but we can't get caught doing that. Nobody knows where we are exactly, and if someone wants to hurt us over there, we have no way to escape. I don't even know where we are. Do you?"

"No," she admitted. "But we should hurry. I can't keep Greta waiting any longer."

Ruby had no idea why Nikki felt so responsible for her friend's disappearance, but she didn't blame her. Nikki just needed someone to remind her to be careful. "What do you think? How far away is the house?"

"A hundred yards, maybe two hundred? I could be over there in a few seconds, grab those two, and run away again."

"But they can't run as fast as you can. And neither can I. We should think of a distraction. And it would really be better if it wasn't just the two of us."

"Yeah, but I guess we can't change that right now." Nikki was getting impatient. It definitely wasn't a good time to suggest her ideal plan: mark the way back to the pack and come back on the day with reinforcements.

"Maybe we can sneak a little closer and look through a window to see what's going on in there." Nikki was about to leave, but Ruby stopped her. "Once we get there, though, we have to be careful not to talk too loud. We don't know who or what lives in there and how well they can hear. Whether they might be expecting someone already."

Nodding seriously, Nikki looked back in the direction of the light. "Come on, we should hurry. If they turn off the light, we won't have a chance to see anything."

This time Ruby let her run, doing her best to keep up. But because she didn't want to make any noise at the same time, she was soon hanging a few feet behind Nikki.

"I don't see anyone," Nikki whispered as Ruby hid behind some bush beside her.

Ruby also bothered to look in the window, but she had no hopes. If Nikki, with her incredibly good eyes, couldn't recognize anyone, her chances were even slimmer. All she could make out was a sparsely furnished living room, with a long table and many chairs at it. A clock hung on the opposite wall, and the door in the right corner was so far over that Ruby could only make out that it was open, not what else was behind it. "Let's wait a minute. Maybe someone will show up." On the one hand, Ruby hoped so; on the other, she was afraid of it.

"Stay here," Nikki replied, and started moving.

"Wait, Nikki. Don't!" But Nikki had already crept off. Ruby had to hand it to her: she was very fast and very quiet, but maybe any sounds were just drowned out by the loud pounding of her heart. At least, that's how it felt.

Even though the girl had only taken a few steps and ducked behind a bush, Ruby was worried that someone would catch her. Besides, she couldn't make out her facial expression. Was Nikki perhaps seeing something? Would she make plans and rush toward the house without checking with Ruby? Or would she move right on to see more? Maybe even get closer? Put herself and Ruby at risk? Do something stupid? Ruby had to stop her.

"Nikki," Ruby whispered, but of course she didn't hear her. Or didn't want to hear her. There was probably no other way. She had to stay close to her.

With her back arched and as silently as possible, Ruby tried to sneak up to Nikki. She quickly realized that she wasn't nearly as elegant or quiet. But as long as no one caught her, that wasn't a problem. After a few steps, Nikki noticed her attempt and tried to stop her from coming over with gestures, but Ruby had advanced so far in the meantime that there was no turning back for her. Only three more steps, then she was behind Nikki's bush, and safe, but it seemed to her like a hundred, that's how loud her heart was beating.

And then it happened: Her foot caught on something - probably a root - and she fell lengthwise onto the ground. How could she mess this up? It made her want to scream. But that wouldn't help either. She quickly scrambled to her feet and sprinted over to Nikki. It didn't matter at all if she made any noise now. If anyone in the house had heard her, they would come out now anyway, or deem it unimportant. And these few steps didn't make much of a difference anymore either.

Nikki knew better than to scold her friend now, too. Instead, she gave her an angry look. And they both held their breath. Hoping, praying that nothing would happen.

But they were unlucky. Voices came from inside, and a few seconds later the front door opened. "What's going on?" a high-pitched voice called out. "Who's out there?"

Nothing but a couple of owls answered the person. Unfortunately, the two girls couldn't make out a figure, from their crouched position behind the bush. And as much as Ruby would have liked to stretch just a little to see what was going on, Nikki held her hand tightly. As soon as Ruby would do something stupid, Nikki could stop her.

Whispers came from the direction of the house. There was more than one person. At least two, talking quietly. After a while, even the whispers disappeared.

Ruby stared at Nikki with wide eyes, silently trying to tell her that she would like to look. But at the same time, she did not move an inch. The fear that they might get caught after all was too great.

It felt like hours until Nikki finally stretched her neck, cautiously looking toward the house. "There's no one left," she whispered even more quietly than before. "And if they're holding Hannes and Greta captive, they now know someone's looking for them, too." She sounded disappointed, but Ruby couldn't focus on that right now. Her fear was still pervasive.

"Have you seen them?" she asked, barely audible.

"No," Nikki replied, far more relaxed than the other girl. "But they didn't exactly sound dangerous."

"One was definitely a woman," Ruby said, and Nikki nodded in agreement.

"I think so, too. But I thought they were with criminals or a witch, not a group of women living alone in the woods."

Ruby remained silent, but she was thinking exactly the same thing. This was either completely harmless, or much more dangerous than they had believed. "We really should go back," she urged Nikki. "And come back tomorrow."

A rustle behind them made them both freeze.

"Well, look who we have here."

TWENTY-SEVEN

House in the Woods

The two girls looked at each other in shock, but when they turned to the person and finally saw who was standing there, a sound like a suppressed laugh escaped Nikki. Ruby tried to keep up her anxious expression. Making fun of the two dwarves in front of them certainly wouldn't help.

"Sorry ... sorry if we scared you, we got lost and then we saw the light from your house..." Even if Ruby hated it, she had become really good at lying. It was probably also quite believable that her voice was still shaking with anxiety. At least one of the men bought her story without question.

"Oh, you poor children. Come inside with us for now, I'm sure we'll find a way to get you home," one of the dwarves said. The one who was not shooting them angry looks. His long beard was clearly visible as grey even in the darkness, and his face showed deep wrinkles.

The second one did not seem quite so friendly. He was barely taller than the other, his face was not quite as wrinkled, but his folded arms clearly showed his ill will. He turned to his friend. "Oh, don't believe everything you're told." The younger of the two seemed extremely angry at the night's disturbance and continued to give the girls nasty looks. "Why are you hiding if you're supposed to just be lost?"

Unsure, Nikki looked over at Ruby, but her expression showed no guilt as she offered an explanation to the two dwarves. "We heard that there were children disappearing in the village, and because we've never been to that part of the forest, we didn't know if you might be ... well, if there was someone evil living in that house. We just wanted to take a quick look inside to see if maybe it was a witch or thieves." She pointed to the window, and the living room behind it. "But we couldn't see anyone, so we were out here discussing what to do next."

In Ruby's opinion, Nikki was doing a pretty good job. Admittedly, it was the truth, after all. Except for the getting lost part. At least Ruby hoped Nikki still knew the way back.

Even the two dwarves seemed to slowly realize that there was no danger to be expected from the two young girls. "Come on, let's go inside," the younger one then said in a gruff tone, not even looking at them on the way to the front door. The other, however, was already pestering them with questions, which they both tried to answer carefully.

Ruby noticed that Nikki was quite attentive even as they entered the living room. Probably because they still couldn't say for sure whether Hannes and Greta weren't trapped in there after all. Ruby also looked around, but couldn't see anything unusual.

The friendly older dwarf introduced himself as Pluto and urged them to sit down at the tiny table. "You must be hungry. I'll get you some of our soup."

When he was gone, more dwarves entered the living room, looking at the newcomers with wide eyes. Silence reigned for a while, until Pluto came back, introducing them.

"This is Ron, Joey, Fridolin, Christoph, Theodor and Olaf. Don't worry, they're quite friendly once you get to know them." All of them wore different clothes and didn't bear any remarkable resemblance to each other even as they were, except for their height, but Ruby still couldn't remember who was who. Especially when they then also broke out of their formation and sat down at the table.

They began to speak. So fast and jumbled that the girls couldn't get a word in and had trouble keeping up.

"Who are these girls?" The dwarf who said this looked almost as grumpy as the one outside. Maybe it was the same one? Ruby wasn't quite sure.

"Why are they here?" It sounded more innocent, almost excited. The dwarf had a pointed nose and red cheeks. Was it Christoph? Or Fridolin?

"She's sitting in my seat." Accusingly, Joey pointed at Ruby, who immediately wanted to get up. But Pluto pushed her back into the chair.

"Don't hold it against him," Pluto said with perfect conviction, "we don't often have visitors."

The two girls said nothing in response, and under Joey's angry look, Ruby still felt the need to get up and let him sit down. But with Pluto's warm hands still on her shoulders, she had no way to do that. Finally Joey grabbed an uncomfortable looking stool from the corner and sat down on it, sighing loudly.

"So, who are you two?" Pluto's question was friendly, and the girls looked at each other unobtrusively.

"I'm Nikki," the dark-haired one finally said. "And this is Ruby."

A series of ohs rang out around the room.

"Ruby?" the pointy-nosed one said, eyes wide. "Are you Little Red Riding Hood? Granny Annie's granddaughter?"

"That's who I am," Ruby brought out cautiously, shyly brushing an auburn strand from her face. How did they know her?

"Do you know where she lives? Maybe you can point us in the right direction so we can find our way home!" Nikki said excitedly, and Ruby forgot for a moment that it was a lie. Nikki was probably just trying to get back before the next morning.

"No, I don't know," one of the dwarves replied. "The forest has a magic that makes it hard to find what you want to find."

"I'm sorry," Pluto added. "But we heard about the missing children. How many are there?" Suddenly all the dwarves seemed to look at them with interest, some even leaning forward so as not to miss a word.

"Well, I guess there are seven in all? Eight? But just yesterday two new kids disappeared and no one saw them. Even the ones who live near the forest..." Ruby had to pause for a moment. She couldn't tell that people who lived *in* the forest didn't know about it either. She had no idea if there were more people in the forest. But the identity of her friends was to remain secret. "No one has seen them," she finally continued. "It's like they fell off the face of the earth. I walk through the forest every day and I've never seen another person there. And for children to suddenly just disappear is ... terrible."

The dwarves looked at her. "We've only heard about it," said one of the ones whose name Ruby couldn't remember. Olaf? They all seemed a little more open-minded about the girls by now. "Not many have passed our house." He faltered. And looked around at his friends. Apparently, they too had a secret they would prefer to keep to themselves.

"There were two or three a few months ago. We heard them outside, but no one knocked on our door. I mean, we were tired and didn't know what they were up to. If we had known they were missing children, of course we would have invited them in. It's terrible what's happening to these children." The dwarves took turns talking. But it still became a coherent story. These men seemed to have lived together for so long and knew each other so well that they could easily complete each other's sentences.

"It's not your fault," Nikki assured them. "So many children have gone missing and no one from the village or the forest could help them. You couldn't have known they needed help."

A few of the dwarves seemed visibly relieved at this assurance. But the others still looked doubtful. Among them was Pluto. "We should have helped them. Next time we will invite them in. Give them a safe place to stay. Unfortunately, they can't live with us. We barely have room as it is."

"There are seven of you," Ruby retorted. "No one expects you to take in the children, but maybe ... maybe sending them toward the village would help. During the day, of course," she added quickly.

"We'll be sure to do that." The pointy nose nodded enthusiastically.

"Then I'm glad we found you," Pluto said now. "Who knows what else would have happened to you tonight? Is that why you're out so late? Looking for someone?"

Ruby looked questioningly at Nikki. "Yeah, we're looking for two friends," she admitted. "Hannes and Greta. They live in the village, and..." Ruby actually wanted to say that it was Nikki's best friend. But she knew it wasn't her place to reveal that.

"Well, that's not so smart. In the middle of the night." Olaf nevertheless threw them a pitying smile. "Perhaps you'd best continue your search during the day?"

A beep sounded from the other room, and Pluto looked delightedly at the two girls. "Your soup is ready!" He disappeared through the door that appeared to lead to the kitchen, and returned a short time after with two large bowls, which he placed in front of them.

Now that the smell was flooding her nose, Ruby actually felt quite hungry. As she picked up the spoon, she saw Nikki doing the same.

"So, it's settled, you two are staying here tonight," Pluto announced solemnly, and the girls had no chance to talk their way out of it.

TWENTY-EIGHT

The Morning After

Although it was very early in the morning when Ruby finally went back to the village and through the front door, her mom was already awake. "Where the hell have you been?" she asked, and Ruby was so horrified to hear her swear that she didn't have an answer ready at first.

Her mouth opened, but only a croak made it out. "I..." Catherine stared at her so angrily that Ruby hardly dared to tell her a lie, much less the truth.

"You weren't with that boy you kissed, were you?" Her wide eyes awaited an answer, but before her daughter could reply, she was already speaking on. "Ruby! That's just stupid!"

Never before had her mother called her stupid, and Ruby had trouble holding back tears. "I wasn't with him," she brought out shakily.

"Don't lie to me!" she thundered, and the girl visibly flinched. "You can't just sneak out at night. It's dangerous out there! You can't just do whatever you want!"

"I was just..." Ruby was about to tell her mother the truth. That Hannes and Greta had disappeared and needed her help. That she didn't because she was stupid. And that it wasn't dangerous out there, that she was the only one who could know. Instead, she couldn't even get a complete sentence out.

"You just what, Ruby? I was worried as hell. You can't just disappear! Do you even know how many kids get lost in this forest?" Her voice grew only slightly softer, but no less angry.

"I'm not a child," Ruby replied through clenched teeth.

"You're my child. And you're not just going out into the woods in the middle of the night. You're going to go to Granny's today, do your chores, and then come right back. No detours, no excuses, do you understand me?"

Ruby said nothing. She was being stubborn. Just like her Granny had said. And suddenly it didn't sound so bad.

"Do you understand me?" repeated Catherine, knowing full well that her daughter would not break such a promise – if she made it.

"What if someone needs my help?" Ruby asked tensely.

"It's not your job to save anyone. You have to think of yourself. And about Granny. If you get lost too, then..." She didn't dare finish the sentence, but she didn't have to. Ruby already had enough of a guilty conscience.

"I won't get lost," she kept insisting.

Her mom didn't want to get upset any longer. Sighing, she glanced at the clock. "You're coming straight home," she ordered with a grim look before turning away. End of conversation.

When Ruby finally left the house, her mom was long gone. Today she had left for work extra early, even forgetting to give Ruby her speech. That she should be polite and knock and stuff. Ruby didn't know what was worse: that she wasn't allowed to help Hannes and Greta anymore, or that her mom was so mad at her that she wouldn't even talk to her.

In all the drama, she must have also forgotten about Ben, who had wisely closed the living room door that night. In her anger, Catherine would have blamed her for his disappearance as well. All right, somehow that was indeed her fault.

The way to the forest seemed much too long to her. Somehow, she had the feeling that everyone was staring at her. That they had heard the argument with her mom or could tell by looking at her that she was still close to tears. To keep herself busy, she looked around among the happily chattering kids on the way to school. It took her a few minutes to realize that she was looking out for Hannes and Greta. And they wouldn't be going to school today.

An eternity later, she saw familiar silhouettes emerging from behind the trees. Relieved, she greeted the pack. It was good to see them all again. And it distracted her from thinking about the fight with her mom.

"Are you guys okay?" she asked, addressing Luke and Leo, oblivious of the fact that the rest of the pack might not have known about their trip.

"Well, sure," Luke answered calmly. "But we weren't the ones who disappeared all night, either."

Ruby looked around for her partner in crime but couldn't spot her. "Where's...?"

Luke grinned. "Nikki's asleep. She'd apparently had quite a wild night. Was babbling about dwarves and soup when she arrived this morning, completely exhausted."

"So, what was going on?" Leo asked in his usual calm way.

Ruby couldn't hold back a short laugh. "Oh, we were with dwarves, and they gave us soup." She was amused by the puzzled faces. "They wouldn't let us go, in the middle of the night, but I'm afraid their beds weren't really comfortable."

The boys just nodded, and Ruby laughed. "You guys didn't have any better luck?"

"Well...", Luke began.

"Well?" repeated Ruby tensely.

Leo cleared his throat, looking around at the others. Ruby didn't know if the rest of the pack knew about this. Or should know about it. Both of the night's outing and of Hannes and Greta's disappearance. "We found a house," she said.

"But unlike you guys, we didn't rush right in," Luke teased her.

"We didn't rush in," she objected. However, Ruby wasn't sure if it was better that they got caught. More likely, it wasn't.

The two boys laughed.

"So, what was up with the house?", Ruby changed the subject again.

With an expectant look, Luke let Leo take the floor. "It was pretty far out, so we'd never seen it before. But when we arrived yesterday, it was dark. Well, not completely dark. There was a woman in the house who lit some candles, and that allowed us to see her. I didn't recognize her, though. Who knows who it was."

Impatiently, Luke took the floor. "We were waiting. For her to go to bed. And for us to maybe scout the house. But she was up forever. I think all night. So we made a plan. How we can keep watching the house and find out if Hannes and Greta are in there."

Ruby was excited. If this woman was still up that late at night, she must have had a secret. And if it was a secret, then maybe that was what they were going to uncover. Hope flooded through her. Nikki and she had just discovered the wrong house yesterday, so what? Surely the next one would be the right one. "When are you guys going back there? I want to go with you." Her mother's words were completely forgotten.

"It's way too dangerous," Leo objected.

"It wasn't too dangerous last night," Ruby countered, crossing her arms defiantly. "And then we had no idea what we'd run into. Now we have an approach. There's a house. Come on, we have to do something!"

Luke nodded. He was on her side. But Leo was not so convinced. No wonder! He kept worrying way too much about others. "It was too dangerous last night, too. You should have just stayed home. We'll work it out."

His words reminded her far too much of what her mother had said. "It's not your decision," Ruby replied stubbornly, and Luke discreetly left the two of them alone. Arguing.

"But it's my responsibility," he countered with conviction. "If something happens to you, then..." He couldn't finish the sentence. He didn't have to. After all, Ruby had already heard a variation of it from her mom this morning. "I don't want anything to happen to you."

"That makes two of us," she replied, pushing her lower lip forward. " Still. You can't tell me not to go. I have to do something; I can't just wait for you to save them."

"Hey," Zola interjected with a friendly smile. "You guys okay?"

Ruby hadn't even noticed that she was getting loud. Or that Zola and her brother were out with the group again today. Now she looked at the black-haired beauty with her lips pressed together. "It's all right." And with one last glance at Leo, she quickened her steps. She didn't want to walk between them. And certainly not to argue out all the reasons why she shouldn't look for her friends. With Leo. *And Zola.*

Against her expectations, Zola closed in on her. "Hey, I really didn't mean to interrupt. Is everything okay with you? I know Leo can be pretty ... intense sometimes."

"Intense," Ruby repeated. That was a good word for him. It reminded her of the looks he gave her sometimes. And how much she wanted to kiss him then. And maybe it reminded Zola of the same thing. She shook off the thought. "Yes, it's all right." She didn't want to talk to Zola about him. Even though maybe she only meant well.

TWENTY-NINE

Second Try

Granny was in a bad mood, but so was Ruby, therefore she didn't care at all today. The girl avoided her grandmother as best she could, and she in turn trudged into her bedroom quite promptly. Instead of worrying too much about how she could make up for Granny's mood, Ruby took the chance and ran out into the woods as soon as she could be sure her grandmother wouldn't get up again.

Her steps were quicker than usual, because instead of being sad and hurt about the fight with her mother, she was now just angry. At her, and at Leo. And somehow at Zola, too.

With too much momentum, she opened her book, accidently tearing one of the pages. Her mood changed immediately. The book really had nothing to do with her mood. And it was one of the most valuable things she owned. So she smoothed out the page and carefully turned to the one she had last read.

Unlike the previous few days, today it was not at all difficult for her to disappear into the words. On the contrary, when a certain boy dropped down next to her, she had her share of trouble breaking away.

"Hey, Red," Leo greeted her. He didn't sound quite as light-hearted and carefree as usual, but he did sound a lot calmer than she could appreciate.

"What are you doing here?" she asked, looking at him piercingly. "Shouldn't you be watching the new house with the others?" He had made it clear that the pack would do it without her. And during the day. So now.

His hand rested reassuringly on hers. He had heard the angry undertone in her voice. "That's why I'm here. You should come with me."

Ruby's eyes snapped open at this unexpected revelation. Instantly, her anger was gone. "You want me to ... come with you?" Almost laughing, she said, "You said..."

"It was stupid of me. They're your friends, too. I shouldn't have shut you out just because I ... because I'm worried about you."

The words silenced her. At least for a moment. A million thoughts flashed through her mind. That he was worried about her. That he actually wanted her there. And that she should probably apologize to him, too. Not just for the fact that she had snapped at him like that. Then the moment was over. "Let's go then. Let's not waste time."

On the way, Leo told her that Nikki had taken off on her own. "And I knew it! I knew it was going to happen! Luke told her about the house, and of course she couldn't wait. When we walked with you to Granny Annie's this morning, she snuck away. And I knew this was going to happen!" Ruby could hear the anger and disappointment in his voice. And she could absolutely understand it. How many times had she asked Nikki to wait for the others? To make a plan? To not just run ahead? And yet she had done all that.

"Well, anyway, Luke's taking care of the pack now. Apparently, they overheard what happened, and Corey and Shawn want to go on a rescue mission. And everyone else, of course, isn't exactly quiet either." Leo sighed. "It's quite a mess."

That's probably why I get to help him, she thought, and just a second later she regretted it. She could imagine the worst things. That he was with Zola, lying to her, and so on. But he had given her no real reason to doubt him. She had to keep reminding herself of that.

It felt like they were walking for half an hour, and surely it was only because Ruby was so slow. Still, it was surprising how close the house was to Granny's. If she hadn't known better, Ruby was sure she should know the residents.

But when they actually stood in front of the house, Ruby didn't recognize it. She had never seen it before in her life. The brown walls looked like gingerbread, with white windowsills and frames. Colorful garlands hung from the door like lollipops and the glass seemed unnaturally blue. There were cakes and cookies on the windowsills, as if someone had put them there to cool down.

To all appearances, a woman who liked to bake had to live there. Why she would kidnap children was a mystery to Ruby. However, she did not see such a woman. She saw no woman at all. And Nikki was nowhere to be found either.

As they got closer to the house, Leo made her duck behind a bush. Even if the surroundings didn't look dangerous at all, you never knew.

"Now what?" whispered Ruby when nothing happened for a few minutes. Her feet were tingly in this unnatural position and the rest of her wasn't exactly great either. Like Leo, she was trying to stay alert, but her eyes were burning when she kept them open for too long.

"We'll wait," Leo replied quietly. "Maybe Nikki went inside, maybe she's somewhere else right now. We can't just walk into the house or blow our cover and look for her out here."

"So we just sit here?" Ruby asked, a little annoyed. She tried so hard to suppress it, but sitting around didn't seem like much help. What if something was going on in there? Just because they couldn't see it didn't mean it was nothing.

Ruby straightened up. Nikki had wanted to come here. She hadn't just gone anywhere else. So either she was in the house or something had happened to her. Ruby hoped for the former.

"Stay here," she hissed to Leo, who was also trying to get up. Probably to stop her from doing what she was going to do next. But Ruby would not be dissuaded. With long strides, she headed for the house. On the one hand, she finally wanted to know what was going on, but on the other hand, she was so scared that her heart was beating up to her throat.

"Everything will be all right," she said to herself before knocking on the wondrous door. It didn't seem to be made of wood, and somehow Ruby couldn't shake the thought that it really was gingerbread. But maybe that was just her hunger talking.

An old woman opened the door, and immediately stared at her with narrowed eyes. "What are you doing here?" At that, she emphasized the *you* as if she knew her, and worse, didn't like her.

Yes, what was Ruby doing here? Looking for her lost friends? Finding out if a child thief lived here? None of which she could say out loud.

"I'm Ruby, Granny Annie's granddaughter? I was just wondering if you'd seen some swans." It was a poor excuse, but Ruby really couldn't think of anything better to say right now. "You know, they were destroying my Granny's vegetable bed, and I thought maybe they'd come by here too." Glancing at the pastries outside the windows, she couldn't help but think that the swans could definitely have made good prey here. Better one than in Granny's garden, anyway.

"Oh my child, there is magic in this forest that you will never understand. You'd better mind your own business." Obviously the story didn't impress her at all, and before Ruby could object, the old woman slammed the door in her face.

Yet again one of those hints. Why did this woman think she was too stupid to understand something like swans? And what did swans have to do with magic?

With reverent steps she went back to her bush, behind which Leo was still waiting. He must have heard everything because his eyes tightened questioningly. "Swans?" he asked, as if Ruby knew more about them. "The swans are magical?"

This time Ruby managed to make a joke. "Maybe they really are princes, like Mara said."

Leo laughed softly. "I'm sure they are."

With a more serious expression again, Ruby cleared her throat. "I haven't heard anything from the house. If they were in there, you'd hear them, wouldn't you?"

"Yes," Leo left an incredibly long pause, "unless she's holding them captive."

A shiver ran through Ruby. She hadn't wanted to think about what might have happened to the children, what must have been going on inside the house. All the terrible things... But she didn't want to believe it. Wouldn't believe it.

And when Greta suddenly appeared, she almost cried out in relief. Disappointment overcame her when the girl stepped up to the old woman's front door, and was let in. It closed behind her, before anything else could happen. "What?!", Ruby exclaimed a little too loudly, but fortunately nothing was stirring inside. The old woman certainly hadn't heard her. Leo put a reassuring hand on her arm.

THIRTY

Nikki & Greta: What happened in the Woods

(Two hours ago)

Nikki didn't feel bad about sneaking away. After all, Greta was her best friend. She couldn't just sit around. Rest, as Leo had suggested she do. No, even if she could rest under these circumstances, she would want to save her friends first.

Now she was running through the forest. No matter what the others said, she was awake and so strong, she could still beat them all if she wanted to. The house had to be close by. All morning she'd had to listen to Luke tell her that he and Leo had found the right house, while she'd had dwarves pouring soup on her. What could she have done? And then she had to beg him to tell her where this wondrous house that smelled like food was. Food! Luke had probably just made that part up. After all, food was his second favorite subject. After himself, of course.

A small clearing opened up in front of her, only a few trees were really close to the house, but there were bushes with berries to hide behind.

Nikki took her position there. And shortly after, the door actually opened.

She didn't know what she had expected. Pirates, perhaps, or a witch, but certainly not the small, petite Greta. Ducking her head under the woman's arm opening the door for her, she walked out, only lifting her eyes when she reached the trees.

Nikki excitedly kept looking between the house and Greta. She had to make sure the old woman didn't see her when she followed Greta. And she had to catch up with her friend.

The door had long since closed, but who was to say that the old woman wasn't peering through the window to see if the girl was doing her job? With her back bowed, Nikki let herself disappear behind the trees, following Greta until they were far enough from the house.

"Greta!" She didn't want to shout, but she couldn't stop herself. The other girl turned, startled, but then her expression brightened.

"Nikki?" Hers was a whisper, and anxiously she looked in the direction from which she had come. "What are you doing here?" There was definite relief in her voice. But equally, fear.

"Looking for you." Nikki couldn't hide her joy. "Come on, we have to get out of here." But when she reached for Greta's hand, the other girl quickly shook it off.

"I can't, she has Hannes."

Of course. Nikki had wondered why they weren't together. The old woman had to keep him with her as insurance, knowing full well that Greta wouldn't leave without her brother. She put her arms around her friend, who was close to bursting into tears. The last hours must have taken a toll on her. While Nikki didn't see any physical bruises, that didn't mean anything. "We're going to be okay," Nikki assured her, "We're going to be okay."

It was barely five minutes later before Greta had regained her composure. "If I come back without wood, the witch will get suspicious. But I don't want to collect wood for her ... Do you know what she said?"

Silently, Nikki shook her head and brushed one of the many tangled strands from her face. She didn't like to imagine all the things the old woman had said.

"She roasts children. She throws them in the oven and roasts them until they're crispy." Disgust made her pause. "And she feeds Hannes an incredible amount. Forces him ... forces him to eat more and more. I think..." she swallowed hard, "I think she wants him to..."

Nikki was glad she didn't finish the sentence. The idea sent shivers down her spine. "We'll get you out of this. I promise." She thought hard, but couldn't think of a grandiose plan. Maybe she did need some sleep.

"But how?" asked Greta desperately. "The witch can do magic, and she's strong. Stronger than she looks. She pulled my arm when I wouldn't help her, and look." She pushed her sleeve up, exposing a bluish-purple spot on her upper arm. "I wouldn't have believed it myself if I hadn't been there."

"Oh my goodness!" Nikki had seen bruises like this before; after all, she lived with a lot of kids and two brothers. But she never expected to see one on Greta's delicate body.

Without meaning to, she stepped closer to her friend again, and as she put her hand on Greta's back, her drive disappeared and turned to fear.

"We've got to get you out of there somehow!" Nikki's gaze remained glued to Greta's eyes for a moment too long. Then she hastily turned away. "You ... I mean," she added quickly as Greta opened her mouth. Of course, her brother! How could Nikki have forgotten him again?

"And how?" Greta didn't sound like she was one hundred percent on the job either. While there was exasperation mixed into her voice, there was equal confusion.

Nikki felt the same way. "We'll outsmart the witch. Get her to free Hannes, and get you two out of there. Let me think..." She forced herself not to think about Greta – not directly, anyway – and instead come up with a plan. The other girl, meanwhile, half-heartedly began gathering sticks from the ground, not quite managing to avoid the occasional glance at Nikki.

Without looking at Greta, Nikki dropped to the ground. Her legs were outstretched, and with her arms she propped herself up. It felt good to sit, Nikki could think much better right away. "You go back to the house, act like nothing happened. Letting on absolutely nothing. I'll wait outside and watch through the window to see what happens. When the witch isn't looking, you open the door, just a little bit, so I can just walk in, and when it's time, you give me a sign, and I ... uh ... overpower her?"

This time, the two looked at each other, and laughed. It was a liberating laugh. One that came from their being completely overwhelmed, but somehow made everything better. "Or something like that," Nikki added, giggling.

Even though they were in an awkward situation, they couldn't keep suppressing the laughter. Greta dropped her sticks and joined Nikki on the floor. "Yeah, you know, I do a little dance to keep the old lady distracted..."

"And then I'll sneak into the house."

"Hey, if you join in the dance, maybe we'll get her so upset she'll let us go willingly."

The two held their bellies. Chances were with Nikki, it was indeed sleep deprivation. And with Greta, the trauma. But maybe they had just missed laughing together.

It was hard for them to regroup. And when it occurred to Greta that she would soon have to go back, they still hadn't made a proper plan. And she hadn't gathered enough wood either. So now, as they picked themselves up with heavy hearts, and together collected branches of all sizes, they talked a little more seriously about their plan.

"You have to manage to open the door for me," Nikki said urgently. "We'll get everything else done somehow, but if I can't get into the house, I can't help you ... you ...."

Greta nodded eagerly and bent for another stick. "I'm afraid she'll notice something," she admitted. "And hex Hannes and me ... and you, too." For a moment, the two just looked into each other's eyes.

"That won't happen," Nikki assured her after a few seconds, though she wasn't so sure herself. But maybe if she just told herself enough, everything would be okay. Unhappy, she realized that Greta had taken the route to the house. Even though they were walking slowly, Nikki could already feel the parting. "I'll save you ... I promise."

When Nikki could already see the clearing where the house stood, Greta turned to her once more. "You should hide now," she said, also taking the wood her friend had collected.

As Greta continued, Nikki ducked behind the trees and bushes until she spotted a familiar person not too far away. Her brother.

THIRTY-ONE

Witch in the Witchhouse

So you have a plan?", Ruby asked the other girl whispering. Leo didn't seem thrilled. Which Ruby couldn't blame him for, after all Nikki had run off and hadn't told anyone.

"Something like that...," Nikki said. She'd told her story in a nutshell and hadn't gotten around to mentioning that she'd gotten too lost in Greta's eyes to come up with a real plan.

Fortunately, Nikki didn't have to elaborate, when she noticed movement in the window. "Is that her? The witch?" she drew the others' attention in that direction as well.

"Yes," Ruby replied, suddenly wide awake. Something was indeed moving behind the window pane. And it wasn't Greta's slender figure moving ponderously across the room.

Nikki couldn't stay sitting next to Leo, who would probably tell her at any moment not to make any rash decisions. "I need to get closer," she stated, quickly making her way over.

"Don't!" interjected Leo, but by then she had ducked and scurried behind a thinner bush farther ahead that would offer her no real protection if the witch peered out.

Ruby put a hand on Leo's shoulder before he could follow his sister. "She knows what she's doing." Her calm voice surprised herself. She was at least as worried about Nikki as Leo was, but she knew that lecturing her out here wouldn't help either of them.

He shook his head, his lips pressed together.

Ruby wondered if Leo and Nikki would see what was going on inside the house, because from her vantage point, and with her comparably poor eyesight, all she saw standing behind the window was an old woman in a long blue-green robe. How she would have liked to follow Nikki and get a better picture! But she did not want to take any chances. She had to trust that Nikki's plan was working.

Tired, Ruby rubbed her eyes. Her knees ached and her right foot tingled because of her strange squatting position. Her eyes watered and her attention kept slipping. At some point she looked through the window and wondered why no one was standing there. Where had the witch gone? Had she simply disappeared from her field of vision or had she left the room? Did Hannes and Greta now have a chance to get away?

She could see Nikki stretching her neck as well, but unlike Ruby, she seemed much more interested in the front door than the window. What was she up to?

And all of a sudden, Nikki ran. Ran to the door and disappeared behind it. Ruby's breath caught in her throat. Dumbfounded, she turned to Leo, who in turn was staring at the door. He had no idea what was happening there either.

"We've got to do something!" Ruby urged him when she was finally able to regain her composure.

"We can't just go in without a plan..." he began, but she interrupted him.

"Nikki's in there. What if the old lady gets her? What if something terrible happens?"

"You said yourself, Nikki knows what she's doing." He wasn't as relaxed as his words suggested either, and while it made sense what he was saying, they were both having a hard time doing nothing. Ruby felt herself wanting to rush after Nikki. And Leo could tell by simply looking at her. "Just take it easy, Ruby. Getting inside..."

She didn't hear the rest. Instead, like Nikki before, she took off running and made a stop behind the much-too-thin bush. No sooner had she crouched behind it than Leo was beside her. "What are you doing? You're putting her in danger if you-"

"Shhhh!", Ruby went, her attention on the window and what was going on behind it. Something was stirring there. And violently so. She tried to rush toward the house, but Leo's reflexes were quicker. He held her by the arm, forcing her to pause a moment longer.

"That's not the witch. That's Greta."

Indeed! The young girl moved quickly, running to one corner of the room, and back to the other. Ruby couldn't quite make out what exactly she was doing. Had she spotted Nikki already? Were they just about to escape, or was she still helping the old woman with the household chores?

"What's happening?" Ruby asked, stretching her neck.

"That's what I'd like to know," a terrible voice demanded behind them.

Wide-eyed, Ruby turned, and perceived Leo jumping up and positioning himself protectively in front of her. It was the witch!

"Oh, a wolf." Condescendingly, she looked at Leo. "Do you really think you can fight me? Be able to defeat me? Magic made you, and magic can destroy you. Remember that, my boy." With a swipe of her hand, she catapulted Leo ten feet to the left. Fearfully, Ruby stared after him, watching as he struggled to get back up. Although she wasn't sure, she believed the old woman hadn't even touched him.

"And now on to you," the witch continued, and Ruby felt herself rising to her feet without having given her body the command. She wanted to run away, but she couldn't. "The girl who pretends to help everyone and then befriends a dangerous pack of wolves."

"They're not dangerous...", Ruby wanted to interject, but the witch forced her to be quiet.

"Tell that to your Granny. She's not too keen on them. For good reason." Her voice suddenly sugary, the witch looked like she was waiting for Ruby's reaction. The girl frowned. Then she defiantly pushed her lower lip forward, wanting to repeat herself. But the witch beat her to it.

Grinning meanly, she looked down at Ruby. "You're wrong about them. You'll see."

Ruby couldn't get a word out. What did this old woman know that she didn't? And why did she believe her?

"Come inside now," the witch demanded, "I have some other friends of yours to take care of."

Everything in Ruby strained against the witch's request, but her legs did as they were asked and followed the old woman into the house. The door slammed shut without her seeing Leo again, and her two friends stared at the newcomers in disbelief. Stared at *her* in disbelief.

"What are you doing here?" asked Greta, confused.

The witch made it impossible to answer. "Greta, preheat the oven," she thundered. Then her voice became sweet and vicious in equal measure. "It's time to eat."

As wide as Greta's eyes were, Ruby almost believed they were about to pop out of her head. "I..." stammered Greta, unable to move. "No!"

Surprised, the witch paused in her movement. "No?"

Nikki, standing in a corner of the room next to Hannes who was in an actual life-sized cage, seemed to secretly be cheering Greta on. When Greta gave her a shy look, she nodded encouragingly. "No," Greta repeated calmly.

The witch took certain steps toward the girl, but Ruby could see how Greta didn't flinch one bit. Only her shoulders lifted slightly. What would the witch do next? Would she hurt Greta?

"Hey!", Ruby heard herself say. She had no idea what came next, but at least she had the witch's attention. The latter now turned to her, and somehow managed to look even more threatening than before. Ruby's breath caught in her throat.

When she made no sound, a smug smile settled on the witch's lips. "What do you want, Little Red?"

"A deal." She didn't know where the determination in her voice came from, or why she suddenly felt no fear. What was that even supposed to mean? A deal? Why would she make a deal with a witch?

"A deal?" the old woman echoed. "But I already have what I want," she laughed.

Ruby tried to make her expression as superior as possible, even though she had no idea what she was doing. "I knew a witch who helped people, healed them when they were sick. This witch was good and wise. Another one created shapeshifter. Wolves. Made these innocent people be driven out of their homes. She was terrible and cruel. What is it you can do? Nothing!"

The old woman gasped indignantly. “How dare you say...?”

When Greta interjected, the old woman turned to her. "She's right after all. All you do is attract harmless children. You make your house look like candy, but you can't do much else."

The witch's brows drew ever closer together and her hands balled into fists. "You don't have a clue! None of you do! I'm a powerful witch. I can control fire."

"Fire," Greta giggled, and Ruby was surprised at how little she let the witch scare her. "I've never seen you make fire before, and when it burns, it doesn't burn much."

Suddenly, a small flame blazed in the witch's hand. With anger in her eyes, she looked first at Greta and then at Ruby. "Who else wants to say something?" She looked around between the two until she suddenly got an answer from a completely different corner.

"Me." Hannes stood in the middle of his wooden cage, his arms folded in front of his chest, his lower lip was pushed forward defiantly. "You've kept us prisoners here, but you can't do anything. You want Greta to be like you, and you just let her do your dirty work. What do you want? When are you going to let us go? Just let us go!"

"Alright! Go!" she shouted, and her small fire became a gigantic one. With an energetic wave of her hand, she threw a hot flame at Hannes. Nikki next to him could still jump aside, but Hannes himself could only move backwards in his cage. When the flame went out, he still held his arms in front of his face, and everyone stared at him in horror. How could the witch want to burn him? Use her fire against him?

For a frightening second, Ruby thought he was hurt. Badly hurt. But then she realized that his face, hands and arms were unharmed. Only the cage had sustained some damage. The bars in front were black and smoking, much less sturdy than before.

Greta was not as frozen as the other girls. She jumped, without thinking, onto the old woman's back, but didn't manage to knock her over. Instead, she hung on her neck, one, two, three seconds, until the witch shook her off.

THIRTY-TWO

Fire

Greta let out a small cry of pain, which probably stemmed more from surprise than from an actual injury. The old woman straightened up, stretched her back and directed her nasty gaze at Greta, who was lying on the ground. But before she could say anything, or summon her terrible fire, Nikki lunged at her.

The unexpected attack threw the old woman to the ground. She almost stumbled over Greta, but the girl was able to push herself aside quick enough.

"Get out of here!" Nikki shouted, as she leapt at the witch again. The attempt to push her to the ground failed as the old woman let a flame shoot out of her hand, grazing Nikki's hip. Nikki was strong, but so was the old woman.

Ruby didn't stir until Nikki gave her a look that allowed no argument. She didn't want to leave her friend here alone. But she couldn't let this opportunity, which Nikki had deliberately created, pass either.

Not knowing if the cage would actually break, she kicked the blackened bars behind which Hannes was still trapped. The wood cracked and fell to the floor, another kick and there was a good opening. She helped the boy out and shooed him toward the door. When she tried to grab Greta as well, she shook her head. The girl straightened up and waited for the right moment to attack the witch.

Ruby didn't waste any time. She'd rather have Greta in here with Nikki than have one of the girls alone. Hannes, however, saw it differently. As soon as he realized his sister wasn't with him, he resisted Ruby's efforts to push him out of the house. But fortunately, the ten-year-old was no stronger than she was, and Leo was already waiting behind the door, putting an arm around his shoulder.

"Where's Nikki? And Greta?" he asked Ruby, and no sooner had he uttered the words than a scream came from inside the house. A battle cry. Nikki's battle cry.

At the noise, Hannes wanted to run back into the house, but Leo fortunately had a firm grip on him. "I have to get to Greta!" he cried desperately, trying to shake off Leo's hands.

"It's too dangerous," Leo told him, but that didn't help.

"Greta can't save herself if she has to save you too," Ruby agreed, and this time Hannes' defensive movements slowed. "We'll give them two minutes. One hundred and twenty seconds. If they don't come out then, we'll go get them."

Hannes let himself be pulled along, and a few steps from the house they stopped. Beside her, Ruby heard Hannes quietly counting the seconds. It seemed to reassure him. She too was afraid for the two girls, but she couldn't let it show. For Hannes' sake. Because then he wouldn't be able to wait out here anymore.

Nikki, who had wrapped her arms and legs around the old woman, lost sight of Greta for a moment. Where was she? In her worry she became careless, and the witch managed to overpower her. How could an old woman be so strong?

She felt the cold wooden floor against her back and the witch's sharp fingernails digging into the skin of her arms. But it didn't take long until she heard Greta's battle cry. And felt a strange liquid on the hand that clutched the old woman. Somehow it seemed hot and cold at the same time, but Nikki knew better than to hold out and see what would happen.

As the witch frantically let go of her, Nikki was able to roll off the floor and pick herself up. In fact, she found that the old woman was far too busy with the liquid to even try to lunge at Greta. The latter was standing right in front of the witch, with a rounded bottle in her hand, looking in awe at what was happening.

When Nikki called Greta's name, she broke free of her trance, but she didn't immediately run to her friend. Instead, she went to one of the closets once again. Nikki was getting restless. What was she doing there? The old woman could attack again at any moment! They had to get out of there!

Fortunately, Greta was back quickly and took Nikki's hand. Then she turned to the witch once more, and threw something in her direction. While she was already rushing off, she shouted "Run!", and it took Nikki a moment to realize that it was directed at her.

The two were out of the house before anything remarkable happened, but Greta didn't pause as she ran into her waiting friends outside. "Run!" she shouted to them, too.

And not long after, they all knew why. They had just reached the first big oak trees – both Nikki and Leo had made sure they stayed together – when a rather unspectacular, quiet bang came from the direction of the house. As they turned, dark plumes of smoke rose into the air.

"Fire," Hannes whispered in shock, shuddering.

"What happened?" asked Ruby, while Leo took a step towards the house and said "We have to put it out before it spreads. And burns down the whole forest."

Nikki turned to Greta with a questioning look. What had happened? What had that liquid been? And had she actually thrown a match at the old woman? But Nikki didn't ask any of these questions out loud.

Hannes clung to his sister, although he was actually too old for that. But he was afraid, you could see it in his face.

Greta caringly put her arm around him and remained calm. "It was a magic potion," she explained. "It doesn't spread any further. It only burns what was touched by the potion."

Leo frowned doubtfully, but didn't take another step toward the clearing. And Ruby didn't quite know what to say in response either.

Smiling, Nikki hugged Greta. No one had to know that the liquid had also landed on her hand. She had wiped it off on her pants anyway, so nothing could happen, right?

Then she wrapped the trembling Hannes in a hug. "Your sister is a hero," she whispered to him, and when she broke away, he even smiled a little.

"I know." Hannes now also seemed a little more relaxed.

After Leo made sure that the fire did not indeed consume the entire house and the surrounding forest, they left this site of horror together. Nikki took the siblings to the wolf village while Leo took Ruby to Granny's house.

When no one was looking, Nikki took Greta's hand, and for a while they walked through the forest like that. Carefree and happy.

THIRTY-THREE

Little Red Riding Hood

Leo radiated a calmness that Ruby definitely needed. The two walked quietly through the woods, and although she was relieved that Greta and Hannes were okay, she was worried about them. What would happen to them now? Would they be able to go back to the village?

It felt like it had only been a few moments when they stopped at the three oak trees. Ruby didn't even have time to think about the fact that she had started across the garden earlier. At some point they must have been walking in circles. Still, the burning house seemed way too close by.

Coming to a halt, Leo pulled her into a long hug, and she buried her head in his shoulder. It was so peaceful. So calm. Ruby didn't want to break away. But eventually she did.

Leo's hand passed over her cheek. "I'll see you tonight," he promised.

She nodded slowly. She knew he would be there. He would always be there.

For a few moments, she watched him walk past the house in the direction of the garden. She had never noticed him doing that. When she had long lost sight of him, she finally pulled herself together. Ruby was still jittery when she arrived at the house. She almost missed the open door. "What's going on?" she whispered softly to herself.

She took the first step into the house. But when she saw broken vases and the shoe rack fallen over, she went back outside right away. Frantically, she looked. For someone. Anyone. Why had she waited until Leo was gone? If he were still around right now, he could help her.

She took a deep breath. This time, as she entered the house, she made sure to keep her movements as careful and quiet as possible. Taking deep breaths, she tried to calm herself. There was probably no one in here anymore. Whoever had been raging in this house had to be long gone. At least that's what she hoped.

Ruby noticed again that she wasn't as light on her feet as Nikki. As she walked down the hall, she nearly knocked over a vase. And almost ran into a small table that was standing crooked in the hallway. And she always managed to avoid all that only at the last moment.

At first she went into the kitchen, where she could smell the sweet scent of the pastries from the days before. In fact, she couldn't think of any other reason why her Granny's house should be broken into, except for her treats. But the kitchen was fine. Untouched. While the hallway looked like a war zone, the kitchen had remained intact. Whoever had been in here had apparently had no interest in this room.

The next room was the living room. And here it looked more like a break-in. The cushions that usually were carefully arranged on the couch were now scattered all over the room. Various books, magazines and Granny's glasses lay on the floor, too.

But again, there was no sign of Granny. Or of a burglar.

Ruby's heart was beating loudly. So loud that she was afraid whoever had broken in here might hear it. But that was nonsense. No one could hear it. And even if someone had snuck in here, they'd probably be gone by now.

Carefully she crossed the living room. To her grandmother's bedroom. The door was merely ajar, which was strange. Usually the door always stayed closed. Granny liked her privacy. Even when she was not in the room, she made sure to keep this door shut. Without exception. Ruby had rarely been in her bedroom. Mostly when Granny had been sick and had had no other choice than to let her granddaughter in.

Hesitantly, Ruby stopped in front of it. She couldn't see what was going on in the room. And when she pricked up her ears, she didn't hear a sound. Was that a good sign or a bad sign?

Slowly and with a trembling hand she opened the door. But what she saw made her freeze.

A wolf with black fur, big ears and pointed teeth was standing in front of her grandmother's bed. When he turned to her, she saw the blood on his mouth and couldn't help but scream out loud. It sounded wrong, given the almost peaceful stillness the house was in.

For a moment, the wolf just eyed her silently. Then he bared his teeth.

When he took the first step towards her, she spotted Granny lying on the bed behind him. Her beige sleeping robe was soaked in blood, and her eyes were closed. But Ruby had no time to imagine what had happened here, because the wolf was coming towards her with big steps. So slowly, as if he knew it scared the shit out of her.

That's when the girl broke free from her motionlessness. Thankfully. She stumbled backward a few steps, and before the animal could catch up with her, she ran as fast as she could through the living room, crossed the hall, and ran into the kitchen. She locked the door, even though she doubted it could stop this beast for long.

"Help!" she screamed loudly as the beast slammed into the door for the first time. It didn't seem very steady already, and Ruby looked around. She could escape through the back door. Through the garden and into the woods, hoping that someone would help her. But there was a much greater chance that the wolf would catch up with her and tear her to pieces.

For the second time, the beast's body banged against the door, making the whole wall shake. Some plates fell to the floor with a loud crush.

Ruby had to make a decision.

Now.

She ran out, not looking back. Through the garden, completely disregarding the well-tended vegetable beds, and jumped the fence in one leap. She had just disappeared behind the first trees when she heard the wolf burst into the kitchen. More crashing, but Ruby did not pause. She had to run. As fast as she could!

Could wolves climb trees? She had no idea, but somehow she believed that this wolf was not quite normal. This was still the Fairy Tale Forest, after all. Magic and all. Hadn't the witch said something about that? There is magic in this forest that you will never understand. Was it perhaps this magic she had been talking about?

She ran, though her lungs burned and her legs ached. Ran until she saw a familiar face rushing toward her.

"Red!"

She didn't want to stop, but he held her by the shoulders, and they both almost fell.

"What happened?!" Leo's face showed his shock, and hers probably mirrored it.

"A wolf!" she gasped. Her voice was trembling. And so were her legs. But she ordered them to hang on.

Out of the corner of her eye, she saw other members of the pack arrive, Luke and Philippa, Mike and Shawn. In their features she saw confusion and alertness. "He's coming."

She turned, looking anxiously in the direction from which she expected the beast. It took longer than she had expected. But all around her, the pack stood ready to attack.

Silence.

Ruby looked around questioningly, and it seemed the pack also became impatient, but remained alert.

The girl turned to Leo. "Do you hear anyone?"

Silently, he shook his head, continuing to look toward the house.

"Granny!" exclaimed Ruby in horror. If the wolf wasn't after her anymore, he was probably taking care of her grandmother by now. And from the looks of her earlier, he didn't have much left to do.

Leo held her by the arm before she could rush off headfirst. But as he spoke, he turned to the rest of the pack. "Everyone in formation, stay behind me, ready for attack. Transformations only if absolutely necessary." With a wave of his hand, he set them all in motion. "Stay behind me," he murmured to Ruby in a much gentler voice. There was no time and no point in contradicting him. And behind him she felt a lot safer. Even if her legs were still shaking.

It felt like an eternity, that's how slowly and carefully they walked to Granny Annie's house. And when they got there, it looked almost peaceful. Only a few patches of the vegetable beds were trampled, and the back door to the ruined kitchen was half open.

Ruby was about to run when she saw the kitchen. Had the wolf pounced on her grandmother again when she had been too far away? She tried to remember what she had seen before she had run away. Had Granny still been moving? Had she still been breathing?

The silence pressed on her ears. Why did it have to be so terribly quiet? And why were they walking so slowly?

A few more steps and they would be at the door. Ruby half expected Leo to stop her. That he would tell her it was too dangerous. Maybe it really was. But that wouldn't stop Ruby.

But Leo remained silent. Quiet. Attentive. He went through the door first, and Luke motioned Shawn to stay outside with Mike. Luke and Philippa stepped over the threshold behind Leo and Ruby.

By now, chaos reigned throughout the house. Ruby recognized Granny's favorite cup shattered among the shards on the kitchen floor and almost sobbed out loud, but managed to hold it back.

The door was broken off its hinges and lying on the stove top. To get into the hallway, one had to climb over it, and although there seemed to be nothing easier for the pack, Ruby tumbled over it with a much too loud crash.

No one said anything, but attentive eyes were on her. While Philippa helped her up, Leo crept cautiously into the living room. His eyes scanned the room, but like Ruby before, he only found chaos. When the frightened girl arrived beside him, she pointed with a trembling hand to Granny's bedroom door, which by now was wide open.

Ruby spotted her grandmother, just as blood-soaked as before, and couldn't help but run to her. This time Leo couldn't stop her.

He was close behind her as she crossed the small room, bending over her Granny. But unlike her, he looked around. Checked to see if there were any hidden dangers anywhere. A wolf, for example.

Nothing.

"Keep a lookout," he said to Luke and Philippa, who instantly moved back through the living room and positioned themselves by the hallway. Only then did Leo turn back to Ruby. The sight of Granny Annie shocked him. Her eyes were closed, and her tattered nightgown was so bloody he couldn't tell where fabric ended and skin began.

He would have expected Ruby to be completely unraveled. Rigid with fear. But her horrified expression lasted only a moment. Then she swallowed the unnecessary emotion, and put two fingers to her grandmother's intact neck.

"She's alive," she whispered more to herself than to him, breathing a sigh of relief. Then her eyes scanned her grandmother, and eventually the whole room. "Bring me some towels from that closet," she instructed Leo. But he didn't even notice what she said. Only when she looked at him did he catch himself. "Leo!"

As he moved toward the closet, she examined Granny's head. A small bloodstain also appeared on her pillow, and Ruby concluded that the back of her head was bleeding. Pushing aside the greyish hair, she discovered a small wound that, compared to the stomach injury, was nothing at all.

Before Leo was back, Mike came to her window, which they only now realized was open. "There's a hunter heading here," he reported tensely. He turned to Leo, who was absently putting the towels down next to Ruby. "We have to go," he said emphatically.

But Leo's gaze rested on Ruby. "You guys go. I'll stay here and help Red."

Mike nodded and moved away. Luke and Philippa did the same. Ruby's worried gaze shifted back and forth between her Granny and Leo. "You have to go, too. I can handle it." If anyone saw him here, they would think it was his fault.

But Leo didn't move. He picked up the stack of towels and held them out to Ruby. "What am I supposed to do now?"

There was no time to argue. Ruby had no idea what she was doing, but the fear of watching her grandmother die was too great to do nothing.

"The wolf probably scratched or bit her. We need to see how deep the wound is." As Ruby pushed aside the fabric of Granny's nightgown, touching the jagged skin, she gagged.

"Scratch marks," Leo commented dryly.

"Now is that good or bad?" she asked with a pained smile, but only got a concerned look back from Leo.

Sounds rang out from the hallway. "Hey!" a deep male voice called out. "Whoever's here, I'm armed!"

Heavy footsteps made their way through the living room.

"It's me, Ruby," the girl called back. "Come here quick! It's Granny."

Sure enough, the footsteps quickened until Hunter Joe stood in the room with them. Ruby had known him since childhood. He would occasionally bring Granny a rabbit or pigeons. His son Peter had played with her back then, when Ruby didn't have to do so much around the house and garden. Hunter Joe frowned at the sight of Leo. "And who are you?" He almost pointed the rifle at Leo, and Ruby had to stand up to get his attention.

"A friend," she answered simply.

Joe's gaze fell on Granny Annie and his jaw dropped. "What happened?"

"A wolf attacked her. I distracted him when I arrived, but she..." As Ruby spoke, the man stood beside the bed. His eyes had seen quite a bit of blood. People's, too. But he would never have believed that he would one day see Granny Annie like this.

"Go get some sewing kit," he ordered, not responding to her story. "Go on, she'll bleed to death."

Ruby's weak legs carried her into the living room, where a sewing box stood beside the bookshelf. She also found the bandage kit nearby. When she got them back to the hunter, he didn’t even look at her, being preoccupied with Granny’s wounds. "You better get out, this isn't pretty."

At first Ruby wanted to protest, but the very idea of the needle digging into Granny's skin made her feel sick. Silently, she left the room, and Leo followed her. She didn't have to say anything; he just put his arms around her.

"Everything will be all right," he murmured, and she just had to believe him.

THIRTY-FOUR

The End?

Everything happened as if in a dream. The hunter did his work and Leo held Ruby in a tight hug the whole time. Around them the chaos of the past battle, and outside the chirping of ignorant birds.

More time passed.

More nothing happened.

Hunter Joe called Ruby into the other room, and she reluctantly broke away from Leo. What would the man tell her? How bad was it?

Leo was right behind her as she moved toward her Granny's bed. Joe's voice reached her as if through a long tunnel. "She's weak, but she's alive." Hearing no more, Ruby dropped to her knees beside her Granny and reached for her motionless hand.

Granny had hardly any color in her face and her breathing was very shallow.

But she was alive.

The hunter walked through the garden. Seemed to be looking for traces of the wolf. And Leo leaned against the door with a wary look. Close enough to be with her, and far enough away to keep track.

Briefly, Ruby felt her Granny's eyes flutter. But when she looked again, she found that wasn't the case. Her grandmother remained motionless while outside the forest grew darker and darker.

"Do you want me to take you home?", Leo brought her out of her thoughts. He had crossed the room with quick steps, and was now squatting beside her.

"I can't leave now," Ruby replied tonelessly, not even averting her eyes from Granny.

Leo pressed a kiss to the top of her head, and only a few minutes later did she realize he was gone. When sudden noises came from the kitchen, she finally looked around. Her tired eyes recognized Shawn, Mike and Philippa working on the destroyed door. And when she looked closer, she saw Nikki coming towards her as well.

The girl sat down next to Ruby and hugged her. "Are you okay?" Nikki's hands were warm, Ruby's were not. "I'm sorry, I shouldn't have asked that. Do you need anything? Leo told me what happened. He and Mara will take care of some food and the rest of the house."

It was hard for her to even listen to Nikki. The shock was still deep in her bones. "You guys don't have to do this."

Of course they did anyway. And Nikki sat beside her as she refused the food, as the first of the cleanup crew advanced into the living room, and as Granny opened her eyes.

"Granny!"

For a few seconds, everyone paused. It even seemed like Nikki was holding her breath next to her, but Granny's gaze went nowhere and her eyes closed as quickly as they had opened.

Nikki gently put her arm around her, and the rest of the world stood still.

It wasn't until Ruby's stomach gave a distinct growl, and Nikki and Leo repeatedly put some food in front of her, that she slowly slumped down. Her hands shook as she reluctantly took the first bite. And then realized she couldn't eat.

Suddenly, she remembered something. "Mom," she whispered softly.

For the first time in hours, Ruby turned directly to Nikki and looked at her. "You have to tell Mom."

"Me?" she exclaimed in horror. "But I have to go to the village to do that. They'll recognize me."

She saw the fear in Nikki's eyes, but she allowed no argument. She almost knocked over her plate as she walked to the living room cupboard. Though she didn't bother checking, she could feel everyone watching her.

When she came back, she was carrying one of her own sweaters in her hand. With a hood. "Put this on. Everyone will just think you're me. And here," she handed Nikki her red leather jacket. And immediately felt even more defenseless than before. "No one will talk to you on the way to the house anyway. If there's anyone there at all. Tell Mom that Granny ... tell her what happened. And make sure she doesn't come here." Ruby let her eyes wander from the bedroom to the living room to the very back of the kitchen. It looked almost normal. Everything destroyed was repaired or put away. The floor was visible again, and there was no sign of the earlier chaos. Instead, pack members were standing and sitting around everywhere.

Finally, Nikki agreed. She looked around at the others, who all looked away as if on cue, then put on the sweater and jacket and left the house.

Ruby knew she would get to Catherine quickly. That she could explain it to her. That she could convince her not to come here.

And yet, an hour later, they were both standing in Granny's living room.

As soon as Catherine saw Granny Annie, she rushed toward the bed. And from then on, Ruby's memories were rather hazy. The pack disappeared, and her mom took care of both her mother and her traumatized daughter. She didn't ask Ruby what had happened. Maybe Nikki had already told her. Maybe it didn't matter.

At one point, Ruby was lying on the sofa, snuggled in blankets. The pack had long since disappeared, pretty much since her mom had shown up. Hadn't said a word, just left. And the house had suddenly felt colder.

As much as she would have liked to, Ruby couldn't sleep. And every time she looked up, she found that her mom didn't either. Instead, she was taking care of Granny. Stood next to her at her bedside. Took care of the house. Went into the kitchen and cleaned up.

She was probably afraid. Afraid like Ruby. Afraid that if she closed her eyes, something terrible might happen. Which, of course, was complete nonsense. Even if they kept their eyes open, something terrible could happen.

It had to be the early hours of the morning, because it was no longer completely dark outside, but not quite light yet either, and a light rain was pattering on the roof. Catherine had finally fallen asleep as well, and Ruby, who had been slumbering on and off, took this as an opportunity to get some fresh air. Without having to explain herself to her mom.

The kitchen was cleared of shards and tidied up, but the door was leaning against the narrow wall instead of hanging on its hinges. As Ruby walked through, she had to push the memories of the previous day far away. Fortunately, the back door of the house was locked, even though it had never been before. That made Ruby feel safer in the house, even though she was about to leave it.

Fear coursed through her as she stepped outside, and she looked around carefully. At the same time, the fresh air did her so much good that she didn't even notice the rain. Instead of going back into the dry house, she joined the two chickens. They were still sleeping on their perch, but at least it was dry in the coop.

Leaning against the wooden wall, she sat there and stared through the open barn door toward the forest. She never thought she would feel fear at the sight. That there were actually dangerous wolves out there. The thought of the wolf and his bloody mouth gave her goose bumps. And she wondered where he was now. If he'd hurt anyone else by now.

A movement came from the forest, and Ruby realized it was Leo coming toward her. His hair and clothes were wet, and his eyes red. He sat down beside her, and she rested her head on his shoulder.

"Did you get some sleep?" he asked her, and his voice sounded rougher than usual.

"Not really. Have you?"

"No."

"Were you out there all night?"

"Not just me." Ruby's questioning look made him laugh, a low, dark laugh. A beautiful sound. "Did you really think we'd all just leave? Half of us stayed here to keep an eye on you, the younger ones went back to the village."

Silence reigned for a while, and Ruby closed her eyes. She didn't want to think about what had happened and how it would all turn out. Instead, she wanted to stay here. In the chicken coop. With Leo. While a new, not-yet-broken day began.

Ruby lifted her head and opened her eyes. The coop made her feel safe, even if she knew she couldn't stay here forever. She sighed, and Leo immediately turned to her. "A hell of a lot has happened," she forced herself to say, thinking about the pact they still hadn't quite finished. But she didn't want to talk about it. Not now. Not here. "How are Hannes and Greta?" Ruby hoped hearing from her friends would distract her.

"They're asleep. They're in our village, being well cared for by Nikki." He smiled at the thought. *Well cared for* probably meant that even while her friends slept, Nikki sat beside them and watched over them. That she read their every wish and worry from their eyes and did everything she could to make sure they were okay.

"Nikki loves her," Ruby whispered. "Greta." She had noticed it especially when they had rescued the siblings in the witch's house. The looks, the hand-holding, the concern. But really, she'd known all along.

He nodded slowly. His arm held her a little tighter. "And Greta loves her."

"You know?" asked Ruby, surprised.

Again, Leo smiled, and again Ruby felt a little safer in his arms. "Of course I do. She's my sister. She's always loved Greta. She's loved Greta when we lived in the village. She's loved Greta when they were kids. She loved Greta when she didn't even know she loved Greta."

He took her face in his hands and looked deep into her eyes. "I loved you, too, when I didn't even know I loved you. And I never stopped doing it. When I saw you again in the forest after we were banished, it was the happiest day of my life. I never want to feel the way I did when I thought I lost you."

Speechless, Ruby looked at him. Her heart was pounding up to her throat, and if she hadn't been sitting, her knees would have given out. She leaned over and kissed him as gently as she had ever done. Somehow it felt so much more intense than anything she had felt before. Their lips parted, but Ruby stayed as close to him as she could.

"You'll never lose me. I won't let that happen. Ever."

Acknowledgements

This book would never have been possible without the Internet. No, seriously. Without the internet and social media, I would never have had the confidence to self-publish a book. So many wonderful role models who have done it before me and shared their experiences. So many who support and help.

And you. You chose to buy and read this book, and for that I am unbelievably grateful!

Great thanks also to the wonderful Ellen who designed the cover, and who – you guessed it – I found on TikTok (Ellen S. Art). It turned out wonderfully!

I don't want to drag this out too long, because let's be real: nobody even reads the acknowledgements, so lastly, I want to thank my friends and my sisters (you know who you are) who I told about this book and who didn't call me crazy for wanting to write, even encouraged and helped me through it. Love you all!

www.ingramcontent.com/pod-product-compliance
Lightning Source LLC
LaVergne TN
LVHW091402190726
843491LV00006B/1225

* 9 7 8 3 9 1 0 6 4 2 0 1 0 *